YURI VYNNYCHUK

THE NIGHT REPORTER: A 1938 LVIV MURDER MYSTERY

This book has been published with the support
of the Translate Ukraine Translation Program

**UKRAINIAN
//IIIBOOK
INSTITUTE**

THE NIGHT REPORTER:
A 1938 LVIV MURDER MYSTERY

by Yuri Vynnychuk

Translated from the Ukrainian
by Michael M. Naydan and Alla Perminova

Edited by Ludmilla A. Trigos

This book has been published with the support
of the Translate Ukraine Translation Program

**UKRAINIAN
//IIIBOOK
INSTITUTE**

Cover art:
© Olha Fedoruk, "Stare misto" (2016) and "Nich nad starym mistom" (2005)

Book cover and interior book design by Max Mendor

Publishers Maxim Hodak & Max Mendor

© 2021, Glagoslav Publications

www.glagoslav.com

ISBN: 978-1-914337-28-4

First published in English by Glagoslav Publications in October 2021

A catalogue record for this book is available from the British Library.

YURI VYNNYCHUK

THE NIGHT REPORTER: A 1938 LVIV MURDER MYSTERY

TRANSLATED FROM THE UKRAINIAN
BY MICHAEL M. NAYDAN AND ALLA PERMINOVA

GLAGOSLAV PUBLICATIONS

CONTENTS

A NOTE ON THE TRANSLATION

"Translation is the art of failure."
– Umberto Eco

Those who have ever questioned Umberto Eco's statement about translation being the art of failure would suspend all doubts once exposed to the task of translating any of Yuri Vynnychuk's works into any language – be it structurally and culturally remote English, German, and French or the more kindred Polish and Russian. And it is not only because any literary work is, according to Lawrence Venuti, an asymptote – a line that a curve of translation infinitely approaches but never crosses. The thing is that any of Yuri Vynnychuk's works is merely not "any." It is always a unique outlier that evades generalizations and escapes the traps of classifications. It is small wonder that throughout the entire project our minds seemed to have been haunted by Eco's voice repeating *"I told you so... I told you so...,"* especially when we had to spend hours upon hours dismantling the author's densely idiomatic style, dissecting the polyphony of his registers, resorting to countless resources, online dictionaries, etc., while chasing the meaning of *batyar*[1] slang and deciphering the contaminated speech of his characters. We groped for adequate means in the English language to convey the spirit

....

[1]   Infamous young hellraisers in the city of Lviv, who appeared in the late nineteenth century and developed their own subculture and slang. They were active through the first half of the twentieth century. They were shady young wheeler-dealers who dressed in a dapper way and hung out together in cafes and bars.

of the original and create asymptotic equivalence rather than a dynamic (Eugene Nida) one. Just like perfection itself, the latter proves to be unattainable, because "no man ever steps in the same river twice, for it's not the same river and he's not the same man" (Heraclitus).

Translating **Vynny**chuk (Винничук) one is doomed to feeling "**vyn-ny**m/винним" – guilty for all the inevitable losses that happen on the way of transferring his unfathomable literary world condensed in this particular work – *The Night Reporter* (Нічний репортер). Rendering the synesthetic plasticity of his kinesthetic, acoustic and olfactory images could be compared to an attempt to give a verbal account of a pantomime, a symphony, and a perfume at the same time. Therefore, translating Vynnychuk is not only an interlinguistic, but also an intersemiotic endeavor, with which Roman Jakobson would surely agree. It is like subtitling a movie with a very elaborate script in which the actors' speech is so swift, and the scenes change so fast that you cannot but cite Faust's'words "Verweile doch, du bist so schön" (Ah, linger on, though art so fair!).

Nevertheless, the feeling of **vyn**-a (вин-*а* – guilt) in translating **Vyn**-ny-chuk did not prevent us from being **vynakhidlyvymy** (*винахідливими* – inventive) while balancing between foreignization and domestication strategies as well as literality and co-creativity. There were many question marks and gaps that were filled with the help and advice of our friend and colleague Svitlana Budzhak-Jones and the author himself, for which we express our heartfelt gratitude. By a remarkable turn of events or just by pure accident (the law of literary attraction must have come into play), the Universe seemed to be prompting answers to our questions by letting us stumble onto various sources of information (books, movies, and websites) that resulted in being of high value in the execution of our translation. One such helpful hand stretched by the Universe was the 1941 movie *The Maltese Falcon* based on the 1930 Dashiell Hammett novel by the same name. We watched it and took notes on linguistic features to get a sense of the kind of language used in English around the time the action of Vynnychuk's novel takes place (1938). As much as possible, we strove to exclude contemporary English slang such as "dude" in the current sense of the word or "bro" that were not widely in use in 1938. With no disrespect intended, we also opted for what would now be politically incorrect slang such as "dame" and "chick" to maintain the flavor of vocabulary in use circa 1938. However, a highbrow translation scholar might still not agree with all such decisions. Therefore, we'll return to Umberto Eco's words and make them even shorter and simpler – TRANSLATION IS THE (AN) ART.

Alla Perminova

INTRODUCTION

Yuri Vynnychuk's novel *The Night Reporter* reminds us considerably of Dashiell Hammett's *The Maltese Falcon* (1930) as well as the world-famous 1941 John Ford movie. While the statuette of the Maltese falcon comprises the Hitchkockian McGuffin in the movie as well as in the novel, Vynnychuk's McGuffin is a missing notebook that will unlock the secret to a series of apparent murders of members of a powerful business syndicate in Lviv, Ukraine in 1938. Like Hammett's Sam Spade, Vynnychuk's protagonist Marko Krylovych is a handsome man who has considerable success with the ladies. Commitment issues and his rough and tumble life keep him from settling down. He is an investigative reporter of the seedy, nighttime underworld of Lviv. The crooks, who use violent methods to acquire the notebook, visually are reminiscent of the fat man Syndney Greenstreet and his two oddball henchmen, particularly the one played by Peter Lorre, from the movie. Instead of a single femme fatale love interest as found in *The Maltese Falcon*, Vynnychuk's protagonist has several possibilities, including the rich wife of the politically powerful murdered candidate for president of the city government Yan Tomashevych. *The Night Reporter* is unapologetically retro-masculininist (the way the world was in 1938 for better or for worse). It is a novel whose events happen over five days, so the action is compressed in a brief time period like that of the movie *Three Days of the Condor*, which like the movie adds to the dramatic tension of the novel. All the action occurs in September 1938 in the picturesque city of Lviv, which was then called Lvov and under Polish control. Vynnychuk artfully recreates the time and place of the tense atmosphere of Lviv of that era just a short time before the Nazi invasion.

While plot elements are significant in the novel, Vynnychuk's prose is equally about texture, the subtlety of dialectal linguistic features and the

MICHAEL NAYDAN

nuances of his characters' speech, who come from various socio-ethnic layers of society, including, among others, criminals, *batyars*, prostitutes, shopkeepers, waitresses, members of the police and secret services, and the rich and powerful. They each speak in their own distinctive way. While there is minimalist description in the novel, the plot presses forward mostly in dialogic fashion. It unravels like a slowly peeled onion or a nesting doll that reveals bits and pieces of the story from various perspectives until you arrive at the denouement and the final reveal. The narrative is told from the first-person perspective of the protagonist with more and more of what truly happened in what people tell him in conversations as well as in his various interactions with them. He above all else is a relentless seeker of the truth with a lofty sense of scruples (though with his flaws – smoking, drinking, fighting, and an excessive interest in the ladies).

The novel fuses two genres: the detective story and the spy novel. It follows the trail of the mystery of a string of murders related to a syndicate of individuals controlling the Association of Brewers, each of whom dies under questionable circumstances. The reporter plays the dual role of muckraking journalist and that of a detective, secretly deputized by the police commissioner to investigate the mystery. He meets several possible love interests over the course of his dangerous investigation. Will he get the girl? And if he does, which one does he get? Or is he incapable of being tied down by just one woman? You'll have to read the novel to the very end to find that out.

Vynnychuk began writing the novel in 1979 when it was impossible to publish such a work under Soviet censorship and published it only recently in 2019. While he revised it some forty years later, it represents an important point in his early development as a storyteller. Vynnychuk became infamous for his lighthearted *Maidens of the Night* about a pimp and two Odesan prostitutes, which he began to write at virtually the same time as *The Night Reporter*. The former delves into the underbelly of underground Lviv in contemporary times. The latter does the same, but in the more distant prewar Galician past, the examination of which becomes an essential passion for Vynnychuk's oeuvre. *The Night Reporter* is a compelling journey into the world of that fascinating multicultural past of Lviv.

Michael Naydan

AUTHOR'S PREFACE

I started writing this novel in 1979, and in 1980 I finished it along with a planned sequel. I didn't have high hopes for publication. I couldn't write a crime novel about the Soviet era in the way the situation required at the time. It would have been very boring for me and, ultimately, I didn't read anything about any courageous police investigators. I was brought up on foreign detective novels and read tons of them, mostly in Polish and Czech.

At that time, the first part of my novella *Maidens of the Night* was already lying in my desk drawer going nowhere. The authorities wouldn't let me publish it. Then piles of paper copied from the new story were added to it, and I was too lazy to reprint the entire text. I printed out only one section and sent it to the magazine *Dnipro* in Kyiv and dropped it off at the magazine *October* in Lviv. The editor of *Dnipro*, Volodymyr Drozd, told me he wasn't interested in a story about Lviv. Roman Ivanychuk, who headed the prose department at *October*, said it wasn't suitable for them either.

The piles of paper had to wait for better times. So, I forgot about them. However, since the 1990s it would have been possible to publish all of it. But I had certain doubts about whether it was worth publishing. So I recently dove back into those piles of paper, began to reread them, and saw that it actually was quite a decent story. I typed it into my computer, refined it, enriched it with realities I had no idea about in the Soviet era, and here it is for you.

My hero is a journalist who gets into various and sometimes dangerous adventures. He drinks and smokes. And he smokes because I also smoked at that time. My passion for cigarettes lasted only four years, and I was seduced into smoking by a girl with whom I had a fling. The affair ended, and my smoking ended with it.

But I just couldn't say goodbye to my hero, because all my habits coincided too much with his. How could I not drink if the hero of the story is a tippler? Together we are a single whole. And when he falls into the arms of an elegant babe, I fall into her arms with him. Fortunately, when they smack him on the noggin, I don't have to take painkillers.

Now with inconsolable distress I look at another pile of paper, where the continuation of this tale has been hidden, and I'm pondering whether I should undertake completing and reprinting it....

Yuri Vynnychuk

THE NIGHT REPORTER: A 1938 LVIV MURDER MYSTERY

THE FIRST DAY
THURSDAY
SEPTEMBER 22, 1938

CHAPTER 1

It was a drizzly, though still warm, September day. The forest is floating in the window, beyond that – there are sprawling pastures and white geese near streams. Boys are crawling among the reeds, groping for fish in the water. The landscape is commonplace to the point of tedium, but there's still nothing to do because I've already leafed through the newspaper, which I took with me on the train. I have nothing to do but look out the window, and as soon as I look away, my eyes catch sight of an old lady all in black, still wearing a black kerchief. Maybe she's going to a funeral or coming from one. Her lips are tightly pursed, her gaze blank; she's all deeply inside herself. Next to her there's a traveling salesman with a suitcase stuffed with all sorts of wares, or rather trinkets, with which he goes from door to door and grinds out the same spiel over and over again, because he's not capable of anything else, and then, upon returning home, makes excuses to his wife for getting buggered again, for spending more for the trip than he earned. A young fat dame with wide hips and an enormous bust sits down next to me. She's moaning and snoring heavily like a blacksmith's bellows. Her snoring's lulling me to sleep, and I feel like closing my eyes and not thinking about anything. From time to time she shudders, looks around timidly, and for some reason straightens out her long skirt and hides back in her shell again. The salesman asks if he can read my newspaper. I say by all means and give it to him. He buries himself in the first page and wags his head sadly. There's nothing good in the news, that's for sure.

"September 22, 1938. The Italians continue to fight in Ethiopia," he reads aloud under his breath for some reason. "Ethiopian guerrilla units are holding off significant forces of the Italian army. Emperor Haile Selassie, who was forced to leave his homeland, delivered a speech in Geneva. That's good, that's good," he shakes his head, "that they're holding off the

Italian army. Hitler can't take advantage of it fully. On the Yablonovskys, in a part of Lviv densely populated by Germans, the appearance on the street of a young man dressed in shorts and white knee stockings caused a sensation. Aha," he raises up his finger, "Hitler's fashion has already come to us. Soon these kinds of young guys will become much more visible, fashion is contagious ... Eh.... In the Community Hall a *viche*[2] was held in support of the autonomy of Transcarpathian Ukraine. Hullo," he becomes furious, "they've been tempted by autonomy. What good comes from autonomy here. Did you hear? They tried to free Bandera[3] again. But the police aren't snoozing, no. 'Conspiracy Exposed!' But there's good news too: 'Six Jews were beaten at the Foreign Trade Academy, and at the University – two more.' It's time to show them their place. Have you heard there's a government plan to resettle all the Jews in Uganda? What a great idea!"

Without sensing any answer or approval from anyone present, he thoughtfully folded the newspaper and put it on the table. Finally, there's peace and quiet.

Uganda! Yes, yes, a fashionable topic recently. They're discussing all the details of the future resettlement really seriously. Our newspaper also has written about it, and I even interviewed a *tzaddik*[4] who was outraged by these rumors and denied that the Jews were waiting to leave for Uganda.

My trip to Stanislaviv is as unexpected as it is secretive. Yesterday I had no idea about what I heard this morning. And it all started with a phone call and someone's insinuating whisper, asking if I'd like to know how Tomashevych's career advanced, how he became rich, and now has become the likeliest candidate for the office of president of the city government. Well, to be honest, I could give a damn about all these Tomashevyches, who, like flowers rising up from dung, suddenly blossom lavishly, because the scent of shit hasn't dissipated from them, but after the editor grabbed me by the chest and shook me, all the bottles I had downed over the last month when I was in a weightless state began to ring in my head, I was

....

[2]   A traditional Ukrainian community-wide meeting to make political decisions.

[3]   Ukrainian nationalist leader Stepan Bandera, who was eventually assassinated in exile by a Soviet agent in Berlin in 1959.

[4]   According to Webster's dictionary, "the spiritual leader of a modern Hasidic community."

forced to come to my senses. Otherwise, I would have been booted out of the newspaper again. I had to do some digging and write about something that would stir fresh interest in the newspaper. No wonder I was nicknamed the "night reporter," because in fact I used to hang out in various seedy pubs and dive bars, in casinos, in dens of iniquity and bordellos, got smacked in the chops, and even had my gut sliced with a blade, fell covered in barf in the gutter, because, there was no other way to get something interesting or of a sensational nature than to hang out with the kinds of people I hung out with. Of course, so that they wouldn't have any suspicions about me, I needed to be like them. I had to speak their language, drink what they were drinking, swear like them, laugh rowdily like them, mingle with prostitutes in pubs, allow them to pat me on the head, and not just my head, kiss me on the ears and neck. I needed to smoke opium in a bordello, so that I could wheedle out something useful, and then, so that it would all not vanish in the wind I'd go to the outhouse and in the dim light of a light bulb jot down key words, the meaning of which no one other than I would have comprehended. And little by little I became so involved that I didn't have any need for company either. I became my own company – and that was the worst.

But then I came to my senses. I sat in front of the mirror, looked at the unshaven face of a thirty-six-year-old man who had never achieved anything decent in his life, but who found so many problems on his ass and got in so many pickles in a short period of time that another person would never be able to get in this many pickles in a lifetime. I looked into the mirror and sighed heavily: "Marko, you have to fight your way out of this swamp you've dragged yourself into. You have to!"

Just the day before, the editor ordered everyone to prepare materials for the election and dig up as much dirt as deeply as possible on everyone, regardless of personal preferences. At the same time, he looked sympathetically at my mug wearied by life, because I hadn't yet made a foray into politics. My sphere of interest was narrowed to clients from beneath a dark star. It was easier for me with them. Among them I could be myself. Even when they battered my ugly mug, the next day they slapped down a bottle of booze on the table, hugged me, and said: "You Matska,[5] just don't be angry! 'kay? Yes, 'kay, cause why not, 'kay?"

....

5   A diminutive form for the name Marko.

Well, it just happened that I immediately took an interest in Toma-shevych, although if it hadn't been for that call, I wouldn't give a damn. Though his rapid ascent surprised more than a few journalists and forced them to try to solve this mystery, they did so without success. An unknown person offered to meet in Jesuit Park.[6] I was supposed to take a stroll, and he would approach me. That's perfect. I shaved, sprayed on some cologne from a little left at the bottom of a bottle, put on a clean, though haphazardly ironed light blue shirt, a dark blue jacket over it, polished my black lace-up boots, and looked in the mirror again. Hey! A really handsome man was looking at me, who always had wild success with women until his breath began to reek so badly that it would scare away crows. Just a week without alcohol – and here's the result for you! I'm the same again as I used to be.

The morning was sloppy and the park deserted. Water was dripping from the trees. Muddy mirrors of puddles lay underfoot and reflected the gloomy sky. There were thick crowns of trees and doused lanterns. I walked back and forth with my hands behind my back, when suddenly I heard the same insinuating whisper behind me:

"Don't look back, *Pan*[7] Krylovych." Walk slowly ahead. So, if you're in-terested in Tomashevych, you have to find out where his shady deals began. The notary Yosyp Martyniuk, who knows a lot, will help you with this, because he actually witnessed Tomashevych suddenly becoming rich. And he continues to get richer, but thanks to this.... Take it." Here I felt that something like a folder was placed into my hand. "Don't look back. Count to twenty and then you can look back."

In the puddle I saw a dark figure in a raincoat with a raised collar and a hat. He was a tall, broad-shouldered man. He was holding his left hand in his raincoat pocket with his thumb sticking out. He, too, apparently must have noticed his reflection, though it was not as clear nor as murky as the

....

6   Now called Ivan Franko Park (author's note) in front of Ivan Franko University.

7   In the Ukrainian and Polish cultures, the words "pan" (Mr. – pronounced "pahn"), "pani" (Mrs. – pronounced "pahnee"), and "panna" (Miss – pronounced "pahna") are used with a person's first or last name as a sign of respect. The words are also used with professions such as "Pan Inzhener [Mr. Engineer]," "Pan Doktor [Mr. Doctor]," and even "Pan Shimon [Mr. Doorman]." The wives of people in professions would also be addressed in the same way: *Pani* Inzhener [Mrs. Engineer], etc. We've opted to maintain this Ukrainian form of address to convey a part of the cultural realia.

puddle itself, and turned sharply, making his way out of the park. I opened the folder and saw intimate photographs of an elderly gentleman hugging half-naked girls in a bordello. The gentleman's face was scratched over so that there was no way to recognize him. What did these photographs mean? As he said: "... continues to get rich, but thanks to this...?" So, is this about blackmail? Is Tomashevych blackmailing this gentleman? To whom were these photographs sent with a ransom offer? But this wasn't the man whose reflection I saw in the puddle, because he's thin and tall, while the gentleman in the pictures is fat....

I looked around: the park was deserted again.

CHAPTER 2

That's interesting! I've known Martyniuk for a long time, but I've never heard a word from him about Tomashevych. I had no idea that he had ever been involved with him, and, in the end, I was not interested in him. However, this unexpected clue tore me from my seat. That very morning I started off for the notary. I was convinced that he wouldn't mess with me, that he'd tell me everything he knew, at least for the sake of the memory of our friendship from our school days.

Martyniuk had his office on Legioniv Street. In the morning this particular street was not as crowded as in the evening, when the Korso promenade was flooded with hundreds of citizens who went for a walk and showed themselves, when you had to look closely at everyone coming from the other direction, so as not to miss any greetings and politely convey salutations. Now you could walk fast without encountering anyone, but I was in no hurry. I wondered if I should tell the editor-in-chief today what I was going to do, and I came to the conclusion that it was better not to do so until the article was already written, if, of course, it does get written, because perhaps all this isn't worth anything. Maybe Tomashevych is just an ordinary careerist, about whom the same claims can be made as hundreds of others.

I entered the gate and went upstairs. There were no signs on the door. Martyniuk hung up no advertising and worked just with a narrow circle of well-to-do clients, which was enough for him to make a living. To be honest, I wouldn't want to have anything to do with him, because the dark world he frequented wouldn't bode well. But the matter at hand, that's one thing, and to nicely chat about someone – that's another.

"Hey there, night reporter!" He shouted out, walking toward me with open arms. This habit of his to pretend to be infinitely happy with someone's visit, evidently, had remained with him.

"Don't play stupid," I cooled him down. "You probably can sniff out that I haven't come for a friendly chat or with an offer to go out for a shot."

"Well...," he dropped his hands, and little by little his happy theater mask began to slide off his face. "Sit down and don't beat around the bush. Spill the beans."

He was sniffling and evidently had a cold.

"I'll spill them," I said, sitting down in a chair as I took out a notebook. "I'm interested in Tomashevych. As it turns out, you used to be involved with him."

He looked at me with surprise.

"It'd be interesting to know who apprised you of this?"

"You know, we reporters happen upon quite unexpected contacts. I don't know who the man is, but in as much as our editor ordered us to dig up stuff about all the candidates for president of the city government, a tip from a stranger came to me just in time. Why not figure out how Tomashevych rapidly rose to the top?"

"And you need my information, of course, not to sing his praises. Do you want to knock him from the top? Do you have any personal accounts to settle?"

"No, nothing of the sort. It doesn't seem to be purely about his career."

"Lord! There are hundreds of people who don't have a squeaky-clean career. But how can I be of help to you? I was involved with him six years ago. After that, I never had anything to do with him again. Will such ancient information really help you somehow?"

"That was the beginning of his career. Six years ago. We have to start somewhere. I want to go forward from that point."

"But listen...," he spread his hands apart, "I haven't kept any material since that time. And to reconstruct it from memory...."

"Well, please don't complain to me about your memory if you can recite Ovid by heart in Latin for an hour."

He smiled – he was pleased that I recalled his unique memory.

"Okay. In 1932, the Galician Joint-Stock Association of Brewers took over the Association of Tavernkeepers that didn't object and was happily acquired by them. It was a really unpopular union, because most of the tavernkeepers refused to join it. It was more profitable for them to become a small cog in a large wheel. And the Brewery Association, founded in 1897, was and is the largest in Poland in terms of the number of employees and the amount of capital. In terms of beer production, Lviv now exceeds all other Polish cities. When I read these documents for the first time, I thought this merger happened all too quickly. The law, which established rules for mergers, was passed only a year before and had many loopholes. One of these, in fact, was used by the merger's organizers.

"Wait a second," I interrupted, "explain how the thought to do it even occurred to you. Whom did you represent?"

"The head of the Association of Tavernkeepers hired me. I had to maintain the legality of the merger and protect their interests."

"Okay. Go on."

"The main loophole was that according to the regulations of the Association of Tavernkeepers, female tavern-owners did not have the right to vote at all, although they belonged to that union. Therefore, only full-fledged male members were invited to the meeting where the vote on the merger of the two organizations took place. And no one noticed that the second paragraph of the current law requires a vote of all members, regardless of the statutes of individual organizations."

"Were you present at that meeting?"

"I was supposed to be," he nodded. "But I wasn't. The chairman of the Association of Tavernkeepers sent me an invitation, but for unknown reasons I didn't receive it. After some time, I was sent a copy of the memorandum. That is after everything had already taken place. Thus, I was unable to intervene in time and to follow the legitimacy of the process of the merger. But even in the memorandum I found a bunch of incongruities. The mere fact that the conditions of the second paragraph were not complied with called into question the entire legality of the merger of the two organizations. But what happened at that meeting isn't what interested me. I was preoccupied with the events that took place before and after it. As I studied the accounts of the Association of Tavernkeepers for the past five years, I wondered whether Mr. Tomashevych should be a free man or admire the sky through black gratings.

"You've yet to tell me what role he played there."

"Tomashevych was their secretary and cashier. And now pay attention for a moment," with these words Martyniuk got up, went to a cabinet, and opened the doors. I saw straight rows of folders with glued-on labels. He took out one of them, flipped through it for a moment and continued: "Here it is... The membership fee was sixty-five *zloty*[8] per year. The income from yearly membership fees amounted to an average of about twenty thousand *zloty*. The expense – lighting, heat, taxes, insurance, postage for correspondence, expenses for participation in conferences, etc. – less than twelve thousand."

"So, they saved eight thousand every year."

"Yes. All this went into their fund. When the Association of Tavern-keepers was supposed to merge with the Association of Brewers, the last balance was... I'll tell you in a second...," he leafed through several pages, "47,920 *zloty*. This is from the last annual report of Tomashevych to the head of the Association. Interestingly, he didn't report to the registrar of the associations, because his Association was unregistered."

"And how did you become suspicious that the reports were falsified?"

"Not right off the bat. Of course, they had the look of being a bit amateurish, but they were authentic. In order for you to understand what concerned me in them, I had to look at the balance sheets. The merger of both societies took place in the fall. The terms of the merger were signed in November. And under this circumstance, Tomashevych's Association had to prepare its balance sheet."

"It's clear to me. However, I still don't understand what's the root of the problem here."

Martyniuk smiled, obviously enjoying the fact that I swallowed the worm.

"It's a question of their fund. In the draft report, it had 47,920 *zloty*. And in the protocol of transfer of the fund of tavernkeepers to the fund of brewers twenty-two thousand disappeared. The difference was alleged to have gone for the costs of the merger."

"But that makes sense. They needed lawyers...."

"As I said, the Association saved eight thousand annually. The account recorded a report for 1931. The year 1932 wasn't involved, but it was almost a full year, and we can easily add to those forty-seven thousand another eight. Now take away the pre-merger account from this amount. There would be 33,920 *zloty*. But they couldn't sustain such expenses in any way. And most importantly... there were no costs at all for that one year."

....

[8]   The Polish monetary unit. Lviv was under Polish rule at the time.

YURI VYNNYCHUK

"How is that?..," I was taken by surprise.

"The Association of Brewers took all costs on themselves. Few people knew about it. But Tomashevych was in the know about all these activities."

"And nobody noticed anything?"

"It was not so easy to catch. To do that required three independent pieces of information. The first would be a draft report of the Association of Tavernkeepers, which only the head saw. The second would be the annual report, which was sent to the registrar of the associations and was seen only by the registrar, because the Association of Brewers was registered. And the third would be the merger agreement. So, there was no single person who would see all these documents together. Each of them was seen by different people.

"But did you see them?"

"Only after I got suspicious of Tomashevych's machinations. And who would become suspicious, because of course it wouldn't occur to check all these documents. Especially since there was another incentive," he said with a mysterious expression. "Tomashevych's association lost some members every year. Not many, but his membership still was in decline. This was one of the reasons that they wanted to merge with the breweries. The second reason was that the price of Lviv's beer rose. It was more profitable to import it from outside of the city, so the city treasury was losing income. Thus, it was in the city's interest to hasten the merger of the companies so that the tavernkeepers could receive benefits. However, most of the taverns were outside the Association, and the interests of the city and the interests of individual taverns failed to coincide. The tavernkeepers had no patriotic interests in filling the city coffers. It was easier for them to bring beer from other cities or say, sell beer from Sambir under a fake Czech label. Therefore, when the idea of the merger became known, the tavernkeepers lost a bunch of members. What does that mean? The fact that that year could not result in that much profit."

"That is, there might not have been a surplus of eight thousand in income?"

"Yes."

My enthusiasm began to wane. It turned out that everything that was turned upside down several minutes ago was now taking on a natural appearance.

"In a word," I sighed, "we're back to scratch."

"Not at all."

"You won't argue that if one side decides to cover all the costs of a particular transaction, it doesn't mean that the other side will not have any costs at all. Tomashevych could have had a number of problems. Maybe he needed to travel to different cities where there were branches of the Association? Those could be the costs."

"You can dig up tens of similar versions. But I figured out something else. A few months before the merger, Tomashevych nearly went to court due to a debt to the bank. And the debt was just thirty thousand."

"And where did those funds go?"

"Maybe to buy a villa in Bryukhovychi. I just don't know."

I whistled in surprise, although the feeling never left me that Martyniuk would introduce some clarifications now, and the case would no longer be criminal again. But he was silent.

"Why don't you go finish?" He shrugged his shoulders.

"That's it."

"How is that?" I didn't believe him.

"Just like this. I completed my mission. They no longer needed my services."

"You said you were hired by the head of the tavernkeepers."

"Yes, but after the merger the leadership of the Association changed. They elected another man as chairman."

I sensed that he was losing interest in our conversation and would prefer to get rid of me. But all this was little like Martyniuk, whom I always knew as a fanatic.

"And you just walked away from the matter?" I asked him.

"What was left for me to do?"

"If I hadn't known you for so many years, I might have believed you."

"Do you think I continued digging into it?"

"Of course. Otherwise, it would be unlike you. You have to finish telling the truth. You won't get rid of me so easily."

"Well, just say one thing to you damn writers...."

"I give you my word that none of what you say further will come to light if you insist on it."

"You're getting excited for nothing. My activity in this matter really stopped then. Only once I came to my office and found an unbelievable mess. Everything was smashed – my desk, chairs, a cabinet. Some papers were torn up, others were scattered, and those relating to both societies completely disappeared. Then that evening I was jumped in a dark alley, and they kicked the crap out of me to their heart's content.

This was something new and smelled rotten. I sensed that I was probably straying into a dangerous place. But was this the first time something like this happened to me?

"So, we'll have to start from scratch," I sighed. "I need to find all three documents, then find out how many members the Association lost during the reporting period, and finally if Tomashevych kept the costs associated with the merger, and which ones."

"There is one document. I'll give you a copy. It was at my house when my office was ransacked. It concerns the debt that Tomashevych paid just before the merger."

"And where is that document?"

He rubbed the flat of his hand against his chin.

"I need to remember. Call later. You'll have to do a lot of digging yourself. But it's not such an easy task. Tomashevych is a much more important figure now than when I was working with him. And yet even then he found an opportunity to harm me. And now.... I won't try to dissuade you, but in my opinion, this is all hopeless. What will come of it if you're able to obtain his six-year-old machinations? It won't explain the genesis of his rise or his current financial situation. There was always someone behind him; that was clear to me for a long time. Someone from the upper echelons is still either dependent on him or has obligations to him. They won't let you make a move."

"And what happened to Tomashevych after the merger?"

"He left there and started working for a company that sold malt and hops. And soon became its director in chief, and then a National Democrat. He joined the People's Democracy Party.... Well, he ended up in the city government, because thanks to him the party gained about ten more seats. They value him. And who knows whether he'll soon become president of the city government."

"That seems to be the point. And that's all you know about him?"

"I'm saying: I wasn't interested in him any longer. Only once, about two years ago, I was approached about a case in the low country in Zamarstyniv.

There was a pasture. And Tomashevych bought it four years ago for grazing, because, apparently, he was planning to breed alpine goats. And it was written up in statements. But suddenly construction began in the lowlands. No one had ever seen any alpine goats there. People who had houses on both sides of the lowlands began to complain. I filed those complaints for them, but they lost the lawsuit."

"Did Tomashevych begin construction?"

"No. He resold the pasture as a construction site, earning ten times more for its resale."

I put down the folder in front of him.

"Here, take a look."

He opened it with surprise and began to look at the photographs with interest. I told him about the meeting in the park. His conclusion was the same as mine: Tomashevych was obviously blackmailing his political opponents. How he managed to obtain these photographs from the brothel is unknown, but here they are in all their beauty.

"Now can you see that I have to do everything in my power to prevent him from becoming president of the city government?" I asked, closing up the folder.

"It's your business. Knocking your head against the wall also has benefits. You become hard-headed. As for your teeth, I'm not sure."

I got up and was about to leave when he seemed to have collected himself and remembered something, hesitating whether he should say it.

"Wait," he said thoughtfully. "So that my conscience doesn't torment me, I'll tell you something else. You asked me about the members, but nothing about the shareholders."

Were the shareholders not simultaneously members?" I was surprised.

"They were. There were five shareholders in total. By the terms of the agreement, the shares of a deceased shareholder became the property of the living ones. Six months ago, three of them died. Suddenly. One after another."

"So, there are two left... And all the shares have been transferred to them?"

"Yes."

"And who are they?"

"You know one of them."

"You don't say! Tomashevych, really?"

"One and the same."

"Who's the other?"

"That's unknown. The names of the shareholders were kept secret. They became known only on the day of their death."

"How did you find out Tomashevych's name?"

"The matter looked like this. The court's medical examination, despite certain suspicions of the police, did not find anything criminal in those sudden deaths. Just human carelessness, the confluence of coincidences, etc. Witold Pogorzelski crashed his car – sped off a bridge into the Dniester River. Roman Korda slipped during an ice storm and struck his head against a curb. Then Jan Fursa turned to me and asked for advice. He suspected that something was wrong here. Fear gripped him. But it would have been ridiculous to go to the police with such suspicions. I advised him not to leave the house at all and not to let anyone in. When asked whom he suspected, he looked at me so expressively that I guessed and said questioningly, "Tomashevych?" And I saw him become startled. "Is he also a shareholder?" I asked him. He nodded. He didn't want to name the other one. And two months later he died from smoke inhalation – his chimney got clogged with soot. Those entire two months he sat at home."

"That is, all deaths are tragic."

"Open any newspaper," Martyniuk said carelessly, "these are everyday cases that few people pay attention to. Oh, if you please: just this night an entire family died – a father and his daughter with her two girlfriends. They lit the stove with charcoal and forgot to open the flue."

"So wait...," I thought. "Then two shareholders are still alive. Did the Association of Brewers buy their shares?"

"The shares yes. But the shareholders owned four more stone apartment buildings and three restaurants. The members of the Association knew nothing about it. Although all this was acquired during the existence of the Association."

"Did Fursa tell you about that?"

"Yes."

"So, someone is still under threat...."

"If you think that one of these two organized their murders, then that is really brazen. You won't be able to convince the police of this."

"Who were the people that died?"

"These people had nothing to do with the tavernkeepers, like Toma-shevych himself, although they considered him a modest secretary. All the others were bank employees, the military, businessmen. They created the Association with the sole purpose of making money. The company was legal, but the shareholders were secret. Nothing like this is possible for us today, but during Austrian times such incidents happened. Moreover, one of the shareholders *Pan* Korda, belonged to the imperial family. After the war, no one paid attention to it, and everything remained as it was."

CHAPTER 3

The street was still wet and gloomy, a mist was drizzling, but so timidly that people rarely opened their umbrellas, preferring to use them as walking sticks. Passers-by on the sidewalks jumped out of the way from cars when a heavy spray flew out of puddles from under their wheels. A tall man in a gray raincoat and a gray hat, pulled down nearly over his eyes, stood near the gate from which I had exited. He looked at me from under his eyebrows as if he were about to say something to me. Something about him was familiar. Wasn't he the guy who gave me the folder with the photographs? He was standing to my right. I couldn't see his left hand. I pretended not to notice anything, waited a moment until I got enough courage to approach and lit a cigarette. But he didn't move, only occasionally turning his head in my direction, but somehow as if for no reason, as though by accident.

I tossed my cigarette butt in a trashcan, crossed the road, crossed Legioniv Street, and went up Syktuska[9] Street. Something was bothering me, something was giving me no peace. I looked around and caught sight of him again. He was walking hunched over with his hands in his pockets, as if he had gone deep inside himself and his problems. But, obviously, he was watching me.

That morning I just drank up my coffee and had nothing to eat when the stranger called. Now I decided to go to Musyalovych's dining room. I hung my raincoat and umbrella on a chair at a free table and approached the buffet. Two young ladies, who were chattering briskly about a dance to which they had been invited, were standing in front of me, but they hadn't yet decided on their dresses. They ordered tongue in aspic along with salads and puff pastries for tea. I was quite hungry, so I took tomato

---

[9]   Now called Doroshenko Street (author's note).

THE NIGHT REPORTER

soup, a cutlet with stewed cabbage and beets, paid at the checkout and was stunned: the same strange man was already sitting at the table I occupied even though there were several free tables. I placed the tray down on the table, sat down, and looked at him. His face was as gray as his raincoat, his eyes were anxious, but his movements were confident and determined. His anxiety was not born of fear, but of the habitual state of a beast of prey who must always be on guard.

"I know you noticed I was watching you," he said in a raspy voice. "But I didn't want to talk on the street."

"You spoke to me in the park," I replied, noticing that he had his left hand in his pocket with his thumb sticking out. "Do you have any other business with me?"

He coughed, covering his mouth with a handkerchief. Then he answered: "Um ... rather quite the opposite. You need me."

"Where do you get such certainty?"

"A gut feeling, *Pan* Krylovych. A gut feeling ... and it never fails me."

"Who the hell are you?"

"I'm a member of an organization that monitors the observance of justice. We defend the rights of workers."

I could see that he was making fun of me and didn't look like a worker at all.

"Oh! Somehow I've never heard of such an organization."

I got bored and started eating. He watched the movement of my spoon for a moment, then resumed his speech.

"We've just started our activities."

"Good," I nodded. "Explain to me – who is that in these photographs from the bordello that Tomashevych is using for blackmail?"

"I won't tell you that. He's not blackmailing just one person, but several."

"What are you after?"

"Justice. He has to be stopped."

"And how can I be sure that you are exactly who you pretend to be? Maybe you're just Tomashevych's man?"

"Today you'll have the opportunity to see. I'll give you an address in Stanislaviv.[10] The person you will contact will help to collect materials."

....

[10]   Now called Ivano-Frankivsk (author's note). It is about a three-hour train ride from Lviv.

YURI VYNNYCHUK

"It turns out you've deprived me of any kind of initiative. Do you think that I won't be able to get to the essence of the matter on my own?"

"You'll get there, but it will take much longer. We just want to help you. You'll have to rummage around too long by yourself. And the elections aren't far off. Can you imagine what will happen to the state when all sorts of Tomashevyches take crucial posts?"

"Aha! Then you're also involved in politics."

"Well, I can't deny it. We weren't sure this matter would interest you."

"You still can't be sure."

"Your visit to Martyniuk speaks for itself. And today you'll be traveling to Stanislaviv."

His cockiness was getting on my nerves, but I was already hooked. I was caught and to protest would be in vain and not in my interests.

"Some of your tracking methods aren't like those of a workers' organization," I said indignantly.

"I think you'll forgive us for this little bit of offhandedness. Times change, methods change, everything progresses. Noticing that he was about to leave, I asked:

"Where should I look for you?"

"We'll be able to find you ourselves."

He got up and coughed again, and while he was walking to the door, I heard a strange crunching sound. It seemed that his shoes were making the sound, and on the table where the elbow of his right arm had rested, a small piece of paper was left. I reached for the basket of sliced bread and grabbed the note, hiding it in my pocket. I did it as imperceptibly as possible, although I wasn't sure why I was so careful. But if the stranger didn't just hand me the note, there were probably some reasons for that. Having finished the delectation of their puffy fritters, both young ladies exited the pub and continued to chatter. I was left in the dining hall alone. At the buffet, a beautiful young cashier adjusted her hairdo, staring in the mirror and pursing her lips that were already full even without doing that. What was there to be wary of here?

I finished eating, unfolded the note, and read it: "Stanislaviv. 38 Vovchynetska Street, *Pan* Dutchak." Then I asked permission to call. The cashier raised her eyebrows:

"This isn't a telephone station," she laughed apologetically and handed me the phone.

Then she didn't take her eyes off me, but my call was far from interesting, because I called the station to find out when the train was leaving for Stanislaviv. When I hung up, the cashier said:

"In this kind of weather?" She shook her head. "They've said that there's a heavy downpour there. There's even lightning."

"That's nothing. Business is business."

"And the Bystritsa River's flooded its banks. So much that the roads were flooded."

It seemed like the cashier was trying to persuade me not to go anywhere. Maybe she belongs to the secret organization?

"Who do you work for?" I asked her.

"Who? For Musyalovych! Don't you know? There are three of us here from eight in the morning until ten, because the place is full already. From ten to one I'm here alone, and then there are three of us again after that. But right at eleven, it's already empty. And that's called a dining room?"

She sighed. She had lush chestnut-colored hair with a bronze sheen and big eyes. Her straight little nose and upper lip were slightly turned up. It would be impossible for such a beauty not to have suitors.

"And when do you close?" I asked her. The cashier looked at me with interest:

"What of it? Do you want to invite me out for coffee? At eight in the evening."

"You guessed right. What's your name?"

"Yasya ... uh ... that is Yaryna. My girlfriends call me Yasya here."

I switched from Polish to Ukrainian:

"Well, you see, a name shows who you are in reality. And I was thinking you were pretending to be Polish."

"No way, where do you get that! Why should I pretend? I also have nicknames for them here: Gasya, Nusya, Visya...."

She laughed, showing off her beautiful white teeth.

"Good, Yasya, I'll drop by to pick you up and take you for coffee. If you're in the same good mood as you are now."

"I'm always in a good mood."

CHAPTER 4

My memories of this morning were interrupted by the conductor's shout:

"Stanislaviv Station!"

Everyone was rushing about, compartment doors started banging. The platform was greeting arrivals with loud music and puddles. Cleaners were sweeping the water onto the tracks. The downpour had long since subsided, but its traces were everywhere. The clouds parted, and the sun was lapping up puddles, and the earth steamed. Leaving the main hall of the station, I asked a passerby, a respectable gentleman with a small, waxed mustache:

"Pardon me, how do I get to Vovchynetska Street?"

"Oh, it's here, if you please, right behind the bridge. Go past the train station, then turn right under the bridge and – then go straight. And that's Vovchynetska."

The street turned out to be long, with mostly small houses on it, smothered by the gardens and sometimes by hedges. There were several carts near the tavern; horses were slowly chewing oats from bags tied around their necks and driving away the flies with their tails. I walked slowly, enjoying the sunny day. Soon I stopped at a house that you couldn't differentiate from the others.

"Does *Pan* Dutchak live here?" I asked an old woman who was puttering in a little garden. At first she looked at me intently, then shouted somewhere into the sky:

"Misko! Go downstairs! Someone has come to you!"

A shaggy head protruded from a small window in the attic.

"You've come for me? And who is it?"

"I'm from Lviv."

"Ah, it's you.... Come in. I'll be with you in a second."

I walked into the courtyard. A man about sixty years old looked out from the door and invited me into the house.

"Is your name Marko?"

"Yes. Did you know I was coming?"

"Yeah... Please come here," he led me into the kitchen and seated me at a table. "Then you're, as I heard, interested in *Pan* Tomashevych...."

"I'm interested in the time when he was the secretary of the Association."

"I worked there and even audited it several times."

"And then, when your Association was supposed to merge with the breweries, did you do an audit that year?"

"Only at the beginning of the year, and then, just right before the merger the audit was not done, because we had to prepare a pile of different papers to settle their affairs. So we left Tomashevych in charge."

"What losses did you suffer then?"

"Well, about twenty thousand *zloty*. Wait a second, I have several documents."

He went out for a moment and returned with a shabby, old folder. It contained all three documents that Martyniuk was talking about. I looked dumbfoundedly at my host.

"You wonder where I got it from? I collected them myself. You see, these copies are even certified by a notary."

"What – did you suspect Tomashevych of fraud?"

"Not only did I suspect. I knew he was cheating. But I had no evidence. He told us that the Association would suffer losses by the merger. And then, after the merger, I learned that all the losses were covered by the Brewers' Association. Then I started scrounging for proof. But when I found it, it was too late. Tomashevych became a bigwig. And I retired and moved to Stanislaviv. I hear that Martyniuk, the notary in Lviv, is engaged in this business. Well, I let go of it. I was interested in Tomashevych when he worked for us. Afterward why would I need him?"

"And what about the turnover of members of the Association of Tavern-keepers? Did a lot of them leave?"

"Yes, some defected, but that year more came in than left."

"How do you explain this?"

"Well, you see, when we were standing on a slippery slope, not knowing whether we would disappear or not, members left. But when the possibility arose to merge with a larger and stronger union, then the membership increased."

"Do you think the merger was beneficial to you?" I asked.

"No," he shook his head. "It was beneficial only formally. We needed to strengthen our own union, but nothing came of it. It was coming apart at the seams."

"Was it Tomashevych who came up with the idea of a merger?"

"Yes. But when he suggested it, he resolved something there and prepared the ground for it. So various benefactors began to visit us to persuade us to decide faster."

"And only men voted at your meeting. Although the new law changed this condition. All members needed to vote, including women."

"The notary Martyniuk was supposed to preserve all legality. But he didn't come to the meeting."

"Did you send him an announcement?"

"Yes. For some reason, he didn't get it."

"And who precisely sent it?"

"To tell you the truth, the head was supposed to do it, but he charged me. He fell ill right then and didn't go to work. I lived next door to him, so he turned to me. But I didn't know the exact address."

"Why did the head charge that to you, and not immediately to Tomashevych? After all, business correspondence is the secretary's responsibility. Maybe he didn't trust Tomashevych?"

"Who knows. He didn't say anything like that then."

"So, in his absence all business was conducted by the secretary?"

"Yes."

"And he made the preparations for the meeting?"

"The head went to work two days before the meeting. So he was preparing something there."

"Can you say precisely: The Association of Brewers covered all the losses to the penny? Or maybe you still had to cover expenses?"

"I don't know if it's down to the penny. But I know for certain that Tomashevych did not spend anything on lawyers or accountants."

"But he probably went to Warsaw and back. That was necessary."

"He traveled there, but was it necessary? The Association of Brewers not only covered the costs, but also did everything that needed to be done.

Tomashevych only had to prepare documentation on the spot. But we didn't know about it then and thought that he really was running errands. Even if you had to incur losses, then not those kinds. At most two hundred *zloty*, well, at topmost – three hundred. Buy some paper there, folders, this and that ... But those are trifles."

"And what did you hear about the Association's shareholders?"

"I can't tell you that. I only knew Fursa. There were others, that is, those who founded the Association. But what kind of people they were, I didn't know. They only sent instructions or circulars through Tomashevych. He contacted them."

"Well, well, thank you, *Pan* Dutchak. I still want to catch the train to Lviv."

"Do you still want to go today? I'll see you off then." He handed me the folder and accompanied me to the bridge.

CHAPTER 5

Coming right from the train station, I went over to visit Martyniuk again. It was immediately obvious that he got no pleasure from my new visit.

"I've come for that document."

He looked at me mockingly and spread his hands apart:

"Unfortunately, I won't be able to help you with anything."

"How's that?" I was stunned. "You said you have it."

"I had it," he muttered discontentedly.

"And it's gone?"

"Gone."

"Where is it?"

"How would I know? It's gone and that's it." He averted his eyes, pretending to be really busy with something else.

"You're hiding something from me again."

"Rubbish. Six years have passed. Think about it. I used to have that piece of paper. But when? And now it's gone."

"Did you even look for it?"

"Well, I was looking."

"Has it vanished?"

"Maybe so. Right now, I just don't have it."

"And who does?"

"It's in the bank."

"But I'm neither a notary nor a lawyer. I don't have the authority to check bank accounts."

"I warned you – it's hopeless," he glanced expressively at me. "Just think: even if it turns out that Tomashevych really took that money for himself, then when you return it, with how many *zloty* will you make each worker happy? The Association of Brewers has over a thousand members.

As a result, each of them will receive a few dozen *zloty*. Is it worth such a row over this that some Kovalsky will get such a miserable sum back?"

I just couldn't believe that the same Martyniuk was saying this.

"It's amazing how drastically your intentions have changed," I shook my head.

"You're wrong. Everything is as before. And you, by the way, haven't proven anything yet," he continued, smiling. "It might turn out that Tomashevych is as pure as the driven snow. And what then? Either way it's not worth the effort."

"You're using someone else's words. Why didn't you say anything about this this morning?"

"Didn't I say it was hopeless?"

"You did. But you didn't try to convince me. Did they buy you off? When did they manage to do it?"

"You've gone nuts. One day your pigheadedness will lead you to sit in the defendant's box. What are you trying to accomplish?" He was starting to get worked up and nervously strummed his fingers along the desk. "Nothing will come of this! Nothing! Understand? They won't let you put this in action. And you'll get burned."

He was already losing his temper because he couldn't conceal his anxiety and maybe even his fear.

"Don't pretend you're so worried about me," I said sarcastically. "You're actually shaking in your own skin. And these Tomashevyches meanwhile...."

"You're just seething because you're convinced you've come to a dead end. Did you manage to sniff out a lot in Stanislaviv?"

"You can't even imagine. I have all three copies of documents. Certified by a notary."

It sounded like a clap of thunder. Martyniuk suddenly drooped like basil that hadn't been watered for a week. He blinked and blushed more and more intensely.

"How ... how did you manage to do it?"

"What is this – professional jealousy? You had to rummage around for so long, and I got almost all the evidence in a few hours."

"You know yourself that it's not enough," his voice was cracking. I did a good job of tormenting him.

"I'll get the rest even without your help. But you'll give me that document on the payment of the debt. Or get a new copy from the bank."

"That's a fantasy. You need to have approval to obtain a new copy. Who'll give it to me? How can I explain it to them? That I just started getting involved in a long-forgotten matter? And right now, when he's a candidate for president of the city? It's not funny."

"Then give me an old copy."

"But I told you – I don't have one."

"Did you have it in the morning?"

"I thought I did."

"Have you changed your mind now?"

He was already losing patience.

"Listen, I want to live the years left to me in peace," he said gritting his teeth. "It's pointless to jump from a frying pan into a flame. I don't have the zeal I once had. And I stopped being a romantic. Do you understand?"

"No."

"You're an adventurer!" Martyniuk shouted as if someone had stabbed him from behind with an awl. "You're crawling into the swamp yourself and dragging me along with you! They'll snuff me out! With them I've already had...." He choked and with trembling hands pulled out a cigarette and lit it. "And now I don't want to."

"Who are they? Tomashevych's people? They were watching me. Did they call you?" I grabbed him by the lapels of his jacket and shook him with a rage that knocked me off balance. "Tell me! Was it after I left?" Martyniuk nodded. "Did they warn you that it would end badly for you if you were to help me? Yes?"

He nodded again.

I dropped my hands and he fell sluggishly into his chair. His pitiful look cooled me off a little.

"How did they come to know that I was taking up Tomashevych's case?"

"Apparently, they were expecting this to happen. Maybe they found out the plans of their enemies."

"Enemies? Do you have the organization for maintaining justice in mind?"

Martyniuk glanced at me in surprise, studied me with great attentiveness for a moment, as if to make sure I wasn't completely out of my mind, then laughed spasmodically until tears welled in his eyes.

"What's so funny?" I was dumbfounded.

"Were they the ones who sent an informant to you?"

"Yes."

"And they helped you find those documents?"

"Yes. So what?"

"Nothing. That organization simply doesn't exist."

"It was created recently."

"It never was and still doesn't exist. Who would know about it if not me? You swallowed the bait hook, line, and sinker."

"But they actually helped me."

"Only it's unknown for what purpose. Tomashevych not only has influential friends, but also influential enemies. And also from the upper echelon. That's the organization."

"To hell with them. I've been on this and I'm not going to back down."

"Just don't involve me. I've had enough."

"I just need that document. And I swear I'll leave you alone. I understand that you don't keep it here or at home. Tell me where, and I'll go get it myself."

"Well, okay. It's at my brother's in the village," Martyniuk squeezed the words out almost with relief.

His brother was a priest.

"Does he have the same parish?"

"Yes, in Rudno. He hasn't forgotten you. Feel free to go to him. But take care of yourself. They'll definitely have a tail on you. I wouldn't want my brother to have any problems."

"I won't fail you."

"By the way, who gave you those materials?"

"*Pan* Dutchak, a former employee of the Association."

"Dutchak? How did he get them? That's incredible. Something's amiss here. He was probably given specially prepared papers to pass on to you. Dutchak himself could never have acquired them."

"You know, I don't care who, how and from where. The main thing is that I have them. By the way, it turned out that during the reporting period the number of members of the Association of Tavernkeepers not only didn't decrease, but to the contrary increased."

"Get out of here! What a stunt!"

"He gave me that data. Some members left the union, while others joined. In addition, Dutchak is sure that Tomashevych didn't incur any expenses. The brewers covered all costs. So, Tomashevych only had to spend money on office supplies."

"You're lucky. However, that's what makes me suspicious that they may have set traps for you. But it's quite possible. It wasn't so easy for me to get all this information. Someone is helping you. But who? These people can turn out to be not very decent. And who knows if, after having taken advantage of your services, then they'll go after you big time?"

CHAPTER 6

Martyniuk and I often used to go to his brother's house in Rudno, especially on holidays. After all, Christmas, Easter, and the Feast of the Holy Trinity[11] have a special atmosphere particularly somewhere in the countryside rather than in a big city. But before taking the bus, I wandered through the streets for a long time to determine whether there was somebody tailing me. However, I didn't want to betray the fact that I really wanted to break away, so I pretended to be shopping. I bought a bottle of wine in one store, raisins in another, because Father really loves them, and in the third, fourth, and fifth I asked for cheese from New Zealand. In the sixth, I bought Dutch cheese. I often looked around at the beautiful girls, though not at the overly beautiful ones, while at the same time I looked at the passers-by who were walking in my direction. After a while, I began to identify the men who were constantly dragging themselves behind me. They pretended to be fascinated by their conversation and didn't even raise their heads when I looked around. One of them was a fat red-faced stiff with a big round, pumpkin-like head and white hair, and the other was a skinny worm-like short guy who walked as if he were dancing.

It was not easy to get rid of them, but Lviv's gates seemed to be made for just such situations. I walked a few meters along Legioniv Street and dove into the gate at the Grand Hotel, from which there was a direct exit to a parallel street, Gaussman Passage.[12] But I didn't run that way, and instead calmly turned toward the buffet. Knowing that it was a through passage, they rushed to the second exit. Meanwhile I left the hotel and took a taxi. In a few minutes I was on a bus to Rudno.

....

[11]   Celebrated 50 days after Easter Sunday.
[12]   Now called Kryva Lypa Passage (author's note).

The elder Martyniuk, Antin, recognized me immediately, of course. I set the gifts I bought on the table, he uncorked the wine, and we had a nice conversation, remembering the good old days. Then I told him about my investigation, and he took an old Prosvita[13] calendar off the shelf without any further questioning and took out the piece of paper I needed.

"What do you think? Will there be a war?" he asked me afterward, nodding toward a fresh issue of the newspaper *Dilo*, which abounded in alarming news. "You journalists probably know more."

"Who knows, Father? Hitler is unpredictable," I replied. "If there's a war, then maybe this is another chance for us. What do you say?"

He served on all the fronts, fought from 1914 to 1921, but didn't lose faith. "This war will probably be worse than that one," I said.

"Yes... Here's what the *Dilo* correspondent from Germany writes: 'Will there be a war or not? This is the topic of all conversations in cafés, among families, etc., even in Germany, although there isn't any particular pre-war panic outwardly, not on the streets, not in the stores, not in the banks. Everything is going well. However, the German organizational flair is already clear and noticeable everywhere. A census has already been taken for ration cards in case of war. Roles are assigned to each house's inhabitants in case of an air attack. In special courses the civilian population is hastily being taught how to defend itself against bombs and various misfortunes carried by military aircraft. Those who don't yet have gas masks need to purchase them immediately. In the air defense course that I'm taking, a little young guy who should probably be called a 'candidate for promotion,' according to modern Soviet terminology, asks the instructor if Jews will also be allowed to enter the underground air-raid shelters. The teacher patiently explains the difference between anti-Jewish German policy and elementary humanity, and the peculiar thing is that all the listeners make encouraging noises.'" And then he talked about what you had said before: 'A week before the Anschluss [Annexation], Hitler didn't know that he would be able to realize his long-cherished dream so quickly. Schuschnigg's[14] tactical and psychological mistake, the French government's lack of help, and the

---

[13]   A calendar published by the highly patriotic Ukrainian organization Prosvita (Enlightenment) in Lviv from 1870-1939.

[14]   Austrian Chancellor Kurt Schuschnigg, who served from 1934 until the Anschluss in 1938.

fragile relationship between Paris and London prompted him to make an immediate and firm decision (which would be difficult to do in a democracy with its weighty apparatus – parliament, parties, groups, etc.). It is plausible that even in the current crisis, the German Chancellor does not know how he will act in the end.'"

"Well, exactly. Not only is Hitler unpredictable, but so is Stalin. So far, both are building their forces."

"And whose side will we take?" He sighed sadly. "Again, we'll be like grains ground under millstones."

"Well, I guess neither on the German, nor on the Soviet. If we've defended Poland once, we'll defend it a second time. Maybe this time it won't reject us."

"We'll defend only out of desperation, because we won't be able to resist."

"But, I beg your pardon, after Austria it's Czechoslovakia's turn." He raised his index finger. "Mussolini demanded a plebiscite in the Czech Republic not only for Germans but also for Poles, Hungarians, and other nationalities. And this 'other' nationality is the Ukrainians of Transcarpathia. If they succeed, they could declare their independence. What do you think of that?"

"Not a bad opportunity, Father. But the more I read such news, the more I plunge into incurable pessimism."

"But I don't," he shook his head. "I don't. I believe that this time we'll succeed."

I didn't want to disappoint him in his dreams and hopes, and I shifted the conversation to other topics, and then said goodbye. It was two o'clock when I returned to Lviv and called the editorial office from the train station.

"Where are you been gadding about?" *Pan* Editor exploded.

"I dug up shocking material. Leave me a page in tomorrow's issue."

"Go to hell, not a page! Everything's already planned out."

"The elections will begin in three days. My article should appear tomorrow, otherwise it will all be for nothing. Listen, *Pan* Levko, if my article is delayed for even a day, it won't be worth a potato peel any more. All the work will go out the window. Finally, see for yourself. You've known me forever. I won't make a mountain out of a molehill."

All the while I was chattering, he was muttering unhappily. Finally, he squeezed out:

"Well, ok ... but ... when will you get it to me?"

"I'll bring it to the printer's by ten o'clock in the evening."

"You mean it isn't written yet?" He choked with righteous indignation, but before I came to my senses, I said:

"It's almost finished. I have a handwritten rough draft and need to type everything. No worry, I'll bring it before ten."

"You'd better. At ten sharp I'll order them to typeset the page with the planned material."

"Agreed."

Pfu-u-u! Now full speed ahead and get to work.

CHAPTER 7

"Ah, *Pan* Marko, why are you home so early?" A guard, or what in Lviv they call a *shimon* [doorman], greeted me.

"I have work, and I don't work anywhere as well as I do at home."

"Yes-yes, I know that myself. In your own little nest, it's warmer and cozier than anywhere else."

Pan Ambrozyak was a sweet, respectful old man. Sometimes I exchanged several words with him and treated him to a small glass when he used to come to pay his respects at Christmas or Easter. The guards didn't receive pay but were entitled to a service apartment on the ground floor and collected payments from residents for opening the gate after ten o'clock in the evening. That's why, half an hour before ten on the streets of Lviv you could see great animation. Everyone tried to make it home on time, although it was only a sporting passion, not a show of avarice, because the traditional ten *groschen* coin that the doorman received for opening the gate didn't play an important role, because for this amount of money he could buy either two rolls or a head of cabbage, or a kilo of potatoes. The guards also got something from the street musicians and traveling salesmen who were allowed into the yard, but that was all very little money. *Pani Shimonova* [the doorman's wife] earned more by doing the wash and smoking meats for the entire building before the holidays.

Dlugosz Street rises up to the end of St. Mark's Street, and then descends to Supinsky[15] Street, lined on the left side with stone apartment houses, and on the right, a gray wall, behind which extends the university botanical garden, filled with exotic plants. From my window you can see palm, fig

....

[15]   Dlugosz Street is now Cyril and Methodius Street, St. Mark's Street is now Kobylyanska Street, and Supinsky Street is now Kotsyubynsky Street (author's note).

YURI VYNNYCHUK

and lemon trees in the greenhouses, even a really huge baobab, and if you look closely, you can see colorful birds fluttering. Next to each tree is a sign with the Latin name of the plant. It is said that after having seized Lviv, Charles XII leapt over that wall on a horse, but it had to have been a horse with wings.

Now all dogs make a stop under that wall, and when it gets dark, not just dogs. When I was late for school, the steepness of my little street helped me get there on time. At the bottom there is a small shop "Oil, Nails, Soap, Grease, Shoe Polish." When there are no customers, *Pan* Pokizyak sits in front of the entrance on a little bench and greets everyone passing by. My building rose up on the corner of Dlugosz and St. Mark's Street, probably the steepest street in Lviv, where there is an ancient well with delicious water, which saved the residents of Lviv many times during sieges when the city was cut off from the Dobrostany water-pumping system.

My fingers clattered so enthusiastically on the typewriter that I didn't even notice it was getting dark, so I took a break to rest my eyes and, without turning on the light, went to the window and put a cigarette in my mouth. Twilight flowed from the thickets of the botanical garden and filled the street. A small carriage rumbled and stopped under a streetlamp at the very bottom at the beginning of St. Nicholas Street. The driver unfolded a newspaper, and taking advantage of a shaft of light, became engrossed in reading the news. I struck a match and immediately extinguished it when someone's shadow under the wall caught my attention: a man was lurking behind an acacia tree. I grew still, rolling the cigarette in my mouth, and began to look more closely. Someone was walking down from the upper edge of the street. A shadow from behind the acacia tree came out to meet him. It seemed to be the red-faced stiff who had been watching me before. He glanced impatiently at the gate of my house, then at his watch. When the guy coming down the street from above approached, I recognized my second pursuer. Catching up with each other, they exchanged a few words, glanced in my direction, and began to pace back and forth. I wonder who sent them? Tomashevych or that strange organization?

The article was almost ready. Another hour – and I'd have it done. Then I'll read through it, and then I'll have another half an hour on the way to the printing house on Zelena Street. I shuttered the windows, lit up a lamp, and sat down at my desk. At half past nine I folded the typescript four times and hid it under my shirt behind my back. I put on a windbreaker and in an inside pocket I stuffed in a typescript of an article from last year, which surprisingly had the successful title "From the Life of a Swindler."

My gate did not have an exit to a parallel street. I was forced to exit right by my pursuers. I had a police commissioner acquaintance, Roman Obukh, and I was wondering if it wasn't worth calling him to send someone to protect me. However, this escape plan came to me late, because I couldn't catch him in either in the commandant's office or at home, and I couldn't address such a request to anyone else. It might still be possible to call firefighters and report a fire on the street, but this kind of ruse is undertaken only from a telephone booth, not from an apartment. It would cost me too much.

I turned off the light and looked out the window. The two guys weren't pacing any longer, but noticing that the light had gone out, stood opposite my gate and didn't even pretend to be busy chatting. But I wasn't born yesterday – I've already been in similar situations. However, I won't say that it was pleasant. In fact, my street was seldom crowded, which is the reason I liked it – for its tranquility and melancholy mood. But in this situation, there was nothing attractive about it. Now tranquility had become my enemy. No one would come to my aid. It was painful for me to think about what to do. The clock read twenty-five minutes to ten. Well, there was no way to delay.

I opened a small cupboard in the kitchen where cereals were stored and put two handfuls of peas in my pocket. Then I went downstairs, walked up to the gate quietly so the guard wouldn't hear me, and peered out through a narrow crack. My pursuers stood firm. Suddenly it seemed like they could already see me, because the stiff took his hands out of his pockets. There was something in his right hand. Something small. A revolver? I lingered and glanced at my watch – twenty to ten. Time flies like crazy.

The rattle of utensils and the smell of fried potatoes wafted from the doorman's apartment. His wife was scolding him, and he was defending himself lazily. No, I had no desire to involve them in this – you could expect just about anything from those wild men on the street.

My first thought was to open the gate abruptly and fly out like a bullet into the street. But I prevailed over myself and stepped out of the gate quite calmly, without even glancing at them. I walked, and out of the corner of my eye kept watching my pursuers. They started off at the same time as me.

They walked on the opposite sidewalk for a while, but then they started to cross the street, and I lost them from my field of vision. I just heard their footsteps – one set of heavy, elephantlike ones, the other – really light. I sped up my pace. But their steps behind me were getting closer and closer. They were running faster than me. How did they manage to do that? And there still wasn't a living soul on the street. *Pan* Pokizyak had closed his shop and turned off the lights.

Behind my back I could already hear their strained heavy breathing and sniffling. Apparently, we were separated by no more than two meters. I felt heat on my shoulders. Well, it's time... And I jerked away like a stallion in a race. I ran with all the might I could muster, putting all my strength into it. I kept running, and my eyes looked at the saving light of the lamp post at the spot where my street ended, and although the carriage had already left, it still must be crowded there, and I could already discern individual figures, illuminated by shop windows.

I could hear my pursuers panting heavily, closing in on me. Then I threw the peas behind me. One of the guys slipped and plopped down, but quickly rose back on his feet and, pouring out curses, continued the chase. Suddenly someone jumped out in front of me. Having tripped over his leg, I did a stunning somersault, and fell hard on the pavement, gasping. The blow took my breath away. And in a moment, they were searching me all over, and although I hadn't yet fully recovered, I was desperately trying to protect the inside pocket of my windbreaker. This provoked my attackers, and after a short struggle they finally made their way to my pocket and took the papers.

"Here it is!" One of them exclaimed, glancing at the headline.

"Well, what are you waiting for?" The second one added, and the one he was talking to took a swing at me. In his hand was the small object that I had already noticed – a metal pipe.

In a moment he'd lower it onto my poor head and I'd be in Lalaland, dreaming of twinkling stars and flashes of falling meteorites until morning. I threw my hands in front of me – that was all I could do, but the blow was late. Suddenly there was a muffled scream and noisy rattling. Something crunched and someone's body fell on my legs. I crawled back and couldn't believe my eyes: several men were ruthlessly beating each other up. The one who had fallen on my legs, the scrawny, tall guy squatted down, and staggering and spitting blood, ran into the darkness. The stiff struggled to break away from that unfriendly company and also fled. Three strangers out of breath remained beside me. One of them asked:

"Do you have the article?"

"Yes."

I recognized the voice of the guy who had given me Dutchak's address.

"Thank God," he helped me to my feet. "It seems that we managed to get here in time. Did they really pound you?"

"No-no," I said, brushing off my clothes. "I just hit the pavement hard."

"But they pulled something out of your pocket."

"That's an old article. I deliberately hid it in my jacket. And here's the right one." I patted myself on the back.

"Are you going to the printing house?"

I looked at my watch – it was eight to ten.

"If I can make it."

"We'll drop you off by car."

The car was around the corner.

"How did you manage in time?" I asked.

"We were taking a walk nearby. We saw someone's trying to hammer someone. Well, so we ran up."

"You won't tell me where you're from?"

"I've already told you."

"Such an organization doesn't exist."

"And you try to imagine that it does, and everything will fall into place. It's easier that way."

The driver, apparently, was an incredible daredevil. He drove like a mad-man and the brakes were screeching on turns.

"And the ones who attacked me are Tomashevych's people?" I asked. Probably."

"I can imagine their mugs when they bring that article to their boss. What do you think will be his next step?"

"He'll send his boys to the printing house," my savior replied quite casually.

"What?" I grew numb. "Would Tomashevych go even that far?"

"Why not? This time they can bring their heaters. What would you do to them with your bare hands?"

"There's a security guard."

"That old coot? Don't make me laugh."

"Damn... I'll call the police."

"And what? Two grumpy old guys will come, hang around for about an hour, explain that evidently not everyone's at home, and then take off."

"What is a way out?"

"Add a few more words to the end of your article."

"A few words? What kind?"

"Absolutely innocent ones. And I'll be on guard with the boys at the printing house until morning. We have some things we can greet visitors with."

"So, what should I add?"

He dictated, I jotted it down, and was amazed:

"And that's all?"

"Of course. Did you expect something special?"

"Do these words mean anything to you?"

"We want it to be clear – that Tomashevych has left the arena for good. So that no one doubts that he'd face a trial. Well, here we've arrived. Good luck."

"Thank you for everything," I said as I got out of the car. "Will we ever see each other again?"

"Who knows? Lviv is a small world."

The editor was already waiting for me and hurriedly snatched the article from my hands and began to read it, occasionally hmming, cursing, and aha-ing, and after reading the next page, he immediately passed it to the compositors. When he finished, he looked at me with sympathy and sighed:

"Well, I don't know.... I don't know how this is going to end. But if Tomashevych sues, you'll have to go to the slammer this time."

So he hinted at the occasions when he was forced to serve time, because the editors couldn't afford to pay the fine.

I stayed in the printing house all night. We didn't know if anyone tried to stop us, because the compositing machines were drumming so loudly that nothing suspicious reached our ears.

The newspapers appeared at dawn, and I finally breathed a sigh of relief. Everything was behind me. I went to the sink, splashed cold water on my face several times, then wiped myself with a clean sheet of paper and sensed I was just falling off my feet.

"Be well, guys!" I shouted. "Tell the boss not to bother me until noon."

Dawn greeted me with the loud chirping of birds. The city had just begun to wake up. The street sweepers had just stopped rustling their brooms and were scattering to their nooks. I walked with a sense of accomplishment, happily imagining how my article was being read by those who were standing behind Tomashevych and by Tomashevych himself. But that wasn't the end. I had no idea that the end was still really far away and that today was just the beginning of real trouble.

THE SECOND DAY
FRIDAY
SEPTEMBER 23, 1938

CHAPTER 1

I was awakened by a phone call. Damnation! They still wouldn't let me get any sleep, but looking at my watch, I calmed down – it's one! Six hours of sleep is even more than I expected to get. For that reason, I immediately took an unspeakable liking to the unknown person who woke me up just in time. The editor was calling. His voice was gloomy and hoarse. I had the impression that instead of me, that he was the one who spent the whole night at the printing house. His first words made me slump into my chair and feel my blood run cold. I spasmodically swallowed sticky saliva and wheezed:

"Re-repeat that...."

"I repeat: an hour ago Tomashevych was found dead. He shot himself."

"Wait a second, I just...."

I rushed into the bathroom, stuck my head under the faucet, shook it, and felt everything fall into place again. Then I returned and put the phone to my ear again:

"Where was he found?"

"In Bryukhovychi. He has a villa[16] there. Right now your buddy Commissioner Obukh is coming over to see you. I told him you were snoozing at home. Did I make a mistake?" You could sense mockery in his voice.

"Oh, not at all. Sooner or later, he'd find me anyway."

"Marko," he said now with warmth and parental concern.

"What?"

"You're a hero! Do you hear? I'm shaking your mitts."

....

[16]   Here are samples of villas in Lviv designed by architect Mykhailo Kovalchuk: https://photo-lviv.in.ua/villy-scho-jih-zbuduvav-kovalchuk/.

Pops! He knew when to cheer me up and when to smack me on the head. At that moment I could have kissed him.

"Thanks. I didn't know it would turn out like this."

"It's okay. It'd be worse if such a chump made it to the top. The ending hit home – as if you were looking into a crystal ball. Well, great. Will you be in tomorrow?

"Uh-huh."

"Goodbye."

I put the kettle on the burner and had a smoke. How did he say it? "The ending hit home?" I repeated it aloud and then realized: those words at the end! Now I see! Martyniuk was telling the truth: I fell into a cleverly prepared trap. I simply gave Tomashevych a cue how to get out of the situation – to shoot himself. Because those few words had no ambiguity. They sounded completely clear:

"Well, there is only one prospect for *Pan* Tomashevych now. Inexorable, inevitable, and true... the solution was hiding there in a desk drawer."

Of course! But I thought we were talking about prison! And a hint at the fact that verified documents of the candidate for the position of president of the city were kept in a desk drawer. Which he must now destroy and withdraw from the election. That's what I thought. But it wasn't about prison.

I poured myself a cup of coffee and sat by the window. It was drizzling outside the window. In a few minutes Obukh staggered in, wet as a drowned rat.

"I've just come from there," he explained. "I got soaking wet while I was searching around the villa. Give me a bathrobe. Let everything dry out. We're going to have a long conversation. So, make me some coffee too. And a sandwich wouldn't go amiss."

I made him some coffee, spread some butter on bread, and put cheese on top. He changed into my robe and wrapped himself up like a doll.

"I'm as cold as ice. Give me something stronger."

"How about some 'Stock' from Bachevsky's[17]?"

"Just what I need. Did your boss call you?"

"Of course."

"Did you get some sleep?"

....

[17]   Bachevsky's was the leading distillery in Lviv at the time.

"I was at the printing house all night."

"What the devil? They couldn't do it without you, could they?"

"I'll tell you everything now."

"Let me first." He tilted his glass, took a bite of the sandwich, sipped his coffee, and said, "First I need to tell you that you are a top-notch swine. To know each other for so many years, and not a peep from your lips. At least if you had handed me the materials you collected yesterday, I wouldn't have let him slip out of my hands so easily. After all, this isn't how friends do things. Haven't I helped you enough? It seems that we agreed a long time ago to share information. Am I saying something that's incorrect?"

"Yes, but the elections were coming soon, and I was in a hurry. The newspaper needed a scandal."

"That's no excuse. I see you're still playing some kind of superhero. Of course, it's nice to feel like the one who saves the day, but everything has its limitations. If you had half a brain, you'd amount to something, but this way.... In short, you're a good-for-nothing. But what's there here to chew over.... Spill the beans, lay it out in order. I'm listening carefully."

"Everything's in the article."

"Well, don't make pops crazy. We know how it really is. Tell me how you took up the case, where you found the documents, and so on."

"It started with the fact that some stranger called and offered to meet me in Jesuit Park. There he handed me this folder and told me from whom I could learn more about Tomashevych's past."

Obukh took the folder and looked at the pictures with interest.

"Did you see him?" he asked.

"He was standing behind me. However, I looked a little at his reflection in the puddle. But later he approached me openly, apparently after he was convinced that I had swallowed the bait. I got the lowdown from Martyniuk."

I told Obukh everything without hiding even yesterday's incident. He listened without interruption. He always knew how to listen. We used to be like two peas in a pod. As young men we joined the Sixth Rifle Division of the Army of the Ukrainian National Republic under Colonel Marko Bezruchko's command. How old were we then? Fifteen. But our voices were already deepening, our mustaches were growing, and we lied about being eighteen. We survived the siege of Zamostya in 1920, and together we executed raids at night, killing sleepy Budyonny[18] army guys. We received medals for the defense of Zamostya, but we couldn't enter a Ukrainian university because one didn't exist. We were forced to study at the Secret Ukrainian University. Romko studied law and I studied philosophy. When the university was disbanded, we took classes in Prague. Upon our return to Lviv, each followed his own path. I went to work for a newspaper, and Romko, thanks to his front-line service, was able to become a police commissioner. He'll probably make it to retirement as a police commissioner, because he's got no chance to become an inspector, unless he converts to Catholicism. Needless to say, my buddy got me out of jams on more than one occasion, and more than one time he saved my life, because some force constantly pushed me to get into a pickle with a zilch as a reward.

"Yeah, you got burned!" He exclaimed happily after listening to my story. "And I've said many times that your independent actions won't lead to anything good. Well, well, you got into the car with them, and what happened next?"

"While we were riding in the car, I asked what Tomashevych would do now, and the guy said: he's gonna send his boys to the printing house. Of course, I didn't like that...But he offered to be on the look-out all night long with his boys. And for that to happen I needed to add several words."

"Aha! Was it by any chance something like "the solution was hiding in a desk drawer?" I nodded guiltily. "Now can you guess what solution was hidden in his desk drawer?"

"Now I can figure it out – there must have been a revolver. Someone must have known that he kept it in there."

"Hey! You don't have to be as wise as Solomon to figure it out. Most of them keep their weapons there so that they can be within reach." Obukh got up and began to pace the room. He had to hold the robe with his hands, because his athletic body could barely fit in it. "Then you, Marko, have been messed over roy-yally. And look, Martyniuk immediately figured it out. That's a smart boy. Not like you, dumbo. To hell with that!" He stopped in front of me. "I could give you a good whack now! But I still need you. Even

....

[18]   Semyon Budyonny was a Russian Red Army military commander during the Russian Civil War and World War II, who became closely allied to Stalin.

without those missing marbles. And just think! It didn't even occur to you to get in touch with me!"

"What do you mean? It did, when I saw from the window that they were tailing me. I even phoned you."

Obukh poured himself some more cognac and sat down on the couch.

"Ye-es, let's put everything in place. Someone needed Tomashevych to kick the bucket. But delicately and without too much of a ruckus. To kill is complicated, you get into trouble. So, then they decide to stage a suicide. In order to do this, they set on you. And like a greyhound sensing the scent of scandal, you launch an attack. And here you are publishing your bombshell article. Tomashevych reads it, feverishly looking for a way out. Big trouble! Dreams of the presidency are over! Life goes off the rails! But the ending, like every ending, is especially memorable. There's a way out. It's in the desk drawer. Tomashevych goes to the villa, takes the revolver and shoots himself in the mouth."

"In the mouth?"

"Didn't I tell you? But here, my dear friend, not everything fits together. If you were in Tomashevych's shoes would you shoot yourself?"

"Mmm...," I thought. "I don't know."

"Imagine – you're Tomashevych. Your political career has taken a turn for the worse. A trial awaits you. But the court is just a formality. You'll only lose about twenty or thirty thousand *zloty*. And what's such a small amount of money to him now? That's when he was just starting off in his career. That was big money then and it meant a lot to him then. Now with all his estates it's a drop in the ocean. Well, a career.... But with his money! To hell with the career. He can go wherever he wants and start all over again."

"What are you leading to?"

"To you being a dolt of the king of heaven." Those few words that you think played a crucial role are worth diddly-squat. Those guys would have been waiting for you all night anyway. They needed your article to appear at all costs. And do you know why? Because they planned to kill Tomashevych beforehand. Is that clear now? Your article was supposed to explain the reason for his suicide. By the way, it was masterfully prepared. To explain to everyone, but just not to me. I'm not missing that marble."

"But where's the evidence?"

"There is no evidence."

"Then it's just your imagination."

"A criminologist without imagination is like a priest without an incense burner. There, at the villa, I found nothing. But I saw the villa itself. A man who has that kind of wealth won't shoot himself because of some trifle. There were scandals that were much worse, and no one shot himself.

"So, you think he was killed? But for what reason?"

"If I knew that, I'd have figured out who did it. In general, you know, this is just a suspicion. I don't have a penny's worth of evidence. Common sense simply won't let me accept the explanation of suicide."

"Will you do an investigation?"

"He-he! My friend! I'm just simple commissioner Obukh with a salary[19] of three hundred thirty five *zloty* and I do what I'm told by *Pan* Inspector who has a salary of seven hundred *zloty*, and who listens intently to what *Pan* Superintendent tells him with the same salary or *Pan* Chief of Police with a salary of a thousand *zloty*. I was ordered to submit a report on the fact of his suicide today. So, I can't blow hot air. Because tomorrow I have more important things to handle. For example, the church robbery in Vynnyky."

"And have you – already shared your suspicions with anyone?"

"There was no need to share. Our commandant, Inspector Wladyslaw Gozdziewski, and the head of the counterintelligence staff, Konarsky, came across me at the villa as I was rummaging around the building. If you are dealing with a suicide, an obvious suicide, then what fool would look for someone's footprints in the garden?"

"But wait...," I became wary, "the chief of the counterintelligence staff?"

"Can you imagine?"

"Who the devil brought him there?"

"So, I thought about that. Someone had searched the desk at which Tomashevych was sitting. There was a royal mess in the drawers. Scattered folders and papers lay on the floor. On the bookshelf all the books were turned upside down. Someone was looking for something there. In the basement, too, there were traces of a search. Apparently, they were looking for something of interest to counterintelligence. From what I know Tomashevych had frequent contacts with Germany."

....

[19] The amounts would be their monthly salaries.

"Well, well, what about the commandant?"

"He called me and asked: 'What are you doing, ducky?' I say, 'I'm looking for clues.' 'What kind?' 'I don't know yet.' He exchanged glances with the head of counterintelligence and said: 'I want the report on my desk by seven o'clock. About the suicide.' It turned out that he had already talked to doctors and a ballistics expert. They all agreed: Tomashevych shot himself. But, as I understood, he hadn't just talked to them, otherwise he wouldn't have been so confident."

"Didn't you find anything that supported your version?"

"I found some things. Newspapers are distributed to institutions before eight o'clock. At eight o'clock, Tomashevych comes to the office, sits down at his desk, and reviews the press. He does this every day. It's hard to tell when he gets to your article. Most likely immediately, because the beginning of it is already on the front page. The review of the press lasts mostly just half an hour. So, he reads about himself, and then what? Do you think he immediately kindles the desire to shoot himself? He gets up, runs to the car, and rushes to the villa? No. He leaves the office at nine o'clock. What was he doing for so long? Considering his situation? Calling someone? Destroying any papers? There's a pot-bellied stove in the office, but there was no ash on the papers, just combustion... But...." Obukh straightened up and looked at me as if there was a hint written on my forehead.

"But he could have done it before! After all, he already knew about your article. And there was no need to go into a panic at the office. He also seemed to know what the article was about. Why the hell schlepp to the office at all? That very morning, after he was told that they had failed to prevent the issue from coming out, he could have gone to his villa.... Of course, one could think that he was still hesitating, that it was that ending that finished him off. But that's ridiculous. In short, at half past nine he leaves the office. It's raining. But it's just a tiny drizzle. Many people don't pay any attention to such a slight mist at all. And what does our suicide do? He goes to the store and buys an umbrella. And not just any one, the cheapest but the one with a carved handle with gilded spikes on it, you know. And he walks further under the umbrella to his car, so that God forbid he doesn't catch a cold before his death. Then.... On the way, he buys a bouquet of chrysanthemums from a florist, adorned with decorative asparagus and boxwood."

"Do you buy that for yourself for your own death?"

"Of course, it's ridiculous. The road to the villa takes half an hour. His death occurred at half past ten."

"How do you know about the umbrella?"

"Because it was wet, and his clothes were dry. And he didn't even remove the price tag. On the living room table, I found an empty bottle of champagne, four oranges, peels from another four, and an empty box of expensive *Nova Fortuna* [New Fortune] chocolates. There were also two glasses. But only one had been used. On the dresser lay a thick paper bag from *Aiaks* [Ajax], from which he laid out the treats. So, he brought it with him. For what? Was he expecting guests? Who do you think might be treated to champagne, oranges, and sweets?"

"Some dish."

"That's what I think. He has a wonderful selection of booze in his credenza, but he doesn't have any champagne or aperitif. If a man had come for a visit, the host would treat him to what he had, and not bring champagne.... Now the question is: who drank the champagne and ate the candy? Tomashevych or his guest? Furthermore, in the bath I found a wet toothbrush. So, before he died, he had also brushed his teeth. You get that? Everything indicated that he was preparing for a dame to visit."

"The brush could have been wet from that morning."

"No, because he didn't spend the night at the villa. His apartment is downtown in the city center. He brushed his teeth again. Maybe she doesn't like the smell of tobacco. In addition, he also trimmed his mustache! I noticed hairs on the mirror. There were traces of a recently used bottle of cologne and mouthwash on the bottle. Nope, there's no way a dame wasn't there."

"Do you think a woman shot him?"

"Maybe. That also happens."

"So, you decided to investigate it anyway?"

"Officially, no. But unofficially, I'll dig around a little myself. The only thing is that I need your help here. I can't, like you, go from one end of the city to the other searching for evidence. You can go nuts: the commandant's office posted a list of one hundred and forty pubs, where the police should go only because of some risky adventure, but I can't just go in and have a beer. And before getting married, a police officer must present his bride to his superiors along with a certificate of morality."

"Aha! That's why you haven't married yet!" I laughed. "Is there a problem with unmarried young ladies being immoral?"

"Come on! When a pauper gets married at last, even the night goes too fast. There's not enough time to scratch your ass. So, what – will you help?"

"Well, it's not like I don't have enough work."

"Explain to the editor that you're preparing another bombshell. You're a hero today, and the ball is in your court."

He got up and went to the bathroom to change. I sat and thought about it. Maybe it's worth doing. And what if Obukh isn't mistaken?"

He returned merry and animated. He looked out the window – and it had stopped raining.

"Well, that's wonderful," he said, not even waiting for me to agree. Only you know this yourself, be careful. Don't share your speculations with anyone. When you have something – give me a call. Here are the keys to my car. It'll save you a lot of time."

"And you?"

"A police car's enough for me."

"You didn't tell me how you learned about the suicide."

"*Pan* Tsikhovsky called. An older gentleman. He passed by the villa, saw Tomashevych's car, and decided to ask for a ride if he was going to Lviv at that time. Because this had happened more than once. This Tsikhovsky also did various favors for Tomashevych. So, he rang the doorbell and waited, but no one came out. Then he noticed that the door was ajar and went inside. He saw Tomashevych lying there dead and called using the deceased's phone. It was eleven ten. Then he waited for the police."

"Does he live nearby?"

"Yes, but you can't see the villa from his windows. It's surrounded by pine trees. Absolutely no one can see the windows of that villa."

"Where should I start?"

"Drive over to Bryukhovychi. He bought champagne, oranges and sweets on the way. But, first, oranges are very rare in September, and second – they don't have any stickers. Which means they're contraband. Do you know that pub with a colonial goods store on Holosko Street in front of the church?"

"*Pan* Gubsky's?"

"Yes. He always has something special. Actually, mostly contraband. You can also have coffee and a snack there. I used to buy something there, and he also packed it up for me in an *Aiaks* [Ajax] bag."

"A company that no longer exists."

"Right. The company was liquidated, and their products were pilfered by anyone who took the trouble. However, I never see those bags anywhere else."

CHAPTER 2

The editorial office of the Polish newspaper *Wieku Nowego* was noisy. Everyone tried to clap me on the back and shake my hand. I was looking for Gennady Zbezhkhovsky, but he hadn't shown up yet.

"He's probably playing the piano at the Atlas Restaurant."

"No, isn't it too early?" I was surprised.

"Well, then he must be writing something for us, because he's supposed to turn it in by seven."

I went to the Atlas. Despite the fact that it was a long time until evening, the restaurant was buzzing, but not with the usual bohemian voices that appeared later, but with the chirping of merchants and stockbrokers, and the loud voice of the owner, *Pan* Edzyo Tarlersky, triumphed over everyone else's. Genyo really was scratching something on the napkins.

"Genyo, howdy. Are you writing a poem again?"

"Ah, Marko! Howdy. Have a seat, old chap. Actually, I was thinkin' 'bout who to wet my whistle with, because, as you can see, our guys haven't yet dragged their way over here yet. God himself sent you to me today."

"Yup, 'cause I was lookin' for you."

I sat down at the table and nodded to the waiter to bring me some absinthe.

"Hey, man, give me a smoke!" Genyo said, raising his glass.

"Our editor's havin' conniptions today that you don't work for him."

"Remind him that he once booted me out on my butt."

"You think he doesn't remember? He does – that's for sure! He even told me to roll over your way and try to gauge whether you'd come back to us."

"Of course, it's tempting, because you pay more. But it'd be vile to do that to *Novy Chas*[20] [New Time] when they picked me up."

"Yes, you're right. My uncle always used to teach me: hold on to the thicker end of the rope. But you drove a guy to his own death!" He shook his head. "It's a special case. Though cruel."

"You say that as if I wanted to do that."

"You didn't want to? The ending of the article suggests the opposite. But no, I'm not blaming you, God forbid. You saved the state a lot of moolah. Because it would have been forced to cover expenses for the trial, for prison, for food for him. And so a bullet in the trap instead of a pill, and it's kaput."

"But just so you know, that ending doesn't belong to me," I defended myself, not understanding whether he was mocking me or speaking seriously.

"Oh really?" He was genuinely surprised. "Not to you? What – did *Pan* Editor add it? Or the typographers?" It seemed he was still pulling my leg.

"No. They dictated it to me in exchange for guarding us all night until the newspaper was published. To be honest, they very cunningly took advantage of me. Now I'm sorry I got involved. And, if you don't yak about it to anyone, I'll tell you more."

"You know me – I'm dependable. I'm listening carefully." He leaned over to me and shut his eyes.

"There's a suspicion that Tomashevych was killed. The article couldn't in any way incite him to suicide: it only destroyed his ambitions. But life could continue on and on."

I had no doubt that Genyo would spread my words everywhere, whether necessary or unnecessary. But the rumor of murder, not suicide, would be useful for Obukh's investigation. Human opinion sometimes influences such things quite positively.

"You don't say?" Genyo wondered. "Is that so? But I won't make a peep. And why were you looking for me?"

"I wanted to ask something about Tomashevych."

"Get out of here! Doesn't he stop being of interest to you, even after he's died?"

....

[20]   According to an author's note, this was a Ukrainian newspaper that was published from 1923-1939.

"Yes, there's something suspicious. You once visited his villa when he was holding a reception. I remember you dedicated a poem to him."

"Ahhh, but when they pay so well I could dedicate a poem even to a pug. And he had the kind of wife you lick your fingers over."

"Already a widow.... poor thing."

"What poor thing? Lately they haven't been living together."

"What do you mean?"

"Tomashevych took up with a mistress. The dumb stump. To have such a babe and then two-time her? His wife, from a wealthy family, made a peach out of that villa. Irena fitted everything out at her own expense, furnished it with luxurious furniture and carpets, and tidied up the garden. Now it's a feast for the eyes."

"Wait ... So he didn't buy the villa, but his wife did?"

"I'm telling you, you blockhead, she did. When they got married, Tomashevych was only able to buy himself an old barn. He hit it big later."

I felt the whole pyramid of my accusations against Tomashevych slowly beginning to crumble. It's possible that if it had gone to court, it might not have been possible to prove that he had hidden some money. Obukh may be right – there was no reason to commit suicide.

"And then what?" I muttered, completely discouraged.

"Then Irena suspected that he had a mistress, and left him, and demanded the villa back. He refused. Then she hired a private snoop. He followed him with his mistress. There were even some pictures. Irena filed for divorce to get free and have the villa returned to her. But she lost the case."

"Do you know who the snoop was?"

"Why wouldn't I? Bodyo Kvartsyany. When he doesn't drink, you can have a normal chitchat with him. Maybe he'll tell you more. If you pay, of course. Do you know him?"

"I know him. We went to school together, but I haven't talked to him for a long time. Where can I find him?"

"He has an office now on Copernicus Street. If you go now, you'll still find him sober."

I didn't delay. Bodyo changed the location of his office depending on his financial situation. The present one, though downtown, was in a partial basement and looked really sad. A peeling, faded corridor and a wooden floor with worn-out paint led to it. Apparently, things were not going very well for Bodyo. Although there were still funds to pay for a secretary, albeit a terrible one, because a thin middle-aged redheaded woman with big glasses was standing in the door in my way. Her long nose and clenched lips attested to the incurable character of a shrew and to the maternal instinct she had toward her boss.

"You-f-for...," she began, piercing me with a stern look, letting me know with her entire appearance that I had broken something in the coordinated mechanism of this respectable institution, but I interrupted her.

"Yes.... I'm here to see Kvartsyany."

Without adding the word "*pan*," I put her off balance. The hot lava of indignation began to rise from the secret depths of her being.

"But he's busy. Please, sir, it's written on the door when – here she emphasized *Pan* (!!!) – Kvartsyany, is taking visitors. Unless you...."

But I had already squeezed past her body, that had long been yearning for love, and headed for the door that led to the office. Her prattling followed me:

"But please, *pan*! I beg you!"

I didn't pay attention to her spluttering. I found the boss at a desk cluttered with newspapers and folders, and on the open surface he had placed photographs and was studying them, armed with a large magnifying glass. Small, round, with a bulging little belly and sneaky eyes, now he looked like a predator who had hunted a cherished prey and was determining from which end to begin feasting.

"Oh, *Pan* Reporter!" He muttered, in far from a friendly manner, deftly covering the photos with newspapers. "And what has brought you to me? You haven't bothered me in a long time."

I sat across from him and looked curiously around the office, which was filled with cabinets with folders, most of which I thought were empty and were meant to impress clients. A calendar hung on the wall, and next to it in a frame under glass was a private detective's license. Above them there was a portrait of Józef Pilsudski[21] by a provincial painter who used a paintbrush instead of an artist's brush.

"Tomashevych," I said, under the impatient gaze of my host.

....

[21]   Polish statesman (1867-1935) and the first chief of state of the newly independent Poland in 1918.

"Ha-ha-ha!" He couldn't contain himself. "That isn't enough for you?" You drove him to the grave and now you keep digging further?"

He rubbed his fat chin with his hand and studied me with his tiny piercing eyes for a minute. Apparently, he just didn't have enough words to express his indignation at my audacity, and since all the words he needed were scattered somewhere, he had no choice but to think about what I had just told him.

"Who did you imagine yourself to be?" He finally squeezed out. "Who are you, that I would share some information with you just like that? What –you think you have Lady Luck on your side? Eh, ducky, you still have to learn and keep learning. That's why...," he tapped his fingers nervously on the table.

"I'm your potential client – that's who I am." I interrupted his tirade and smiled sweetly.

His eyes bugged out.

"You want to hire me?"

"No. But I'll pay you for what you did a long time ago. Can you imagine how profitable it is to get a fee for something totally unexpected?"

He clearly brightened up and fidgeted in his chair.

"Well, well, what would that be?"

"I'm interested in his mistress."

"Yeah! And how much will you give me?"

"Depending on what I get."

"And it depends on how much you pay," he laughed, rubbing his hands contentedly.

"Well, tell me your price."

"Twenty *zloty*."

He's really not doing very well if he's asking for so little. I was ready to give him more.

"All right," I said. "Agreed. Well, so tell me."

"What are you interested in?"

"When did Tomashevych's wife turn to you?"

"Two months ago. She gave me their photos and explained to me where to find them. But they didn't hide much. At first, they looked like lovers. They sat in pubs, strolled in the park, and went to the villa. Such a, you know, sweet couple. Her name is Emilia. She's still really young. Seventeen or eighteen. She's as beautiful as a doll, and her parents are poor. So, she clung to the rich man with all her heart. She played her role perfectly."

"Do you have the impression that she wasn't in love with him?"

"I wouldn't say impression, but belief. More than once, I noticed that she was looking at some young fellas. Sometimes she even smiled at them when they winked at her or gave signs to suggest that they should get together.... One of them pointed a finger at his watch, then pointed at the same place where they were sitting, and then showed eight fingers. That is, he'd be waiting for her at eight. And she, instead of frowning and turning away, smiled, and tried to explain something, moving her lips silently, and just using gestures. What it was, I couldn't see from my location, but I could see that fella nodding. Apparently, they came to an agreement. They both still kept smiling, and then Tomashevych returned from the water closet, and she bestowed her charming smile on him. Oh-h, I tell you, that's a rogue!"

"Where did that happen?"

"At The Carlton next to the Industrial Museum. Most often met they there, but they still used to go to The Victoria and The Vienna."

"So you don't know how that flirtation ended?"

"No way! I wasn't interested in her."

"And how long did you monitor their meetings?"

"For two weeks."

"What about his wife?"

"Irena, too, by the way, is a doll, I'll tell you. In her early thirties, tall, slender, with a large bust. She planned on winning back the villa and getting a divorce. I helped as much as I could. I don't understand why he latched onto that village girl."

"Is she a village girl?"

"Well, from Kryvchytsi! As a child, she used to take cows to pasture and tend geese."

"So where does she live?"

"He rented her a domicile on Syktuska Street, number six, apartment number four. But she won't stay there long, because who'll keep paying the rent? Unless she does what all former mistresses do when they're jilted, get hired as a maid for a family, then give in to the will of the master of the house, and then get tossed out into the street over a scandal. And on the street – we know what happens...."

"So, do you have a file on them?"

"Of course. I have everything recorded in detail. I always keep copies for myself, because who knows what might happen in the future."

He got up, went to a cabinet, took out a folder, and placed it down in front of me. I opened it. There were records of where and when Tomashevych met his mistress. There were also photos. Lots of photos. Emilia was indeed extraordinarily beautiful. Her face gave the impression of a kind of innocent little angel with dimples on her cheeks and pouty lips. As she sat at a table, her figure with her narrow waist resembled an hourglass.

"I'll take that with me," I said.

"Ehe! Not a chance," he wanted to take the folder, but I deftly raked it onto my lap.

"I'll look it over carefully and return it to you. Don't worry."

"You know, if I trusted everyone this way, I wouldn't be sitting here."

"I'm not everyone. And you know that. Here's your fee. I'll return the folder in two days."

He grimaced but took the money.

"You know," he told me contentedly, "things have gotten better for me. I'm thinking of hiring an assistant. You'd fit in with me."

I left his office with a satisfied look on my face and in return the secretary looked me over with the gaze of a lioness, from whom a chunk of antelope had just been swiped.

CHAPTER 3

I brought the folder home, and then went to Syktuska Street. The old doorman opened the gate and measured me with a studying look:

"Who are you here to see?"

"*Panna* [Miss] Emilia."

"Oh!" He was quite surprised and even adjusted his glasses to get a better look. "Are you from the police?"

"Private detective," I said, pointing to my ID, which Obukh had arranged for me.

The private detective moniker usually commands more respect than that of a journalist or even of a policeman.

"Aha, then you're probably working on the Tomashevych matter?" He guessed.

"So, you've heard already?"

"It was just on the radio."

"Did you know him well?"

"Did I know him?! Know is a strong word. He used to come here to visit from time to time. Such a courteous gentleman. He used to put all ten *groschen* coins in my hand, even though he came during the day. Such woe, such woe. Probably lost at cards? What do you think?" He looked at me hopefully, waiting for something interesting.

"I don't know," I said. "The investigation is still ongoing. But when it's all over, then everything will be in the newspapers, no doubt."

"I'd have no doubt! But, you know, there's an itch to find out everything, as they say, firsthand. Because honestly, I would have voted for him. Because I think this way: if someone is generous to an individual, then he will be generous to everyone. What do you have to say?"

"An original idea. When I hear of something fresh, I'll definitely let you know."

It's always worth being polite to those guards, because they usually know a lot of interesting things. I went up to the second floor and rang the doorbell. From behind the door the sound of a gentle female voice resonated:

"Who is it?"

"Police.

The door opened and before it slammed shut I immediately put my foot over the threshold. A beauty with disheveled chestnut hair gave me a cold look and tried to close the door. She realized I wasn't a policeman, but I had already burst my way inside."

"And it's better for you. I'm a private detective, but I cooperate with the police."

She twirled the ID in front of her as she looked it over, and then returned it.

"And what's that supposed to mean?"

"You understand that private detectives have the same resources as the police. But it's in your best interest to have a chat with me instead of at the commissioner's office."

She retreated showing no enthusiasm and started moving forward, adjusting her robe which was printed with attractive Chinese landscapes – curly pines, huts with curved roofs, mountains in the fog. She was tall and nice looking. The photos I had seen didn't exaggerate her looks. I walked behind her and admired her shapeliness, thanks to which all those landscapes seemingly came to life. Pines swayed, mists floated, mountains steamed, and the huts skipped. In the living room she sat down on the couch and pointed to the armchair for me to sit. On a small table there was an open bottle of cognac, a large box of candy, and a glass. I felt she was already high. Her eyes were red with tears.

"What do you need?" she asked. "Are you the one who followed us?"

"No, I'm not. But I've seen the pictures. I'm interested in something else: were you at the villa this morning?"

"Why would I have been there?"

"And when was the last time you were there?"

"Last week. I've rarely been there at all."

"And when was the last time you saw Tomashevych?"

"The day before yesterday at seven we went to dinner at the Grand Hotel, sat there for about an hour, then he had some kind of business to attend to, and we said goodbye."

"How did you find out about his death?"

"From the radio.... I can't believe that Yanus[22] shot himself.... That bitch drove him to it.... Add also that deceitful article. Why did he do it? He had the kind of lawyers that would have that newspaper shredded along with whoever wrote it."

After those words, she burst into uncontrollable tears. And I thought it would be good for me not to admit who I really was. I waited until she calmed down and poured her some cognac. She shook her head.

"I've had enough.... though...," she took the glass, made a sip, and started sobbing again. "It's her! She killed him.... With her lawsuits and scandals...."

"You mean his wife?"

"Who else could it be!"

"So, you didn't call Tomashevych today?"

"Why should I call him since we agreed on the day after tomorrow. We were supposed to drive to Stryi."

"Why Stryi?"

"He had some business there. And I was going to keep him company."

"Did Tomashevych have another companion like you?"

"I don't know."

"Someone called him at work in the morning, and he immediately drove to the villa. He bought oranges, champagne and chocolate candies. He laid them all out on a table. And waited."

"For me? What are you saying? I can't stand champagne. "Because I.... because of....," she hesitated, "Well, you know."

"You break wind?"

She was embarrassed and nodded. So, it wasn't her who called Tomashevych?

"If it wasn't you, then who was he waiting for at the villa?"

She shrugged. Her lips started to quiver.

"I don't know. Maybe Irena. Maybe she proposed something to him."

....

[22]   Yanek and Yanus are diminutives for the name Yan (Jan in Polish). The Ukrainian language has a penchant for using diminutive forms.

"For example?"

"For example, an amicable agreement."

"How do you imagine that? Tomashevych buys treats, waits for the visit of his wife or some other woman, and suddenly shoots himself without waiting for her to arrive? No. He was waiting for someone. Someone drank champagne, nibbled on those chocolates. Are you going to say that Tomashevych did this?"

She was hiding something. It was evident she was nervous as she fixed the folds of her robe.

"I don't know...," she uttered sadly. "The police declared that it was suicide." She looked at me and squinted.

"And you don't believe it?"

"Not really. Have you read the article?"

"No. On the radio they said that it might have influenced him. But I'm not planning on reading it. Why don't you believe it was suicide?"

"Because he wasn't there alone. Someone else was. Someone was looking for something."

What did Tomashevych like to drink?"

"Everything...."

"What did he drink most often?"

"Cognac, but he drank wine and champagne, though rarely."

"And stuffed himself with candy?"

She smiled.

"No, I didn't notice that about him. But Irena loves candies."

"How do you know?"

"Because Yanus once treated me and said that they were Irena's favorite candy. That she only nibbles on them with wine."

"And champagne?"

"And champagne. She loves champagne."

"And could she have downed a whole bottle?"

She shrugged.

"If I can drink half a bottle of cognac, then why wouldn't she be able to drink a bottle of champagne? And I'm not drunk." She looked at me intently. "Or am I?"

"Seemingly no. What kind of sweets were they.... Irena's favorites...."

She nodded toward the table on which there was a box with the image of a painting by Arkhip Kuindzhi and the inscription "Moonlit Night." I took one oval candy the size of a plum, bit it, and crunched on nuts and raisins.

"Aren't they delicious?" Emilia asked.

"I'm not crazy about candy, but they really are delicious. So, was it easy and effortless for you to adopt Irena's taste?"

"You're saying such a thing? What, I shouldn't eat bread either, because Irena eats it? I just hadn't tried them before.... Only when I met Yanus."

"Tell me more about your suitors. Because it seems to me that such a beautiful girl as you wants something more than the courtship and money of an older gentleman."

Her eyes flashed angrily.

"What suitors? I had no one else. I loved Yanus. What can I do with myself now?" She began to choke up again, tears streaming down her face. "Now I can only find work as a maid...."

"The detective who followed you said that he had seen you more than on one occasion winking at young guys, and you agreed to meet up with one of them on a date. That was at The Carlton."

"Oh my God! That detective of yours just has a wild imagination. I was flirting as a joke. It amused me. So what? And with the one at The Carlton, I was just kidding. He winked and signaled that supposedly, we'd be meeting there at eight o'clock, and in response I pretended that I was saying something to him and moved my lips.... As if I were really saying something. I found it funny how he tried so hard to understand what I wanted to tell him, and I did it to pull his leg. I nodded, then shook my head, in the end I completely confounded him. I just had a lot of fun with that."

She spoke quite convincingly, and I had no reason not to believe her. Why would she risk meeting up with young suitors if she could lose her benefactor over this?

"Did you meet Tomashevych in private at the villa and here?"

She blushed and nodded obediently, as if repenting over something.

"And what will happen to me?" she asked, batting her abundantly long eyelashes. The edges of her bathrobe parted, showing her shapely full thighs in silk stockings. She seemingly didn't notice this, covering her face with her hands.

"You'll need to look for another benefactor," I said, without taking my eyes off her seductive legs, and even wondered if it was worth it for me to apply for this role. But I restrained myself. Not with my moolah.

"He couldn't have just left me.... he couldn't...." she said as she lowered her hands and adjusted her robe.

"I doubt that he managed to write a will."

"Then that whore will take it all," she sighed. "She drank so much of his blood."

"Tell me about her."

"Once, when we were at the villa, she arrived unexpectedly with her driver. He's such a fat crook. I barely managed to hide in the closet and observed through a crack. She came to demand a divorce. And wanted him to get out of the villa because it's all hers."

"Isn't it hers?"

"Well, yes, truth be told, it is, because her parents bought it. But Yanus then also contributed. In a word, they argued, and that crook was standing to the side. But either she gave him a sign, or he himself decided on his own – he went after Yanus and grabbed him by the neck. Yanus jerked away and pulled a pistol from under the desk. The crook retreated. Yanus shouted at them to get out, and they left. If he was killed, it was at her request. If not for the pistol, the crook would have strangled him."

"Well, good," I said, getting up. "If you don't have anything more to add, I'll be going."

She looked at me somewhat strangely, as if she still really wanted to say something to me, but, apparently, she changed her mind and showed me to the door. On the threshold I looked back and asked:

"You don't smoke, do you?"

"No."

"But Tomashevych did."

"What of it?"

"Didn't that bother you?"

"When you love someone, nothing bothers you about them," she said in dismay and looked at me with tears in her eyes. I wanted to pull her close to me, to feel her large, firm breasts against my chest. She must have felt my urge and even took a step forward, looking me straight in the eye. I pressed the latch and left.

CHAPTER 4

In a few minutes I was driving on my way to Bryukhovychi. The drizzling rain was thrashing the windshield. Fog was spreading on the road. The gloomy day gave me a shiver and spoiled my mood. The car bumped up and down as it hit potholes, slipped in mud, and snorted, scattering bits of mud and splashing water in every direction. I glanced in the mirror – looking at me was the tired face of a gazetteer, who managed to make a name for himself thanks to scandalous reports about the life of nighttime Lviv. Day and night knocking about the city, stealing a few hours of sleep from time to time. Only because shellshock at the front deprived me of my ability to sleep as much as other normal people, I've never been able to start a family and I live alone. The girls that fate has brought my way very quickly became disappointed in my lifestyle. They could see that I wasn't the brightest bulb. I don't have and won't be making any big money. And the constant absence of a husband at home would make anyone cry out of boredom. So they cried in desperation and eventually left.

Pan Hubsky's pub and colonial goods store beckoned with its picturesque shop window: in the middle sat a seductive black woman made of chocolate in a swimsuit woven from artificial orchids, and above her a variety of vegetables, nuts, raisins, candied fruits, and lollipops hung from ornamental trees.

"Oh, it must be a blue moon. *Pan* Editor has dropped by! And on a day like this *Pan* Editor needs to explode again like a bright star on our crappy horizon!" The shopkeeper greeted me with a downpour of words. He gave everyone respect, calling an ordinary accountant *Pan* Director, and a railway worker *Pan* Engineer. That's how I became *Pan* Editor.

"You want some coffee of course? I have some fresh from Yemen. And I have a really fine liqueur. You'll lick it to the last drop."

"I trust your taste like I do my own."

"That's great. Please sit down, I'll bring it right away."

There were four tables in the store and nobody else was there. The shop-keeper brought me the coffee and liqueur.

"Where are you going, *Pan* Editor?"

"I have a matter in Bryukhovychi."

"Oh, then, they probably found something sensational again. I'll take a seat next to you," he immediately brightened up as he sat down at the table. "Some time ago I read your article about that rogue. He lured girls to work in America and sold them instead to bordellos. Then you gave him hell. There's nothing else to say. And now you nailed it again! I read it, I read it. Hold on.... To Bryukhovychi? Wow! Then, it's probably on the Tomashevych matter? But isn't the case closed? What's there still to sniff out?"

"Yes... I want to drive over and see exactly where that tragedy played out."

"Aya-yay, such a tragedy. He was such an honorable gentleman – just to live and live and praise God. Why'd such a big shot shoot himself? And just after I finished reading your article on the radio they say: He shot himself! I just couldn't believe it. And you?"

"I can't say so explicitly. We still have much to learn. And how are you doing here? I see that it's empty right now."

"Well, that's 'cause of that rain. But in the evening people will be here. In good weather there's people during the day. Kids rush in for popsicles."

"So today I'm, maybe, the first customer?"

"No, there were already two. Somewhere 'round ten o'clock. First, a handsome gentleman with a neatly trimmed little moustache drove up. Twasn't in vain I called him *Pan* Handsome. He's come to me on more than one occasion to buy something, mostly candy. At my place, you know, you can get different kinds of *tzimmes*.[23] Look – we got bananas, figs, lemons, and dates. Here he came by today and asked for a champagne, oranges, and candies. But he sez: 'the best ya got.' Ya sees, I ain't got no bad ones. I also joked with him: I sees my candy's tasty for you? And he sez: 'Naw, if I had really stuffed myself like that, I already wouldn't be able to fit through the door.' So, he didn't buy it for himself. So's, I wraps it all up nice and fine for

---

[23] A traditional sweet Jewish dish with multiple ingredients and a base of carrots and honey. It is often served at Rosh Hashanah.

him and asks him: mebbe some coffee, 'cause I got coffee with ice cream. He looks at his watch and says: 'good.' He sits down here at this table and starts smoking. I begin makin' the coffee. Do you understand?"

"Wait, you didn't know who it was?"

"Eh, don't be in such a hurry. I didn't know then. As soon as he left, I starts to read the newspaper and I sees – his photo. It was Tomashevych! Just then I found out who that was in my place. But listen some more. After he lit up, and I hands him his coffee, a second car pulls up. A dark blue Packard. And it stops there on the grass. There were four gentlemen and one woman. Three of them and that woman stayed in the car, and one came in here."

"Could you recognize her?" I interrupted him.

"Heck no! Rain, gloom.... Long dark hair, a raincoat with a turned-up collar, dark-colored.... You can't make anything out.... And I don't have things to do: I sit and watch. Here comes the one with the white mane. He looks at the handsome guy who was drinking coffee and says: coffee please. I go to make him coffee. Just as he raises it up to his mug, the other finishes drinking his coffee and gets up to leave. This one sees that the coffee's hot and he can't drink it fast. He leaves it behind and walks to his car. The handsome guy left, and those five followed after him. What a farce. Why order the coffee?... Well, and, actually, then I opens up the newspaper and finds out who it was in my place. And I think.... Just between us. Why are they tracking Tomashevych. About two hours pass, and then – vroom – a police car's zipping to Bryukhovychi, vroom – a second one. I think: Wow! Something's must have happened! After a while those police cars returned. And a little later I see that dark blue Packard. And the same gentlemen are sitting in it. They drive a little past my place and stop. They look in my direction, as if thinking whether to go in or not. And I pretend not to notice them. But they didn't come in. They drove even further where the old mill is. And they stopped there for a minute and drove off to the city.... That's it. But, *Pan* Editor, I beg you to keep what I've told you close to your vest. I don't wanna have nothin' to do with the police. No, why bring that trouble onto my bald head? I don't expect nothin' good from them for me. Why should I do anything good for them, right? And to add to that: those three crooks might return here...."

"Don't be afraid. Nobody will write about that in the newspapers. But they're going to search for them. For your own safety." I stopped at the door already and said: "And give me that same box that Tomashevych bought."

"You won't regret it!" Hubsky was delighted. "If you go to visit a dish, there's no better gift."

In a second he handed me a box of candies, on which were embossed in golden letters "Moonlit Night."

CHAPTER 5

I thought it was time to take a look at that villa. Bryukhovychi began to plunge into twilight. I couldn't see any pedestrians, so there was no one to ask the way to the villa. But I had a map. I had written down the address from Obukh. Lisova Street is truly unique. But I knew that the villa was located on the roadside among pine trees, and, walking along Lisova Street, you need to look carefully. Buildings and the villas here stretched only on one side of the road – on the forest side. Fields extended along on the opposite side. I slowed down and was barely crawling along. Rain was knocking on the car windows. A thick mist was hanging in the air, and the fog began to swirl.

I might not have even noticed him if I had driven faster. He was standing on his knees on the road, in the ditch itself, grabbing his stomach with his hands, and nodded back and forth like a porcelain little Chinese boy. I pulled over and approached him.

The young boy was moaning heavily, and between his fingers blood oozed out into a puddle around his knees. I jumped back in my car and pulled out a towel, though a not very clean one and, as best I could, tied it around his stomach tightly and pulled him out of the wet ditch. I don't know if I did it well. I asked him what was wrong, but he didn't answer and just howled, though sometimes a single word burst out: "White.... white...." Then I rushed to the nearest building. It turned out to be a small bright white hotel with balustrades on a brick porch. I rang the doorbell.

Unhurried, heavy steps reverberated. An older lady opened the door. It was clear that they weren't expecting anyone. I asked for permission to call a doctor and the police.

"The police? What happened?" Said the man standing behind her.

"There's a wounded young boy next to the road."

"So, maybe it's not worth calling the police?" The man nodded to the woman to step away and conspiratorially asked: "Did you hit him hard?"

The woman looked at him with surprise but didn't leave.

"I didn't do it," I said. "He has a wound in his stomach from a knife or bullet. He's bleeding."

"Oh!" The woman became frightened. "I'll call now."

She disappeared. I heard her shout in an excited voice to the telephone operator. Her husband took a flashlight from a shelf and measured me with a heavy gaze.

"Who are you?"

"A reporter."

"Well, of course," he muttered. "You stick your nose everywhere."

"Where do you say he is?"

"He's there, near my car."

He went out, illuminating the way, because the twilight fog had already shrouded everything all around. So, I waited, listening to the woman call the police, several times trying to explain what happened, and then, finally losing patience, calling an ambulance. Her husband returned.

"It seems like he's already pushing up daises," he said dryly.

"He was still alive when I noticed him."

"Did you ask him anything?"

"I tried, but he just moaned."

"Well then.... you have to wait until the police arrive. Come on in."

I followed him to a small sitting room with armchairs. In the corner was a fireplace, in which firewood was smoldering, giving off sparks. There was a coffee pot hung on iron bars over the fire. I sat in an armchair.

"They'll arrive soon," the woman said, sitting down opposite me. "Make me some coffee, too," she addressed her husband as she smiled at me, spreading her arms apart. "This is our hotel."

"In which there's not a living soul except us," said her husband.

"It's not in season yet," the woman sighed. "But, when the snow falls, people will come here for skiing. Since the construction of the ski jump, we get a lot of vacationers. Because it's one of the largest ski jumps in Poland."

"Coffee for you, too?" Her husband asked me.

"Yes, thank you. I was a little unsettled by this circumstance."

"I didn't even want to go look," the woman said. "I worry about everyone so much...."

The man brought a cup of coffee and joined us.

"Did you take a close look at that boy?" I asked him.

"I did."

"And you recognized him?"

"Maybe I did. But I don't want to get involved in this matter. The police, if they need to, will find out for themselves."

"Are you joking, or do you really know him?"

He snorted unhappily, sipping his coffee.

"Slavka, don't joke around like that," his wife said. "If you know him, why beat around the bush?"

"Well, okay, they'll get it out of me anyway. He's a boy who worked for Tomashevych. He was their chief errand boy. He dug up garden beds, planted bushes and trees, and painted what needed to be painted. Felyek was his name."

"So, you heard what happened to Tomashevych?" I asked.

"Why wouldn't I have heard? It was in the evening newspaper."

"Did he live somewhere near you?"

"A little further up the road, about a hundred meters."

"What did you think when you heard about his suicide?"

"What?..." Here he looked at me closely. "Aren't you the one who described his con?" I nodded. He shook his head. "Well, I don't know, I don't know.... whether I'd shoot myself because of something like that. And now this boy...."

"So, you didn't believe it was suicide?"

"What about it? I'm just a little guy. If the police say that it's suicide, I also say it's suicide. I can only say about myself that with that kind of money and property, I'd never shoot myself because of such nonsense. But that's me."

"I'm just not myself today...," the woman said. "I just heard about this tragedy. I couldn't come to my senses. Not that I knew him well, but sometimes we'd see each other, greet each other.... He rented skis from us on more than one occasion.... two pairs...."

"And who was with him?"

"Some girl. She never came inside our place. She was waiting for him by the forest. He brought those skis to her, and then they drove over there – to the ski jump. It was the first time I saw the late Tomashevych, when that horrible murder happened at our neighbor's. When was that, Slavka, in 1932?"

"You have nothing to wag your tongue about," her husband muttered. "In 1931, during the night of December 30-31. I will never forget that horrible scream in the middle of the night...."

They recalled the mysterious case of Gorgonova when at the villa of the architect Henryk Zaremba his seventeen-year-old daughter Liusya's corpse with her head smashed in was discovered in the middle of the night. Suspicions fell on Rita Gorgonova, the governess and at the same time the mistress of the owner, who was originally from Croatia. At first she was given a death sentence, although there was no direct evidence, but because she was pregnant, she was pardoned, and her sentence reduced to eight years.

"Tomashevych was acquainted with Zaremba," the wife explained, "in fact, he bought the villa from him, which he had built to sell. And, when Gorgonova's trial was already going on, another murder happened in our neighborhood, and a young girl was the victim again. Gorgonova's lawyers immediately stated this in court, but the court didn't take this fact into account. Although there was a witness, who saw the likely killer."

"Really?" I was surprised, because not a single newspaper wrote about anyone like that.

"And who's this witness?"

The wife looked at me triumphantly and uttered it syllable by syllable: "Tom-a-shev-ych...." And satisfied by the effect that the last name prompted in me, she continued: "He saw someone who looked like Zaremba's gardener! He saw him run away from the crime scene!"

The gardener did arouse suspicion then, but his place was searched only on the tenth day after Liusya's murder. I remember Obukh tried to act more decisively in that case, but same as now, they did not allow him to do so.

"That's interesting," I said. "So, they didn't hear Tomashevych in court. So, what happened to the gardener?"

"After that second murder which also had signs of rape, he disappeared."

"In the meantime, the investigation was convinced that it was Gorgonova who deprived the girl of her virginity with her finger, mimicking rape."

"That's the way it was. Our son was friends with Stas, Zaremba's son. He heard Tomashevych tell Henryk that he had seen someone similar to the gardener. But Henryk didn't believe it."

"Have you seen that gardener?"

"Why not? I've seen him many times. He was gone for several years and reappeared about two years ago. But he no longer works as a gardener, but as a driver ... for whom might you think?"

"For the life of me, I can't guess."

"None other than for *Pani* Irena Tomashevych!"

"Oho!" I exclaimed. "So, she didn't believe her own husband."

"No one believed him. It's not a big deal if someone looks similar to someone else. Tomashevych couldn't swear that was the guy he had seen."

"Was Zaremba satisfied with the gardener?"

"Yes, he was a really fast worker. He worked as fast as lightning. Although I'd never hire such an antisocial guy. He never greeted or communicated with anyone, lived alone, didn't go out for any fun. Except to the pub. A very suspicious and odious type. He glanced at my daughter like a cat ready to pounce on a mouse. He looked around and drooled too. I even complained to Henryk...."

There was the roar of an engine. Light from the headlights ran across the sitting room. The husband stood up and looked out the window.

"They've arrived."

I gulped down my coffee, burning the inside of my mouth, and stepped out into the yard. An ambulance and a police car were standing on the road. Two orderlies carried the body into the car. A young policeman with a dashing little mustache illuminated me with a flashlight.

"Corporal Radomsky," he gave his name. "So, it's you who found him?"

"Yes."

"Is that your car?"

"It's mine."

"How did you run over him?"

"What are you talking about? Haven't you seen he has a wound in his stomach? Shine the light over there – he was sitting in the roadside ditch. A lot of blood pooled there."

He approached the spot, showed his light on it, but shook his head.

"So, what of it? You could have knocked him over anyway. And he was thrown over there. You'll be coming with us. Do you have any papers?"

I gave him my ID. He took the card unenthusiastically, turned it over and just as carefully looked at the reverse side. However, there was nothing on the back. He returned the document to me and spoke in a bored tone:

"Re-port-er.... Did you know that boy?"

"No."

"I knew him," the hotelier finally intervened, seeing that the policeman had already picked on me. "He's the gardener who worked for Tomashevych. His name was Felyek."

"The same guy who shot himself?" The police officer choked a bit.

"The same one."

"And there – you have it!"

He took out his cigarettes and lit one up. One of the orderlies approached.

"Well, what's up with him there?" The policeman asked.

"Will he live?"

"No. It's too late. He has a bullet wound in the stomach. Then it's you who bandaged it?" he asked as he turned to me.

"Me."

"He's bled to death."

"Oho! Something smells rotten," the policeman shook his head. "When you do the autopsy and remove the bullet, let me know. And you," he turned to me, "do you have a revolver?"

"No," I lied.

"Do you want me to believe you?" A night reporter, without a revolver? You sneak around dive bars and clip joints?"

"You can search me."

"Everything in due course."

The husband and wife returned to the hotel, and the orderlies left. Another police car arrived, out of which Obukh stepped.

"Oh, I was hoping to catch you here," he said to me. "Well, tell me what happened here," he addressed the police officer.

He explained everything he knew to him.

"He couldn't have been sitting in that ditch this entire time," Obukh said. "He would have been noticed during the day. Have you looked around the area?" he asked the policeman.

"I didn't have time."

"Well, let's go take a look."

They illuminated the ditch with flashlights, then moved in the direction of the forest, lighting the way step by step. I followed them. Traces of blood were everywhere. In a few minutes from behind the bushes resounded:

"Here!"

I moved closer. There was crushed, blood-stained grass.

"He had been lying here for a while, and then crawled to the road," said Obukh. "We won't haul out anything now. We need to wait for dawn. And then take a closer look at the place. Let's get going."

"What about him?" The policeman nodded at me.

"What's wrong with him?"

"Is he beyond suspicion?"

"Beyond."

The policeman went to the car with an unhappy face. Obukh asked me quietly:

"Have you been to the villa yet?"

"Not yet. I was on my way there when I came across the boy."

I told him about the shopkeeper, about the private detective and Emilia, about the Zaremba's gardener, and also about what I had managed to hear from the dying boy: "White.... white."

"He must have meant that white-haired crook," I said.

"He, obviously, witnessed a murder. I wonder who those four in the Packard were?" Obukh thought. "We know about two of them: we know they followed you. We know what they look like. Who are the other two? And the chick with them! Who is she? Irena? Emilia? Is there a third unknown woman? Maybe Tomashevych had another mistress, about whom Emilia suspected nothing.... And which of them called Tomashevych over to the villa from his office? Or maybe Emilia's lying?"

"She assures me that she'd never order champagne because she breaks wind from it."

Obukh laughed.

"It's worth it to keep her under surveillance. But so far Tomashevych's wife arouses the most suspicion. Maybe she was in the car."

"She at least had a good motive."

"So, some girl, though I don't exclude Emilia, calls Tomashevych and lures him to the villa. The place is just perfect due to its isolation. The day and time are also chosen in advance: the morning of the day when your article is to be published. But who but Emilia could lure him from the office? A new passion he was courting? But a new passion, I think, would demand a more luscious treat. For example, caviar, oysters, figs.... No, it was someone he knew well. And he knew her tastes because he ordered a particular candy." He thought for a moment and added: "But that toothbrush!"

"It was a young girl who doesn't like the scent of tobacco."

"Of course, the young girl he was waiting for. Emilia says that his wife could have lured him to the villa. For example, agreeing to an amicable settlement."

"Anything is possible. But some other woman could have been waiting for him at that spot. Not specifically the one who had lured him. And if it was the one who was in the car with the killers, it means that she's conspiring with them.... And you know what I think? The ones who followed you and the ones who defended you are from the same circle. There was a staged attack on you, too. Yes, and they threatened Martyniuk only to kindle your interest so that you immediately took up the scent like a greyhound. Because that whole story about the merger of the associations, though scandalous, isn't deadly."

"But Martyniuk was beaten who knows when and they stole the documents about the associations' merger."

"It was at the dawn of Tomashevych's career. He was concerned about his reputation then. I'll tell you another interesting thing: your *Pan* Dutchak died two years before you saw him."

I was stunned.

"How could that be?"

"He never lived in that house. It was a house that was rented just for a day. Someone pretended to be Dutchak and handed over the documents to you."

"Did you drive there?"

"No, I called a friend in the local commandant's office. The Dutchaks lived at a different address, but both are already deceased."

"If you suspect Tomashevych's wife, then I can't imagine how she could have organized such a large team. Someone much more powerful had to have intervened here. Add to that the murder of that boy. Maybe at least now they'll give you this case?"

"No. Sausage is too good for a dog.[24] Tomashevych's case is closed. Period. Suicide, and that's it. Therefore, you are my only hope. You must help me. And as for someone more powerful.... We've kept Irena's father out of the picture. He is a really powerful and wealthy man. If necessary, he'd gather an entire army...," he pressed my hand. "Well, I'm outta here. And you be careful. Do you have a revolver?"

"Of course...."

---

[24] We've opted for a literal translation of the colorful (originally Polish) saying "Ne pro psa kovbasa." Here it means something like "not every dog has his day."

CHAPTER 6

I drove about fifty meters, got out of the car, and then walked on foot. From the description Obukh had given me, I recognized the villa. It was well hidden among the pines – it was a two-story red brick building covered in wild grape vines. The windows at the bottom had bars on them. A path, covered in fine gravel, led to the porch. On both sides there were flowerbeds with the last blooms of autumn. Silver mist dripped between the branches. It was quiet and the cawing of crows echoed from the woods. One window at the bottom was lit up, and there was a gray Wartburg in the courtyard. Evidently, cars entered the courtyard through a separate gate.

I climbed up the steps to the porch with a wrapped box of candy under my arm and rang the bell. A loud bark of a big dog boomed from the house. Then someone opened a peephole and examined me.

A male voice asked:

"Who is it?"

"I'm a private detective. I want to have a chat with *Pani* Tomashevych."

"She has nothing to say to you."

"Better to talk to me than to the police."

"Don't make me laugh. The police closed the case. Who are you really?"

"One case was closed, and another will be opened."

"What kind of case?"

"A hundred meters from here the body of Felyek was found dead. He was shot."

A pause ensued. Someone, apparently a servant, went deep into the house and returned after a minute. The key in the lock creaked and the door opened. The crook, about whom Emilia had spoken was there, and then the housekeeper. He measured me with a look as if he were choosing meat on display. Behind him a really big German Shepherd growled.

"Calm down, Valyus! Stay!"

The dog obediently loped along the corridor and disappeared behind the corner.

I entered the living room, which was brightly lit by chandeliers, and saw the woman of my dreams, adorned with gold bangles, like a Christmas tree. She had a gracious waist, her bosom lifted high, and under the robe, I expected, full thighs and a curvaceous posterior. Her long dark brown hair was gathered in a ponytail and fell on her chest. She silently stretched out her delicate white hand with many rings, nodded toward the couch and spoke in a silky voice:

"Please sit down."

She sat down on an armchair with her legs curled under her. The crook was snorting behind my back.

"This is my driver," she explained. "And guard. You can go," she told him.

I sat down, put the chocolate box on the table. After a second, I heard the driver trudge down to the basement. Apparently, he had a workshop there. I don't think he performed any other functions besides that of driver and guard because he was quite hideous looking.

"Oh, how sweet of you!" said the mistress of the house. You must already know everything about me, *Pan* Night Reporter, if you brought my favorite candies? Well, tell me what brought you to me."

I was surprised.

"Did you recognize me?"

"Of course. I saw you at the magistrate's. I was interested in who was writing such caustic articles. And they showed you to me. And now you pass yourself off as a private detective? Did you think I would despair that you led my husband to suicide?" She laughed, unpacked the box, unwrapped a candy, and put it in her mouth. Her lips moved sensually.

"No, I knew you wouldn't be despairing, *Pani* Irena," I answered, looking away from her lips. "But you're not so naive to think that my article could have driven him to this."

"Of course not. He was hard as granite," she laughed again.

"More precisely, sometimes – like granite, and other times – like a rag."

She went to the credenza, took out a bottle of whiskey and two small glasses.

"You won't refuse to have a drink with me? No? That's good. By the way, you can smoke. I love the scent of tobacco."

I stared at her with surprise. Why did she say that to me? But I took out a cigarette, lit it, and said:

"So, you never forced your husband to brush his teeth before kissing you?"

"Me? What eccentricity! I've never been capricious."

"And how about Emilia?"

"Oh, how should I know how Emilia kisses?"

"Your husband brushed his teeth again, waiting for a visit of an unknown young lady. The day he was killed. Or did Tomashevych have another mistress?"

She smiled mysteriously, looked away to the side, and said:

"There was. That one.... a former one. But he also met up with her from time to time."

"And who was that young maiden?"

"Oh, a young maiden, tell me another fairy story! Maybe her pinky's still maidenly. Agnieszka. She used to work as a waitress."

Agnieszka? I had an acquaintance with that name. She also worked as a waitress. But there could be quite a lot of young ladies named Agnieszka.

"She's no longer working there?" I asked her.

"That was a long time ago when I was still interested in his lovers. I just don't know now.... And by the way," she suddenly changed the topic, "I've wanted to meet you for a long time." She poured out the whiskey and we clinked glasses. "I don't hide that I'm happy about what happened to my husband. But probably you have already ferreted out everything. Right?" I nodded. "And you talked to Emilia?"

"I did.... Poor girl."

"Not so poor. I paid her well."

"You?"

"Of course!" She was eating the candies with delectation, graciously moving her lips. "I dispatched her secretly to Yanek,[25] because I couldn't get rid of him. He had a mistress before her too. But I couldn't control Ag-

....
[25]   Yanek is another diminutive for Yan.

nieszka. So, I picked this one. It's always better to have someone in sight. The girl completed her task, and I'm grateful to her."

"So, Emilia already has heard the news and knows that she's been left without a benefactor."

"Do you feel sorry for her?"

"Why on earth would I?" she chuckled. "We're even. But ... out of gratitude, maybe I'll find her another benefactor. She is pretty, isn't she."

"She's really pretty. And unhappy in her own way. I just feel bad for her."

"Oho! Did you really fall for her?" She laughed consolingly. "Then take her under your wing. The young lady is free as a bird."

"As my buddy said, sausage is too good for a dog."[26]

"But why? Such a good-looking fellow as you...."

"Good looks have nothing to do with anything here. With my salary, I couldn't support a dish like that."

"That's the point! Well, yes.... when a girl gets used to luxury, it's not easy for her to find herself again in...," she got lost in thought, choosing her words.

"Did you mean in poverty?" I suggested.

"Oh, no, no, I don't think your business is that bad. But I suspect you live modestly. I have acquaintances among the bohemians. So, I judge by them."

"When did you arrive at the villa today?" I interrupted her thoughts about my financial status.

"At noon. The police were already here. Actually, they called me."

"Did you tell them you didn't believe it was suicide?"

"Do I look like such a dummy? And where did you get that I don't believe it? Are you trying to catch me slipping up on a word? My God! A stone just fell from my shoulders, and you want to heap another one on me again? I'm talking to you so freely because I want to have my say. But I forbid you to publish anything from our conversation, because I'll deny everything and sue you. Understood?"

Her voice stopped being silky smooth.

"No, I'm not going to write about this until everything becomes absolutely clear."

....

[26] We've opted for the literal translation of the expression here, which suggests here something like "she's out of my league" in this context.

"That's good. Because, first, I'm not asserting that he couldn't have shot himself, and secondly, that he had been shot. True, the killing of Felyek.... That's just too much. Although it could be a coincidence."

"After you received confirmation of your husband's infidelity, you weren't paying Emilia any longer?"

"No. She was supposed to leave him. But she stayed. Well, that's her business. She didn't interest me any longer."

"Was she summoned to court?"

"Of course."

"And she confirmed everything?"

"She confirmed that she was friends with *Pan* Tomashevych. But she denied an intimate relationship. And the photos spoke for themselves. We managed to take pictures of them through the window where they were in their underwear or naked. Those present even laughed at those words of hers."

"The thought never occurred to you that suspicions might have arisen that you were involved in Tomashevych's death?"

Her long eyelashes first dropped, then slowly rose up. She glared at me in surprise.

"No, it never occurred to me. My conscience is clear. I had every chance to win legally.... that is, not entirely legally, but through the courts."

I told her how cunningly I had been led to take an interest in Tomashevych and write my article. She listened intently and didn't interrupt. Her face at first was gloomy, then brightened up, and her robe spread apart on her legs just as happened at Emilia's, baring no less beautiful legs in silk stockings, maybe even the same brand. I wouldn't have minded sitting next to her and continuing our conversation with my hand on her full thighs. When I finished speaking, she got up, went to a desk, took out a folder, and placed it down in front of me.

"What you've said is all very interesting. But here is my alibi."

"What is it?"

"Letters with threats addressed to my husband. They were scaring him into not running for president of the city government of Lviv. They threatened to kill him. If they still decide to open it as a murder case, I have nothing against that."

I opened the folder. The anonymous letters were neither written nor printed – the individual letters were cut out from newspapers. One of the anonymous letters was strange: they warned Tomashevych to be prepared to fulfill a certain task, otherwise his wife would receive spicy photos.

"What photos are they talking about? About the ones that were made at your order?"

"I don't know."

"Did he see them?"

"Yes. One time I threw several in his face."

"Then this threat was simply ridiculous. He knew that you knew about the mistress."

"Of course, he knew. But the one who was doing the threatening might not have known."

She was right.

"When did you find these anonymous letters?"

"A few days ago. I have my own key. I came when he wasn't here. In such cases, I always took care not to frighten the sweet couple. I only came in once when his mistress, apparently, was hiding somewhere. I sensed it by the scent of her perfume. Another time I came again and decided to rummage through his papers, thinking that maybe something might come in handy for the trial. And I found these letters. He threw away the envelopes, leaving just the last three. They were without a return address anyway."

"These need to be given to the police."

"As you wish. I don't care," she said in a casual tone.

"Do you suspect anyone?"

"No. I haven't had contact with his circle of acquaintances lately."

"Did you know that your husband also was blackmailing someone?"

She was surprised.

"Yanek? I'm hearing this for the first time. Who could he be blackmailing?"

"A stranger handed me a folder with photos from a bordello, where you can see an elderly gentleman surrounded by half-naked prostitutes. There is a suspicion that Tomashevych had sent them."

"Who was the gentleman?" She tried, or I thought that she was trying to pretend indifference.

"His face is scratched off."

She finished up her drink and squinted.

"Apparently, I overlooked something in my relationship with him. After all, we haven't been living together lately. If this is related to his candidacy for president of the city government, I don't see any sense in that kind of blackmail. He far outdistanced all the other candidates."

"Is it true that you never wished him dead?"

She smiled with a mysterious look.

"Wanting and ordering are two different things. I actually did want just to take the villa away and break off all relations with him. The upcoming court case in Warsaw gave me hope for this. And he, having won the election, would probably have been more accommodating. As president he had great prospects, plus his shrewdness and keen flair...." She nodded for me to top up the glasses. "No, you know, sometimes I couldn't help telling him to drop dead, but, in fact, I wouldn't want to be involved in anything like that. Do you believe me?"

Her eyes sparkled and she seductively bit her lower lip.

"It's hard not to believe you," I admitted. "But this doesn't remove you from the list of suspects."

"The investigation is closed. Isn't it?" She smiled wryly.

"Yes, you're right. But this is about Tomashevych's murder. But the murder of the boy cannot be hushed up... And one more thing.... Can you tell me what might be of interest to counterintelligence? Was Tomashevych involved in some kind of secret dealings?"

"He often traveled to Germany, met with a German ambassador. He had some business deals with them. But I don't know the details. I was also surprised, what was the chief of counterintelligence doing here?"

"Tell me what prompted you to take the Zaremba's gardener as your driver?"

She shrugged.

"What's so strange about that? I needed someone like that to protect me."

"Like when he almost twisted your husband's neck off?"

"Aha! I thought so!" Irena seemed to rejoice. "So, Emilia was hiding somewhere here."

"So, you didn't believe your husband when he said that he had seen your driver fleeing the scene?"

"It was evening. It was drizzling. From his car he saw some figure near the forest. He couldn't see the face. Therefore, no one took his testimony seriously. Henryk also brushed it aside...."

She paused, putting the glass to her lips. Then she looked at me in a not very friendly way and asked: "Tell me, why are you questioning me in such detail? We agreed that you won't write about this conversation with me!"

"No, I won't entangle you in this. I'm just helping the investigation. For the time being privately. I'd be grateful if you would allow me to drop by again."

She suddenly changed her wary expression to a friendly one:

"Oh, such a courteous guest who comes with my favorite candy, any time."

She accompanied me to the door. I kissed her hand again, which was cold.

"But then again, maybe, you have a warm heart?" I said on my way out, and left without waiting for an answer.

THE THIRD DAY
SATURDAY
SEPTEMBER 24, 1938

CHAPTER 1

I handed Obukh a folder with the anonymous letters and related my conversation with Irena.

"And what about the investigation of the place where the boy was found?" I asked.

"Here, read it," he handed me the report.

"Four tire tracks that were well preserved in the wet ground made it possible to make distinct gypsum castings. A broken bicycle was found in the bushes. Paint from the car's fender was found on the bicycle frame. The Packard is no older than five or six years. Dark blue color. The condition of the tires indicates that the car had been driven up to fifteen thousand kilometers. On the left fender the finish is probably damaged and there must be a dent. Glass fragments from a broken headlight were also collected."

The victim was riding a bicycle. From the tracks of the car, it is clear that the boy was being watched and was run over on purpose. Then he was shot in the stomach and dragged into the bushes. He lay there, unconscious for some time. When he recovered, he crawled out onto the road.

"At about eleven the boy who was later killed brought Tomashevych bushes, which the latter had ordered to plant," Obukh explained. "What does this mean? It points to the fact that he could have seen those who had come to Tomashevych and killed him. From that moment he was doomed."

"What was he doing for so long from eleven o'clock till dusk?"

"He was hiding from the killers. Upon seeing that Tomashevych had been killed, he jumped on the bicycle and took off wherever the road took him. Those guys chased after him. But he turned toward the woods and broke away from them through the forest paths. They apparently called someone else to be on the lookout at paths coming out of the woods. Eventually, when he let his guard down and rode out of the forest, they ran him over. But before that something else happened. The boy made his way from the southern side of the forest to the health sanitarium, where there's a booth with a guard, and he requested to make a phone call. The guard permitted him to do that but didn't fathom anything from that conversation and didn't understand who he called. After all, he's a bit deaf. Felyek called the police but saw that the pursuers were approaching. He again jumped on his bicycle and disappeared into the woods. The guard told them the same thing that he told me...."

"I wonder who he called first?"

"Yes... This whole story doesn't piece together very well... Those who were blackmailing Tomashevych, apparently, are also the ones who killed him. He didn't respond to the blackmail. He didn't withdraw his candidacy; then they resorted to a more cunning plan involving you. But I have a sneaking suspicion that elections didn't play a major role here. There's something else... they were looking for something in his office I wonder what that could be?"

"Apparently the counterintelligence chief knows the solution," I said.

"You're right. But he won't say anything to us about it. Tomashevych's secretary said that he didn't receive any phone calls in the morning. That means to the office. The switchboard operator claimed that there were two calls to his apartment at seven-ten and seven-thirty a.m. Female voices. Different ones. One from a phone booth and the other from a pub on the corner of Kleparivska and Yanivska Streets."

"The legendary pub, praised in song by the *batyars*? Was it already open that early?"

"No, it just never closed. A young woman with long dark hair made the call."

"Fantastic, Emilia and Irena have the same kind of hair. If someone other than them phoned, we have another dish involved."

"The bartender didn't take a good look at her face. Add to that, he was drunk. It seems that you should still have a good chat with Emilia to see whether she hadn't heard of any other mistresses of Tomashevych and an apartment we don't know about? But also run over to Kvartsyany to see whether he came across that Packard. In tracking Tomashevych, he could have noticed it somewhere. And ask him about the apartment, too. Somewhere Tomashevych must have hidden what the unknown murderers were looking for."

"And have they searched that apartment in the city center where he mainly lived?"

"Yes, but without me. They hide all the information from me. However, I still managed to find out something: what they were looking for wasn't there. That's why I thought there might be some other secret domicile."

CHAPTER 2

I found Kvartsyany with a compress on his head and an unhappy look on his face. This time the secretary didn't interfere, because she was busy making coffee.

"What happened to you?" I was surprised by his appearance.

"Oh, shit! You're just what I need now. What the hell are you doing here?"

"Have you forgotten that I'm your client? Tell me then what kind of adventure you had."

"Do you have another twenty *zloty*?"

"I see you have a fixed rate. What? Do you have anything else for sale?"

"He-he, I'll always find something interesting. So, do you?"

"I do."

"Put the money on the table."

"For a pig in a poke?"

"No, not a pig but an entire boar. Didn't you see my head? Put it down and have no doubt. Now you'll hear something interesting."

I took out the money and put it on the table. He folded it neatly and put it away.

"Well, then have a seat."

I sat down. He took a bottle of cognac from under the table and poured it into two glasses. At the same time playfully grinned, as if to let me know that I'd hear some incredible news right now. And it turned out to be exactly that.

"I'm listening," I woke him from his sweet state of euphoria.

"You know me, I don't like to focus my attention just on one single case. When another order floats over to me, I take it without hesitation. And it so happened that – he-he – literally yesterday... let's say, a stranger approached me... that is, he approached me by phone. He didn't give his name. I felt that he was lying, but I didn't say anything. He knew that I was working on the Tomashevych matter. He asked me to break into the villa when no one was there and to look for a folder with valuable papers and a notebook."

"Wow!" I couldn't restrain myself. The news was great. "And what? Did you break in?"

He smiled contentedly again and lit a cigarette.

"You listen now. I'm not just some knucklehead. Okay, I say, but I want the money in advance. I received a letter in two hours. In it there was a down payment – one hundred *zloty* and a note: I'll receive two hundred more when I hand over those papers and the notebook. Well, so be it. From shadowing the lovers, I already knew that there were evenings and nights when there was no one at home in the villa. So as not to dilly-dally, I grabbed my lock picking implements, drove up in the car, but left it behind a bend. I approached the villa and saw that it was lit up. By the house there was the Wartburg that *Pan* Tomashevych drives in. There were silhouettes in the window. Okay. I waited. I stood in the bushes and had a smoke. When I looked: the door opened, and you stepped out. I wanted to stop you and ask what you had forgotten there, but I didn't think I knew yet how my mission would end. You left, and I continued to stand there, waiting and pacing. About two hours later the lady of the house came out with her driver, got in the car, and drove off. Well, then I broke in, lighting my way with a flashlight. At first, I rummaged around in his desk, but there was nothing. His wife had to have done this before me, but she doesn't have my kind of experience. So, from above I could see a folder with photos that I had given to her, another pile of papers from a court case, various petitions, and appeals. In short, there was nothing of interest for me. Then I began to examine the desk more closely and came to the conclusion that there must be a hiding place in it. But where? I tapped all the legs, and one of them was swaying a little. I twisted it once, a second time, and finally carefully unscrewed it. Inside I found a small book with a red cover. The size of two matchboxes put together. There were names in the notebook.... And opposite each name were numbers with dates. I understood that Tomashevych was blackmailing someone. And the numbers were the amounts of money they paid him."

I couldn't control myself and poured myself some more cognac.

"Do you have this notebook?"

"Ho-ho! Hold your horses. I didn't have time to properly look at that notebook, and headlights struck the windows.

A car pulled up. It was the same Wartburg. Irena and her driver got out of the car. I hid the notebook down the back of my sock and thought: what should I do? I ran up the stairs to the second floor, and from there to the attic. I sat down and waited. They entered the house, turned on the light, and I heard: 'Ah, here it is! How could I forget my favorite hat? It's good we returned for it.' And the driver said: 'Have you forgotten anything else? So we don't have to return ten times, as we always do.' And she said: 'And what do I pay you for? Don't worry, I won't come back for anything else.' And they left. I heard the car drive away. I still looked through the attic window. They were gone. I went downstairs. On the ground floor I approached the window and saw that the car had left, but not that far away because it stopped near the road. Wow, I thought something was wrong here. And that was my last wise thought. Because then I got whacked on my head and came to my senses in the bushes near the pine trees. Have you ever slept under pine trees? It's an unforgettable impression. The air is magical. Fortunately, it didn't rain."

The secretary interrupted and brought us coffee. Bodyo waited for her to leave to continue:

"Do you know how I got burned?"

"You didn't lock the door behind you."

"Oh, dang! How did you figure that out?"

"Well, because you didn't want to mess with the lock one more time. You were sure they had left."

"And they, dammit, came back and played that scene. She drove away in the car, and that crook stayed behind and gave me a knock on the dome."

"And you didn't have the notebook any longer?"

"Hey! They didn't find it, although they searched me. But they didn't know why I had broken into the villa and what I had been looking for. And they didn't get to my socks."

"I wonder why they didn't turn you over to the police?"

"E-he-he, not right away! Of course, they recognized me. When I got hit, I fell on my chest on the desk, and slipping, dragged a pile of folders. That still was etched in my memory. Then the film was interrupted. I guess that they decided I had broken in for some folder."

"And what names did you see in the notebook?"

He looked at me quite thoughtfully:

"There were no names. That is obviously what we are talking about is surnames, but in fact there are initials: YR, TM, LH, t.d. That is, t.d.[27], in the sense of so on and not TD [as initials]. But after I got whacked on my head, I didn't want to mention it."

"But do you have the notebook? And will you give it to your client now?"

"Oh no! I'm not that stupid. For those few hundred *zloty*? Once I saw the sums there, I wouldn't give it to anyone. I'll wait. My time hasn't come yet."

"Has the client already called you?"

"Of course. I said I hadn't found anything and would return the money."

"You're lying that you don't know the client. Who is it?"

"Don't rush like that. Maybe you'll find out very soon. Why did you come here?"

"During the time you were following the lovers did you come across a dark blue Packard?"

"Naw, not then. But I've seen it two or three times recently near Tomashevych's office. I thought it was some kind of security he hired when he was under threat."

"How do you know about the threats?"

"I have such an incurable habit of sticking my nose where it doesn't belong. So, I checked the mailbox in his office several times. I would take the letter, come here, steam it open, look through it, seal it up again, and put it back in its place. Regarding this case, I'm meticulous."

"Didn't you not return some letters and give them to Tomashevych's wife?"

Bodyo glanced at me suspiciously.

"Well ... a little bit of extra cash never hurts."

"She didn't give you up. She said she found them herself."

"An upstanding chick. Lucky to have one like that."

"But you're playing with fire. You're better off giving me the notebook, and I'll take it to the police."

"No way! I'm poor as a church mouse. I have to earn enough to feed myself."

....

[27]   *tak dali* in Ukrainian.

"You may not manage to earn anything. When are you meeting with your client?"

"He's supposed to call. Maybe I won't meet with him, because he'll just tell me where to send the envelope with the money."

"Did you hear anything about any other domiciles of Tomashevych?"

"I told you, neither he nor Emilia interested me individually, just as a couple. And they were either at the villa or at Syktuska Street. He never took her to Legioniv Street."

"And the last thing: why didn't you tell me about one of Tomashevych's other mistresses?"

He laughed.

"Did you ever ask?"

"I'm asking now."

"Eh, that'll cost a bit more cash! Good, but that chick ain't worth much – give me ten more *zloty*, and I'll tell you everything."

I put the money on the table. He grabbed it again and lay down a thin little folder in front of me. There were just a few photos in which Tomashevych was strolling around the city with a portly girl.

"Who is she?"

"She's his former squeeze. She has as much to do with Emilia as I have with the Pope in Rome, but, apparently, she can do something that makes it difficult to break up with her, because he met up with her more often than with Emilia."

"And where did he take her?"

"To his place on Legioniv Street."

"Where can I find her?"

"She worked as a waitress in the Bagatelle, but now she works at the Warszawa [Warsaw] Restaurant. Her name's Agnieszka."

"What do you know about her?"

"She's a cunning honey! She knew how to turn more than one head. Irena knew about her but didn't know where she could catch her and her husband. And I couldn't manage to follow them everywhere, because they were in a car, and I was on foot. Then Irena pushed Emilia his way. Well, then Emilia told her where they would be, and I would already be waiting there."

"Didn't Emilia know about Agnieszka?"

"I don't think she did. Tomashevych didn't really go out and about with her. He'd come by car, pick her up, and off they'd go. But with Emilia he was already taking strolls."

"So, Agnieszka must have known about this? She could have seen them somewhere."

"She could have. But he paid her well. You see, with Emilia he played the lover, gave her pocket money, for clothes, for food, and paid for her housing. But he just paid Agnieszka for each time. She had no complaints, and he didn't make any particular plans. Unlike with Emilia."

"Was Emilia planning to marry him?" I wondered.

"She was. Why not? But he didn't want to get divorced. Then she would fume and chafe. I've seen them quarreling many times. She tried to convince him about something, and he'd wave it off. Maybe the role of mistress didn't satisfy her very much. I think that their love affair was coming to an end. Although very slowly."

"When did you realize their affair was ending?"

"Just recently," he muttered, and immediately jumped up, because, apparently, he didn't have any intention of confiding.

"What does recently mean?" I pressed him. "You didn't stop following him?"

Bodyo frowned, lowered his head, and sniffled.

"My head hurts, and you're provoking me here...," he muttered.

"Bodyo, you've already said that you've recently seen a Packard next to the office. Now this.... You continued to follow him? Now on whose order was it?"

"I don't know." He sighed heavily. "They called me and made a proposition. Was I supposed to reject it?"

"Who called? The same guy who asked you to break into the villa?"

"No, it was a different voice."

"What exactly was Tomashevych interested in?"

"His contacts. Well, and then there was that secret apartment. They figure he was hiding something there. But what exactly it was – I wasn't told. I'll just say to you...," he shook his head painfully. "I've dirtied myself up to my ears. Who knows how this will end for me."

"Why do you think so?"

"Well, because someone else was watching Tomashevych. Not only those who were sitting in the Packard – the albino and the worm – as I call them.

There were also the typical investigators, who spoke German. Then I started to think... and got worried....”

“Did you take photographs of them?”

“No way!” He became startled. “Not that bunch! Right away you could see their style and approach to the case. No, I wouldn’t tangle with that kind.”

“Now tell me, dear friend, what exactly testified to the fact that their affair was coming to an end.”

“Oh, how you’ve bamboozled me! And why am I being tormented and punished?...”

“Don’t forget: I’m still your client.”

“Marko, I know you’re not Croesus either. And those *zloty* don’t fall from the sky. My conscience begins to torment me when I’m milking you.”

“Don’t worry. I’ll get that money somewhere else. Go....”

“There were several times when they didn’t see each other for a long time. He forbade her from seeing him at the office or calling him there. Finally, the secretary was warned about it and didn’t allow any private calls to get past her. So, all Emilia had left to do was to call him at his apartment. But even there, either he didn’t pick up the phone or immediately hung up.”

“How do you know about it in such detail?”

Kvartsyany smiled contentedly.

“From her letters.”

“Ah, did you also read through the love letters?”

“More than that, I bribed the postal carrier, so she’d let me know when certain letters would reach the office. And I was already waiting for them at the gate.”

“Wait, why just to the office? She didn’t write to him at home?”

“She did, but she didn’t receive any answers, then attacked him in the office. Sometimes she even stood in front of the entrance waiting for him.”

“What about him?”

“He walked past her with his trap screwed shut.”

“And then what?”

“Then they reconciled. But wait... Add ten more *zloty*.... Because this is beyond my usual rate. I feel like I’m losing my level of proficiency. You know, we have our childhood years and other things. Though we love each other like brothers, we count like Jews.”

I had to lay out another ten *zloty*.

"Okay. Tell me more."

"In those letters, she actually described everything. Her efforts to call him, to ambush him at the office, and her desperate letters. The reason for their quarrels was his reluctance to divorce Irena. He rejected this complete-ly equitable decision in every possible way. And she seethed and seethed and became enraged. But some time passed, and then they again were a pair of doves. But it couldn't last for long. I saw that he was already losing patience when she started to stalk him. He had to hide from her on the days that he would meet up with Agnieszka. But what – he'd get in his car and skedaddle from her, then somewhere he'd pick up that Agnieszka and that's the end, it's over. And so it was an endless cycle, you know? They'd make up, then quarrel."

"And on those days when she couldn't see him, did she meet up with anyone else?"

"I already told you ... eh ... that is, I lied a little when I said, that she in-terested me only as part of a couple. And it really was like that till a certain time while I was working for Irena. But when I started working for the un-known *Pan* X, I was only interested in Tomashevych, but Emilia's intimate life already passed beyond my watchful eye."

"Then you had to know about Tomashevych's secret abode?"

"I didn't notice anything like that. In fact, it also interests those who hired me."

CHAPTER 3

The doorman met me again at the gate on Syktuska Street.

"Have you come for *Panna* Emilia? She's not in."

"And where did she go?"

"She left. At daybreak. She called a taxi. She packed up her things and left."

"She didn't say where she was going?"

"I asked, but she just laughed and said, 'To conquer the world.' Maybe she's doing a film for the cinema. That kind of dish would be welcome any place under the sun. And what have you heard about *Pan* Tomashevych?"

"Not much is new," I replied. "We're still running in place. Tell me, was Emilia home the morning of the day before yesterday?"

"On Friday? No, she took off early in the morning."

"Exactly when?"

"Around seven. I was still surprised because she had never been out so early. She came home that early, but she had never gone out then. And what do you think: will there be a war? Because, I read, the Union of Silesian Rebels has already started enrolling in the Silesian Legion. That must mean something, right?"

"That's not surprising, the border guards have to be vigilant first and foremost."

"And we doormen have already been instructed on how to react during a bombing," he whispered. "Just don't write that in the newspaper."

"Good. And when did Emilia return?"

"That I can't tell you. She came in when I wasn't able to see."

I thanked him, then went to Café President on the corner of Syktuska and Kościuszko Streets and paid for the phone. Bodyo picked up the phone and croaked unhappily:

"Halloo!"

"It's me, Marko. Give me the address of Emilia's parents."

"So what? Has the little birdie flown away? Well, fine, I'll be good today," he named an address in Kryvchytsi. "Take the tram number 2, walk toward Lychakiv Cemetery, and it's a couple of meters from there."

"I have a car."

"Oh! Up and coming in the world? Well, ain't you a shit of a whore's mother? And I still have to keep workin' my ass off!...."

Upper Lychakiv had the scent of fried buckwheat groats, sour horse droppings, and burnt potatoes. Emilia's parents were fixing up a leaning, and in some places, knocked-over fence.

"What happened?" I asked. "Did a car slam through it?"

"May the steering wheel get twisted in their car and in their head!" The old man said.

"Take a gander, he drove all the way to the garden, crushed everything – flowers, bushes ... he turned around and took off. And we have to sin like this on a Holy Sunday...."

"Maybe he was drunk?"

"Naw, he also laughed!"

"Does Emilia happen to be at home?"

They looked at me in surprise and checked me over from head to toe, maybe thinking I was her suitor.

"Emilia? That hoity-toity? She's not here. She dropped by last week. She ran over just for a minute, left some candy for us, and took off."

"So – she's not at home?"

"She left today. Where could she have gone?"

"And who might you be to her?" The old woman interrupted and squinted. I hesitated. Finally, I fired out:

"I'm from the newspaper. Here's my ID." They checked out my ID with disbelief.

"From the newspaper...," the woman rejoiced. "Then write what those cars are doing! Take a gander, lilies used to grow here, then asters, then dahlias ... everything's destroyed ... and I could have made some money on them."

"But what do you need Emilia for?" The old man interrupted. "Will you be writing anything about our Emilia?"

116

"There's going to be a pageant 'Beauty Queen of Lviv.' We want to invite her to take part. She has a really good chance of winning it."

"What does she get from that?"

"There's a cash reward – a thousand *zloty*." Their jaws dropped.

"She has a girlfriend," her mother said immediately. "She visited her on more than one occasion. She lives in Zamarstyniv. Right at the beginning of Sadova Street.[28] It's an old house with a big chestnut tree. Our Emilia! Who would have thought!"

I thanked her and said goodbye. I'm a good liar.

Driving through Zamarstyniv is a pleasure: you crawl like a cockroach, because everywhere there are market tents, slaughterhouses, tons of people, everyone wants to sell you something. They peek through windows, they shout. It's not a street, but a continuous bazaar. It seems that the people of Zamarstyniv are never under a roof, only on bumpy sidewalks and muddied roads. On both sides there are taverns, which are proudly called restaurants, with large drive-in courtyards. The middle of the courtyards boasts of plank-covered wells with pulleys and troughs for watering horses, because everyone leaves their horse carts here, and then goes on foot into the city so as to not pay at the "hoofed" turnpike barrier for using the roads. Those carts are immediately surrounded by speculators and traders, filling the air with incredible noise, and once they buy something, like ants with crumbs, they fly around their courtyards, where on all the porches and balconies washed sheets flutter loudly in the wind.

I left the car before reaching Sadova Street and continued walking along past the pubs, behind the windows of which you could see crowds of people, who often quarreled, tore their clothes and hair, and wrestled from corner to corner. Shady-looking guys gathered on the street in front of the windows, entered the taverns, went out, whispered – this is when Lviv's thieves planned their night excursions. From time to time the door of a particular tavern opened, and with a shout and a scream the community of drunkards poured out, pounding each other with their fists. A striking screaming filled the air. Knives often glistened, blood was shed, and sometimes a corpse was left on the pavement, but no one paid special attention to it. Not a problem, because in a minute everything returned to the way

---

[28] Now called Horodnycha Street (author's note).

it was. Both the powdered and lipsticked prostitutes, from whom stench and the hopeless boredom of cheap hotels wafted, paid no attention to the hurly-burly. They lazily clattered in their worn-out shoes from one corner to the other, waiting for offers.

Suddenly, they stopped and listened, and on the top floor of one of the stone apartment buildings the melody of a tango, passionate and hot as the midday in Andalusia, flowed from an open window. No one else, except for them and the stranger who turned on the radio for the entire street, listened to the magical melody. But it didn't last long, because in a moment the window in the basement opened and the hoarse voice of an angry doorman's wife thundered:

"Will you close the window, you darn *batyar*, or not? You lie in a dirty, unwashed bed all day and even play the radio! It's a pity you didn't go to the café. You've probably run out of money, because your strumpet bought herself a new dress. She'll parade around like a lady from a big house! We know from which house and how you earn your bread, we know! What kind of a *pan* do you think you are – you haven't paid the doorman's fee[29] five times already!"

The maidens of the night giggled. One of them, listening to the tango, snapped at the witch from the basement:

"Shut up, *Pani* Doorwoman! You're barking like a dog at a sparrow. Oh, what nice music!"

The doorman's wife looked contemptuously at both of them, spat, and slammed the window.

I thought that if I walked past the windows that the owners, taking notice of me, might say that Emilia wasn't in. There were no windows in the wall facing Zamarstyniv Street. I climbed over the fence, bent down, went under the windows to the door, and quietly pressed the latch. The door opened. Voices came from inside, both of them female. I recognized Emilia's at once. The child's voice belonged to the baby. I quickly crossed the vestibule and completely surprised them. Her girlfriend was feeding the baby porridge. Emilia was sitting at the table and flipping through a children's book.

"Who are you? What do you want?" The hostess got worked up.

Emilia was silent, her eyes shut with guilt. I smiled politely.

....

[29]   A small fee paid to doormen for opening the gates of apartment buildings after 10 p.m.

"Excuse me for sneaking in so rudely, but I was sure you'd say she's not here. But the matter is quite urgent."

"Do you know him?" Her girlfriend asked. Emilia nodded.

"Who is he?"

"From the newspaper."

"From the news-news-paper?"

No, I didn't say anything about the beauty contest.

"Emilia, I need to talk to you. It's in your interest."

"I know," she said meekly and stood up.

"I won't let her go anywhere!" Her girlfriend started up to her feet, hugging the child close to her chest.

"But we're not going anywhere," I tried to reassure her. "Just to the garden. And not for long."

"Emilia," her friend said, "if something's up – shout!"

Emilia went out with me to the garden with her head drooping. I asked:

"Why did you run away so suddenly?"

"Someone came to me last night."

"Who?"

"I don't know."

"Did it happen to be the one who ordered you to call Tomashevych yesterday morning?"

She looked at me with fear.

"You already know?"

"The police know too. How did it happen?"

"I've never seen him before. I'm so terrified. The day before Yanus was shot, he called me and told me to arrange a meeting with Yanus at the villa. That is, the next day in the morning. He spoke in such a terrifying voice. As if it was very important. But that I should not go there myself."

"When was that?"

"In the afternoon. About three. I said I wasn't planning on doing it. He then told me to call my parents and ask how things were with their fence. Then he hung up. I called and learned that a car had smashed through their fence and crushed the flowers that my mother loves so much. Then he called again and said that the second time the car would run over one of my parents."

She started to sob and leaned against me. I hugged her and sat her down on the bench next to me.

"What happened next?"

"Well, what's next... He said he'd be waiting for me the next morning next to the gate. That I should come out. But I didn't come out."

"And what happened?"

"Nothing happened. I phoned my parents to call the police. My father has an acquaintance at the police station. He came to them and looked after them. But no one bothered them anymore."

"And you?"

"Someone else called me. I didn't pick up the phone. And from the window I saw a really thin tall man walking down the street. He was incredibly ugly and jerking his legs the entire time."

"So, you didn't approach the phone. And if it was Tomashevych?"

"I didn't make any arrangements with him. It couldn't have been him."

"Who summoned him to the villa?"

"I don't know. Somebody else. Maybe Irena. She did her best to get rid of him. I never ordered any food. And I can't imagine how I could lure him to the villa."

"Well, you might as well have said that you got pregnant." She winced.

"No, I'd never lie so vilely. Although I guess he would have been happy since his wife couldn't have children."

She fell silent as she touched the hem of her skirt with her fingers.

"What happened next?"

"I thought it was over and that no one would bother me. However, this morning he calls again and says that I'm a naughty girl. But I can make up for it if I go on a date with him. I said that I won't go out on any dates. In a few minutes he was already knocking on my door. I threatened to call the police. Then he said he'd get me no matter what. When he left the building, I looked out of the window. He seemed to have sensed me looking at him and raised his head abruptly. I barely managed to step back. I wouldn't want to see him again."

"What are you going to do? Hide at your girlfriend's place?"

"I still have some money left. Syanka's husband got killed by a train. There's room for me to live there. I can sew. We'll take care of ourselves. How did you find me?"

"The private detective who had been watching you told me your parents' address. And your parents told me about your friend. Just in case, warn them not to disclose your whereabouts to anyone. At least for the time being. The police are searching for this crook. As soon as they get him, you'll be safe."

"Really?"

She was snuggling up to me like a little child, seeking protection and maybe even nurturing. But what could I offer to such a dish?"

"Have you by any chance heard about any other apartments of Tomashevych? Other than the one he lived in on Legioniv Street?"

"I have. But I don't know where it is."

"Could Tomashevych have had another mistress?"

Her face became slightly tense.

"Oh my God! I didn't see him every day. He could have."

"Well, did you happen to notice, say, any signs of a woman's presence, other than you, in the villa?"

"I did, but what of it? His wife used to go there. How could I know who might have left those traces there?"

"And what kind of signs could there have been?"

"Well, lipstick on a glass ... a hairpin ... women's slippers not where you had put them... But I didn't suspect Yanus of anything. And I didn't pry into his life."

"You told me that the last time you were at the villa was last week."

"Yes. Why?"

"What were you doing Friday morning?" She pondered for a little while.

"In the morning?... Nothing ... I was at home."

"Didn't you go out?"

"I'm saying I was at home. Why?"

"The doorman said you left at about 7 a.m." Emilia blushed.

"Was that on Friday? Yesterday? I thought Friday was the day before yesterday. I'm confused. So, it's Saturday...." She shook her head. "I'm all mixed up."

"So where did you go on Friday?"

"I ... I was in a bad mood. I had had a nightmare about running away from someone and hiding in the woods. I woke up at six, had a quick breakfast, and felt like I couldn't bear staying at home. So, I went out and headed to Jesuit Park. I walked there for about two hours. Then I went to the cinema on Khorunshchyna Street."

"To the Atlantik Cinema?"

"*The Sorceress from Salem* was playing."

"And then?"

"Then I came back home."

"Yesterday morning before and after Tomashevych was killed, a Packard with four men and a woman in it drove to Bryukhovychi and back. Those were the murderers."

Emilia looked at me in surprise:

"Did they really kill him?"

"Yes. And not only him. They also killed another guy, the gardener."

"Felyek?" She wondered.

"Yes. Did you know him?"

"A little."

She buried her face in her palms and started sobbing. I waited for her to calm down and asked:

"Emilia, what was your relationship with Tomashevych in recent times?"

"Why are you asking? Haven't I told you everything?"

"No, you haven't told me that he ignored you from time to time, and that you were pursuing him."

The girl's eyes glared defensively.

"Who told you that?"

"Does it matter? Did Tomashevych say it was time for you to break up?"

"No, he absolutely didn't. We sometimes quarreled. I guess I was too attached to him."

"You wanted him to marry you. And he procrastinated, which irritated you."

"Isn't it a woman's natural desire to start a family?"

"It is. But some people had the impression that your relationship was coming to an end."

Emilia frowned and pursed her lips. Her eyes glistened with tears. I felt sorry for her. I stood up. She looked at me sadly and asked:

"Are you leaving already?"

"Yes. Who do you think that woman in the Packard might be? Apparently, she's the one who lured Tomashevych to the villa."

"I don't know," she sniffled. "I didn't live Yanus's life. I don't know anyone from his surroundings. If someone had forced me to lure him to the villa,

I definitely would have come up with some capricious things that would make him suspicious."

"Like what?"

"Well, for example, I would have also ordered Cuban cigars. He would have guessed something was amiss."

I couldn't help but recognize her cunningness. Since I had nothing else to ask her about, I just asked for permission to use the phone. I wondered how Bodyo was going to return the money and whether his client had bothered him. But Bodyo wasn't there. The secretary said he had already gone home. It was weird. Did he go home in the early afternoon? I asked if anyone had called him, and she confirmed it.

He lived on Vulka Street. He didn't have a phone there, that's why he rented an office.

CHAPTER 4

The *Warszawa* Restaurant was located at 3 Smolka Square. In the middle of the dining room, decorated with white and green marble, there was a fountain with fish swimming in it. Unlike other pubs, where the clientele constantly changed from the day to the night, in *Warszawa* mostly the same people hung out. At night they would sometimes spend what they had earned during the day at the same table. And although they were basically the same group of people all the time, daytime was significantly different from nighttime. During the day, regulars were immersed in newspapers or discussions, without leaving their tables, forming separate groups, each of which lived its own life minding its own business. In the evening, the tables were covered with white tablecloths, the newspapers were folded, the discussions were interrupted, and the groups merged to share a social life. And then the people who had been sitting at the next table all afternoon without paying any attention to their neighbors, would all of a sudden become aware of each other and start exchanging smiles and bows, bathing in a heartfelt atmosphere of mutual friendliness.

In fact, I found this usual daytime picture – most of the tables were occupied by stockbrokers immersed in newspapers. No one was ordering hard liquor yet, only beer. Some were having coffee with cakes. There was a blissful peace and quiet. A young man with a narrow strip of mustache hairs over his lip was bored to death behind the bar. My arrival failed to impress him at all, even as I approached the bar and sat down on a stool.

"What would you like, sir?" he asked idly.

"I'd like to see Agnieszka. Is she working today?"

He glared at me in surprise, moved his lips silently, as if trying to utter a word he had never uttered in his life, and finally muttered:

"Um ... uh ... what's the matter?"

Two weeks ago, I could have asked in turn, "What do you care?" But lately I realized that in such cases politeness still paid off, although I was none too happy about it.

"It's a private matter," I replied in a low voice.

He was even more surprised and said:

"Agnieszka's changing now. I'll let her know you're looking for her." I thanked the guy, restraining myself from asking why she was changing. I wanted to pretend to be a friend of hers. So, I ordered a coffee and sat down at an empty table. The bartender disappeared for a moment, then came out and occupied his previous spot, looking as bored as when I first saw him.

I was hungry, but I didn't have time to wait for a hot meal, so I ordered chicken broth and two paté sandwiches. Just a few minutes after I had finished my meal, a sexy dish in a long glittering dancing gown showed up. Her dark hair was falling in waves along her temples and down to her shoulders. Apparently, Agnieszka had made a career. She was no longer a waitress, but a taxi dancer, who encouraged the clientele to pay for dances. I was gazing at her glide up to me, but it wasn't easy now to recognize the same Agnieszka I used to know. Although she had been attractive before, she was never as beautiful as she was right at that moment.

That night, I was trudging across the railroad bridge in my usual state of inebriation, returning from Levandivka – the middle of Lviv's nowhere, where I had spent the entire evening in a lousy pub with several buddies after a good scrap. Prior to that, Purtsel had called to tell me to help him out with a certain issue. I couldn't say no, because Purtsel had never said no to me either. He was an old chap of mine, a *batyar*, who was respected among the criminal fraternity and gladly joined in any fight, without asking who was fighting for whom and why. When I had to get into a dive bar where no one knew me, I took him with me and then had nothing to worry about. He set a time to meet in a tavern in Levandivka. Besides him, I saw Pretzel, Chains, Gypsum, and Smolder (Pretsl, Tsep, Gips, and Schweler) there. They were all powerful guys. The first two worked as masons and laid cobblestones. Gypsum and Smolder were inseparable; they even owned a small shop in Levandivka adorned with a "Gypsum and Smolder" sign. Both were dependable guys and buddied around with us. They often joined us on various escapades.

This time an extraordinary thing happened. Pretzel's sister Syanka had been grabbed on the street and dragged by force to Kazio Markhevka's bordello, where she was raped and so battered that she ended up in the hospital.

"Not dat she was all dat pure," Pretzel said "But, dem shitbags first raped her and den smashed her face. What da hell's wit dat?"

We agreed to go the bordello and raise hell there, and punch out Kazio's mug at the same time. It was a rather bold venture, because Kazio Markhevka was not a simple guy. He had his own gang, ran three brothels and a gin mill, and it was really risky to get involved with him. But incidences similar to the one with Pretzel's sister were getting more frequent. The police couldn't do anything about it, so we were left with taking up the matter ourselves.

I saw the guys hide brass knuckles in their pockets along with leather sticks filled with lead, and knives. Purtsel gave me a glove with jagged iron nozzles. We boozed it up a little and then set off.

It was winter and the snow was cracking under our feet. Kazio's bordello was located in a small house as long as a barn at the edge of the forest, where even the light of lanterns didn't reach. Drunken screams, singing, and music could be heard from afar. The party was in full swing.

"Remembers," said Purtsel, "We beats up only Kazio and thems who messed up Pretzel's sister. The rest don't matters to us unless they asks for it."

Fat Tonyo was standing at the door. He worked as a butcher for his day job and at nighttime as a doorman at Kazio's.

"What kinds a band's this?" He became enraged. "Who invited yous guys here?"

"Get out of the way, Tonyo," Purtsel said firmly. "Or…."

"Or what?" Tonyo bristled.

"Or you might get whacked. Do yous need dat?"

"Me? Whacked?" He burst out laughing. "By yous?'

At that moment Purtsel threw a left hook and punched Tonyo in the nose. His nose cracked. Blood oozed across his face, but he didn't have enough time to fly into a rage, because Purtsel's right hand nailed him right below his chest. He shrank like a sack from which sand had been poured out. In an instant he was already lying there at the threshold. We stepped over him and went inside. There were two dozen guys and girls spinning in a light tango. Kazio himself was sitting in the corner with his legs crossed, wearing shiny black silver-buckled shoes and smoking an expensive cigar. Gypsum and Smolder blocked the exit and didn't let anyone out. If someone was very intent on getting some fresh air, he would first have to crash flat on the floor and wipe the blood from his trap. Purtsel moved right away to Kazio, whereas Pretzel, Chains, and me were clearing his way from anyone making any attempt to stop us. My glove did itself justice by getting soaked with blood from two of their traps.

Kazio grabbed his pocket and pulled out a gun. But Purtsel hit him with brass knuckles, knocking out his tooth and catching his hand. Meanwhile, Pretzel took the gun, pressed it against Kazio's head and asked:

"Who massacred my sister today?"

Kazio coughed, spitting up blood, and croaked out:

"You, bastards, won't get away with this...."

He didn't have time to elaborate on his deep thought because Pretzel hit him on the noggin with his gun.

"Tell me, asshole, who, 'cause you'll end up not only witout your teeth, but witout your ears, too." While speaking he flashed a razor blade in front of Kazio's terrified eyes.

"He's not here," Kazio wheezed.

Chains jumped up to the server at the buffet, grabbed her by the mop of her curly hair and slammed her mug against the counter with undisguised pleasure – so that she even made slurping sounds.

"And do you know who it was?"

The old lady began to scream with her trap wide open. She groaned and muttered:

"It was blind Lyonio!"

Lyonio got the nickname because he wore sunglasses. He was a pick-pocket and a sadist. None of his visits to a prostitute would end without him beating her up. But since he always paid regularly, all his dirty linen was washed "in the family." But not this time.

"Where's dis Lyonio?" Purtsel asked Kazio.

He shook his head and muttered something indistinct. Pretzel wanted to deck him again, but Chains had already got the old lady to talk. She said that Lyonio was lying with a whore in the last room at the back of the bordello. We left Chains in charge of Kazio and rushed there. We found Lyonio just as he was smacking around the poor girl with both hands. Purtsel tossed him out of bed and began to punch Lyonio's trap with his brass knuckles, first breaking his nose, then his cheekbones and jaws. Then he made sure to knock out all his teeth. Finally, he lopped off both of Lyonio's ears with a razor blade, wrapped them in a newspaper, and put them in his pocket. After that, Lyonio passed out at a very timely moment, because Pretzel was about to lop off another part of his body, even though he was already stained with blood like a butcher in Zamarstyniv. The girl in bed watched all this not without pleasure, wiping tears and blood from her broken nose.

On returning to Kazio, Purtsel said, leaning over his ear:

"Remembers, Kazio, next time yous picks up anutha poor chickie off the street, I'll chops off all the parts that sticks out of youses' body. Haves I made myself clear?" Kazio nodded, and Pretzel showed him Lyonio's ears. "And I'll burn down all three of youses' bordellos."

Kazio's eyes were as wide as saucers. He winced at the sight of the ears, because those ears didn't look very appealing.

"What are we waiting for?" Smolder asked, firing at the oil lamp. The lamp exploded and the burning oil spilled onto the floor. The fire quickly spread through the room. Everyone rushed to the doors and windows in a panic. No one tried to put the fire out, although Kazio screamed "Water! Water!" like crazy.

Purtsel knocked out the window, and we jumped out. The girls and visitors of this cozy establishment also jumped out of other windows. In fact, the fire raged the most in the dance hall, and reached the bedchambers after everyone had fled. So no one died. Everything ended happily and neatly.

It was late at night when I finally broke free from the cesspool of sin and debauchery. My feet from time to time got tangled and I slid on the ice. The wind was tossing snow into my trap, but I thought it was a really good opportunity to sober up while I was walking and didn't look for a carriage. In the distance on the bridge, I saw a dark figure. The wind was blowing her hair around and slashing the hem of her raincoat. She held onto the metal railing looking down, where a steel track glistened against the moon, and snowflakes danced in the streetlamps' light. In the distance, a steam locomotive rumbled, slowly approaching the bridge. The figure began to lean on the railing and even threw one leg over it. Meanwhile the sound of the locomotive puffing out steam was getting louder and louder. I wasn't aware of what I was doing. I just saw a girl in front of me who wanted to throw herself from the bridge underneath the locomotive pulling freight cars. And I rushed to her as fast as I could. At the moment when she was swinging her other leg over to stand on the other side of the railing on the edge of the bridge, I grabbed her and pulled her with such force that we both fell into the snow while the train rumbled beneath us.

She was struggling to get free like a wildcat, screaming and cursing, biting and scratching, but I held her tightly, even though blood was oozing from my cut lip. I let go of her only when the train had disappeared behind a bend, and there was silence again. We were lying in the snow on the bridge, breathing heavily. She stopped squirming and just whimpered sorrowfully on my chest.

"Why? Why?" She muttered, and I stroked her hair trying to console her.

"What's your name?"

"Agnieszka...," she said softly.

I helped her to her feet, pulled out a bottle of *horilka*[30] from my pocket and poured some into her mouth. She gulped it down and coughed, then picked up a handful of the clean snow and ate it. I didn't drink any. I already had enough. Her attractive face and disheveled hair seemed angelic to me. I took her by the arm and led her toward the city. She walked obediently with a doomed look. I put a handkerchief on my torn lip and said:

"If girls jumped from the bridge because of every scoundrel, humanity would cease to exist."

"How do you know he's a scoundrel?" she asked timidly.

"Because only a scoundrel could abandon such a beauty." She looked at me in surprise and said:

"I've never thought that way about myself."

"Now think about it from time to time. Where do you live?"

"Nowhere at the moment," she sighed.

"How come? Did he throw you out on the street without anything?"

"No. One day he just vanished into thin air. And I have nothing to pay for my lodgings. Today they threw me onto the street. I left my things with the guard."

"You need to find a job."

....

[30] Ukrainian vodka. Its name comes from the verb "hority" (to burn). Firewater might be a close literal equivalent in English.

"I don't know how to do anything."

Her helplessness moved me. She looked like a homeless kitten that I wanted to take pity on and cuddle with.

"It's not too difficult to be a waitress," I said. "Any restaurant will take you. They like to hire pretty girls to attract customers. And you'll eventually meet someone there...."

"And what then?" She looked at me with a smile. "A new adventure, new suffering? All men are scoundrels...."

"I've heard that somewhere."

"Because it's true. What happened to your lip?"

"You don't recognize your own work?"

"Did I scratch it?" She sounded so regretful that I wanted her to scratch me somewhere else.

"Who else?"

She gave me a quick peck, licked her lips, and said:

"I'm so sorry. I was in despair...." Then she suddenly startled: "Where are you taking me?"

"There's a cabbie dozing. We'll take a carriage and go to my place."

"Forget that!" She flared up. "I'm not a whore."

"And I'm not a pimp. Tomorrow I'll introduce you to someone who can help you get a job."

"But I won't sleep either with you or with him."

"No, of course you won't."

And that's how we became acquainted. I put her in the bedroom and heard her push an armchair against the door. I lay down on the couch in the study and fell asleep snug as a bug in a rug. In the morning I was awakened by the rattle of utensils in the kitchen and the smell of buckwheat porridge. Having heard me getting up from the couch and getting dressed, she shouted:

"Well, finally you're up! Breakfast's on the table."

Entering the kitchen, I saw clean dishes and steaming porridge with milk on the table.

"Oh," I laughed, "you said you don't know how to do anything."

"Well, I'm good at making porridge. Although it got burnt a little." She watched me intently take a spoonful of porridge and put it in my mouth. "How is it? Is it edible?" she asked timidly.

"First rate," I said, knowing all too well that a man must never dare question any woman's culinary skills. That would never be forgiven. It would be etched in her memory forever and would be mentioned over and over again.

The porridge did have a slightly burnt taste, but not so burnt as to make it inedible. After breakfast, I took her to Genyo Zbezhkhovsky, though not without some regret. It seemed to me that she might have liked to stay with me more, but she was ashamed to admit it. She was glancing at me hopefully and smiling mysteriously, as if provoking me into some conversation, while at the same time successfully demonstrating her cleaning skills. But at that time, I didn't feel like starting a new affair when the wounds from the old one hadn't healed yet. I preferred to remain alone with my spiritual pain.

Just as I thought, the moment Genyo saw this beautiful dish, he started fluttering about and came up with tons of ideas where she might get a job, immediately announcing his incredibly wide and diverse network of connections. But I quickly trimmed those wings, since I understood that Agnieszka's qualifications were not good enough for either a telegraph operator or an editorial secretary. A saleswoman or a waitress would be the best options she could hope for. That was what actually happened. That same day Genyo found a place for her in the Bagatelle on Reytan Street.[31] This pub, actually called Casino de Paris, was famous for its ancient ballroom, which, however, enjoyed a notorious reputation. Although cabaret performances did take place there, besides visitors from other towns and cities, it was also filled with heavenly birds and the daughters of Corinth.[32] The people of Lviv called the pub Bagatelle, and the bar in its basement – Kurvidolek [The Whorepit]. My guess is that Agnieszka didn't last there long because Roiza Pink, who was in charge of the place, didn't need virtuous waitresses. We hadn't seen each other since then. Until the day I came to the Warszawa Restaurant.

"Are you here to see me?" she asked in a sonorous, almost childish voice, possibly not recognizing me.

I confirmed that, asked her to sit down, and smiled. She looked at me closer and cried out:

"God! Is it you? How come I didn't recognize you right away?"

....

[31]   Now called Les Kurbas Street (author's note).

[32]   I.e. prostitutes and women of ill repute.

"Well, that's understandable. I look a lot fresher now than I did that night."

"Oh, yes! I'd say that you even look younger."

"And you don't look any older. How long has it been? A little more than two years?"

"Something like that. What brought you here? Have you been looking for me?"

"How are things with you? Have you found your life's dream?"

Agnieszka laughed.

"No. But I've found some inner peace."

"I'm here regarding the Tomashevych case."

Not a single muscle on her face twitched.

"Are you? But what do I have to do with that?"

"You were involved with him. Don't try to deny it. The police don't know about you yet. So you'd better tell me what you were doing yesterday?"

"When exactly?"

"In the morning until noon."

"Sleeping. I dance here till late."

"Did you call Tomashevych in the morning?"

She looked at me in surprise and bit her lip.

"How do you know?" She finally uttered.

"So, you did. What time was it?"

"Around seven."

"And what did you tell him?"

"What-what... You have to know everything... I told him that my 'Auntie Fanny' had come for a visit, that's why," she nervously crossed her legs. "I said we'd meet in a week.... Because that time of the month lasts a bit...."

"And then?"

"Then I just plopped like a pancake into bed."

"And when did you leave the house that day?"

"Late in the afternoon."

"Will the doorman confirm?"

"We don't have a doorman. I don't live in a stone apartment house ... but in a small hut in Klepariv."

"Do you live alone?"

"Yes. Would you like to come over?" Agnieszka winked mischievously.

"I'll give it some thought... It won't be easy for you without Toma-shevych, will it?"

"It wasn't easy with him either. Though, we did come to an agreement recently."

"On what?"

"That he'd finally leave that shrew."

"Emilia?"

"Yeah."

"Did he promise you that?"

"Yeah. He was fed up with her carping. Get a divorce. Get a divorce … She kept saying. She wanted him to marry her. And why should he get a divorce? It was good for him the way things were. And I didn't demand anything from him. I knew up front what he needed. I did everything to please him. Never got under his skin. I was mostly silent. Guys, you know, prefer silent women to chatterboxes like Emilia. She chattered like a magpie."

"Have you heard her talk?"

"No, but Yan told me about it."

"But you put up with her presence in his life?"

"Why would I care if he was watering at another spring. I don't care."

"Do you smoke?"

"No. Why?"

"When you kissed Tomashevych, did the smell of tobacco bother you?"

"No, he smoked expensive cigarettes. What's the meaning of all these questions?"

"I also need to know about two suspicious characters...."

I described those who were after me and asked if she knew them.

She immediately objected:

"Give me a break. I'm not at the police station. I'm at work. Do you want me to be sacked? We're not supposed to join anyone at the table and just wag our tongues. We're here to make money for the joint."

"By tricking a customer into a treat?"

"You don't seem to know what taxi dancers do, do you?"

"I can order something for you. What would you like to drink?"

"Now, that's another topic. Champagne. A whole bottle, because I'm on a roll."

I ordered it. The waiter opened the bottle and poured the wine into glasses.

"Do you like champagne?"

"Who doesn't?"

"There are some who break wind from it."

"Brea-a-k wind?" She laughed. "Are you saying that somebody might fart from champagne? This is the first time I've heard such a thing."

"Did Tomashevych often buy you champagne?"

"Always when I asked and even when I didn't ask. He knew there had to be champagne. Because I don't like strong drinks, but champagne is just right."

Agnieszka downed the glass and licked her lips. I refilled it, and she gulped it down again quickly.

"And what did Emilia drink?" I asked her.

"How the hell would I know. Probably what everyone drank."

"What exactly?"

"I'm saying: I don't know. I never asked about her. Only lately did he begin to complain about her and confess about it to me. And I didn't push him. If he wants to break up with her – I'm fine with that. If he doesn't – I don't give a damn. With my work schedule I can't take more than two nights off. And if he wants more, then let him look around. As my grandmother used to say, a pecker isn't a pestle, it'll never wear out." She giggled again and nodded for me to pour.

"Did Tomashevych tell you about the scenes that Emilia created?"

"Oh, so you also know about that? He often escaped from her in the car with me. And I also read her letters. They were on his desk. Such calligraphic handwriting, such confessions of love.... Holy cow! I would never-ever be able to come up with something like that. "My beloved Yasya," Agnieszka muttered in a pseudo-theatrical tone, "the jasmine flower of my feelings is losing its petals without the gentle touch of your fingers... The buds of my breasts are bursting with passion...."

"Did he show you those letters?"

"No way! I'm telling you – they were on his desk. While he was bathing, I had nothing better to do but read them. Then I put everything back in order the way it was. I know it's dishonest, but we girls are like that. We're curious about the mistresses of our lovers, and we can't help it." She finished drinking the glass and looked at me with interest: "I like you. Do you happen to have a lover?"

"From time to time."

"In three days, I'll get in shape for you...."

"And you were so inaccessible two years ago!"

"Two years is a long time. I still had some dreams, some convictions.... Then it all went to the dogs. But I'm not a frivolous slut. Maybe I was stupid then for not seducing you. But you got rid of me so fast...."

"All I did was to put you in good hands."

"But not that good. In the Bagatelle they wanted to make me into a courtesan. But you were right – all I have is my beauty. So, I escaped and ended up here. And when Tomashevych appeared with a thick wallet, I stopped resisting and didn't think that I was doing something dishonest... But you also saved me from suicide. Sometimes I think... that even though life isn't always a bed of roses, it's better to be alive than to rest in a remote corner of the cemetery, where suicides are buried, rotting slowly... I'm grateful to you for that."

"When was the last time you were at the villa?"

"Why the last time?" she wondered. "I've never been there."

"And if I tell you that you were seen yesterday morning and afternoon in a car on the road to Bryukhovychi and back?" Here I decided to go too far, carefully watching her facial expression. But it remained unchanged. "In the company of four men. Two of them were the ones I already described."

She was silent for a moment, as if digesting the news, then shrugged.

"I wonder who told you that tale? I was sleeping then like a baby. Well, you know, your champagne's not making its way down my throat anymore. Enough for me."

She got up and walked straight to the bar. The champagne had no effect on her.

CHAPTER 5

Bodyo used to live with his parents. Then his father died, and his mother was a drunkard who wouldn't give him any peace. Sometime later, he settled on Vulka Street where he lived by himself in a small house, whose low windows had settled into the ground. First, I took a tram and then walked the rest of the way to get there. His street had no sidewalk and wasn't paved. I had to walk around puddles, sometimes holding on to the fence. I went into the yard, which was a mess – there were piles of rotted wooden planks from the old floor which Bodyo had replaced with a new one, but for some reason had not burned yet, and rusty buckets and pots from previous owners. His house had not changed since my last visit. There was the very same desolation and absence of a caretaker. The heavy oak door, covered with a steel sheet, was left ajar. I pushed it, and a frightened cat rushed to my feet. Apparently, it wasn't strong enough to squeeze into the opening. I stepped over the threshold and smelled moisture, mold, and death. I entered the dark hall and shouted: "Bohdan! Where are you?" But only the flies answered me with their buzzing. I fumbled for the switch on the wall, but there was no light. I groped my way into the gloomy room, whose windows faced north and were obscured by thick bushes and trees. There were crumbled messy bed sheets on the couch against the wall. Books and paper were scattered on the floor. In the next room, which was used as a study, everything had been turned upside down. Someone had been searching for something, apparently for the notebook, in disbelief that Bodyo hadn't found it. Pale bare feet were sticking out from under the table. I moved closer and saw Bodyo half-sitting and half-lying in a chair, his head and arms dangling to the side. Blood was dripping from his head making a puddle on the floor. There was no point in feeling for his pulse. Bodyo was dead. A fly was crawling on his face. There was an unfinished glass with something yellow on the table in front of him. The ashtray was full of cigarette butts and ashes. I tried to imagine the last minutes of his life. What was he doing? There was a calendar with certain days marked. I turned it over to its unprinted flip side. I could see notes written in ink – numbers and dates. The dates coincided with the days marked in the calendar. But what did they mean? Nothing to me.

The moment I opened the desk drawer, I heard the rustle and the creak in the floorboards behind me. But it was too late. I didn't have time to look back and received such a whack to my head that I passed out right away.

I came to my senses from a bucket of cold water that was poured on my head. I opened my eyes and saw the policemen through the gray mist. Corporal Radomsky, whom I had met before, pointed a pistol and ordered me to get up. To my surprise, I saw a heavy hammer in my hands. There was clotted blood and some hair on it. How cunning.

"This chump seemed suspicious at the outset!" The corporal shook his head. "Wherever he is, there's a corpse. Well, get moving. You'll get your chance to cool off on a bunk in the slammer."

I struggled to my feet, dropping the hammer. The corporal picked it up carefully, wrapping it in a linen napkin he had pulled from the credenza. They were at that moment carrying out Bodyo, and the photographer was packing up his camera. I tried to explain that I couldn't be the murderer, but no one would listen to me. I obediently went to the police car without any resistance, realizing that there was no point in trying to justify yourself if you were caught with a bloody hammer in your hand. I was handcuffed and put in the back of the car. Bars separated the driver from me. On the way, I was thinking that this annoying incident would significantly ruin my plans for the day. Who knew how much it would take to get the police to finally contact Obukh. That was exactly what happened, because as soon as I asked about him in the commandant's office, I was advised to shut up. They took my fingerprints and locked me in a cell with some thief. Seeing my bloodied hands, he immediately huddled in a corner, watching me with frightened eyes. But there was a sink in the cell, so I washed my hands even though they were shackled. An hour passed, I started feeling hungry, but Obukh didn't show up. The thief didn't take his eyes off me. I dozed off. I dreamt of summer, and a river, and willows, and someone calling me from the opposite bank. I opened my eyes – a policeman called me to go for interrogation. I was reluctant to part with such a warm and vivid dream, but I obediently got up and dragged myself down the long, boring corridor to the office. For quite a long while they questioned me patiently about what I was doing on Vulka Street. My explanations made them laugh.

"Tell the truth," the corporal insisted. "You came to steal something. The master of the house caught you, and then you hit him with the hammer. Right?"

"No, that's wrong. What could I steal from someone who could barely make ends meet? Kvartsyany was an old friend of mine. We went to school together."

"You're lying. But we will get to the heart of the matter. We've caught chumps worse than you. And don't you rely on the commissioner. He won't help you here. Your fingerprints are on the hammer."

"If I had come to steal something, where is the thing I stole? And why was I lying on the ground with a bump on the back of my head?"

"Oh, now you're acting like a smarty-pants. Wait, we'll kick your pride out of you. The fact that you didn't manage to steal anything doesn't exonerate you."

"Well, then who knocked me out so that I fainted on the floor?"

"It's really a mystery. But we will solve it. Maybe there was someone else with the master of the house. Let's say his buddy. You hit the master, and he hit you. You fell. He got scared and ran away. But we'll find him, too."

I was locked in the cell again, and I tried to doze off again and restore the same dream I had, but it wouldn't return to me. Right after Obukh showed up, I was rescued. First, I heard his angry voice, then the guard unlocked the cell and released me."

"Can you possibly stop doing things without going out on your own?" He upbraided me. "Why didn't you let me know?"

"But how did I know I'd find a corpse?"

Obukh took me to his office, gave me some tea, and sent an underling for sandwiches. I told him about Emilia and poor Bodyo, then about Agnieszka.

"Well, here's another person," he sighed. "We lost our way in broad daylight, literally among three pines. And one of them is lying. Actually, I visited Kvartsyany's office, and everything was turned upside down there. Fortunately, the secretary had already left, so she was safe. Neighbors called the police when they heard the noise. That's when I sent Radomsky to his house."

"They probably didn't believe he hadn't found anything," I said. "Any news about the criminal case of the murdered boy and the private detective?"

"*Pan* Commandant does not believe that the murders of the boy and Kvartsyany are in any way related to the murder of Tomashevych. But this is only what he says, because in fact somebody must be digging. I haven't found out who yet. Just in case, I'm forbidden to bother the widow with interrogations. But you have a free hand. And I think it's time for you to pay her another visit."

"I will, but tomorrow. Right now, I'll go over to Bodyo's mother. I have a feeling he left something for me there."

"I wish I could keep you company. There's such havoc in the city. Everybody's in a panic. I'll dash over to Legionov Street now. They're already breaking windows over there now. By the way, we managed to find out who Felyek phoned."

"Irena?" I hazarded a guess.

"No, Emilia. But no one picked up the phone."

"She said she had been walking around since morning, then went to the cinema. That's why she didn't answer."

CHAPTER 6

Bodyo's father changed his denomination to Roman Catholic and received a government job on the railroad, and later – an apartment not far from the Austrian three-story stone apartment houses along Horodotska Street built specially for railroad employees. Those were square blocks with bare, spacious courtyards inside. They were called alcazars[33] with good reason. Since the apartments there were so tiny, no one called them houses, but rather "toy houses" as if they were made for dolls.

But Bodyo's father was lucky enough to get a separate house, which, unlike the gray "toy-houses," had a garden where we used to play. Sometimes I would stay overnight and listen to the cacophony of arriving trains, the roar of their train buffers, and the whistling of locomotives, inhaling the smell of smoke and coal. Behind the houses there was the very old Horodotsky Cemetery – the railroad workers' favorite spot to rest, where they liked to sit on the tombs sipping beer, reading newspapers, and playing cards. They would even bring dates there. It was their park, their botanical garden, a place for meetings and farewells, where wild trees and bushes grew. In the middle of the cemetery there was a monument to a bishop who had died of the plague. We used to climb on it and jump onto the soft ground.

This time I went there by car. I drove to the very end of the street and parked the car around the corner. The old woman's house leaned toward the ground on one side. Several sticks supported the walls lined with last year's corn stalk tops. Behind the house, an unkempt garden abounded in wild thickets. As I approached, a flock of sparrows scurried out of the elderberry bushes. Above me, pines were rustling in the wind, and crows were cawing. The courtyard was swampy, and a path of dark, dirty boards led to the door.

....

[33]   A Spanish fortress or palace.

I went into the yard and looked around, but I didn't notice anything special. I lit a cigarette on the porch and stood there facing the street for a few minutes. I didn't want another surprise. But it was quiet everywhere. I threw my cigarette away and knocked. A hoarse female voice told me to go to hell. I entered. It was dark in the entryway.

"Who the hell is there? What the heck do you want?"

"It's me, *Pani* Kvartsyana. May I come in?"

She coughed and said:

"You can't, but come in anyway. Who are you?"

"Your son's friend."

There was coughing again, and the squeaking and creaking of bed springs.

"What do you want from me?"

"I want to talk. May I come in?"

"The door isn't locked."

I entered a spacious but incredibly cluttered room, which consisted of both the kitchen and bedroom. There was a thick odor in the air, a blend of such semitones that one couldn't tell what it was. But something was odiferous. It was something unpleasant and alarming. In the corner of the bed, a disheveled gray head protruded from under the duvet, a sharp nose in the middle of thick wrinkles and thin, pursed lips. There were jars, glasses, bottles, boxes with pills and a half-empty bottle of *horilka* on the chair at her bedside.

"Are you his colleague?" she asked, leaning on her elbows.

"I work for a newspaper."

"You seem to be an honest guy. But nowadays it's not easy to tell who's honest and who isn't. Well, as you can see – I have one foot in the grave. I won't last long. But I'm still alive, and when you're alive you have to keep kicking. You can't imagine how much my medication costs.... I'd better not say." Having noticed me looking at the bottle of *horilka*, she grinned: "He-he, I need to have a drop or two of this on my tongue as well. Would you care for a glass?"

"Thanks, but I have to keep my head sober."

"Well, well. You would never get yourself drunk with an old woman, would you?" She lay down again, staring at the ceiling.

"Besides, I'll be getting behind the wheel."

"It wouldn't hurt. Those who paid me a visit before you also came here by car. So what? They boozed it up and even left half the bottle for me."

"Who were they?"

At that moment I realized what seemed alarming about the room. It was the scent of cigarette smoke.

"Well, curiosity killed the cat, you know."

A thin yellow hand appeared from under the duvet, took the bottle and put it to the mouth. The woman took a deep sip. Some *horilka* ran down her chin and neck. She burped and put the bottle back in place.

"I'm sick, can't you see? And I want to sleep."

"I'm here on business."

"You can kiss my butt, you and your business. Or maybe you're a spy? Eh? Just like those guys?" she turned her head to me. "Say something?"

"I have already said that I work for the newspaper."

"What do you want from me? Give me a holy break, all of you."

She straightened up on the bed again, but her eyes scanned me. "Isn't your name Marko by any chance? Come closer to me."

"Did Bodyo tell you about me?"

"Is it you, Marko-boy?"

Her voice finally softened, and whimpering notes appeared in it.

"Of course. You've known me since childhood. You treated me to dumplings."

"So why on earth are you beating around the bush, *batyar*? Sure enough, Bodyo did tell me about you. He said, you're the only person I can trust. He also told me what you look like now. Finally, I'm able to recognize you. But remind me, what kind of dumplings those were."

"With grated potatoes. Dark, with cracklings."

"Yes, yes, It's you."

"When did he come to you?"

"Early in the afternoon. He didn't say when you would come. But I've been waiting. However, those papers are gone. I don't have them."

"What papers?"

"The ones Bodyo left. He said that if someone offered good money for them that I should give them away."

"Did you give them away?"

"I need medication. So, I gave them away to those goons."

"What did they look like?"

"One – was a sturdy pumpkin-headed blockhead and the other looked like a thief from under a dark star. Probably they're what they look like."

"But you said that Bodyo advised you to trust only me. Why didn't you listen to him?"

"I did, I did. Don't worry, I'm not as stupid as I look. Those papers were not for you. He left a note for you and said when a decent man by the name of Marko comes over, you should just give it to him. See, just give it to him. He must respect you. Of course, I didn't tell those goons about it." She leaned down, reached her hand under the mattress, and pulled out a crumpled piece of paper. "Here you are. He said you would understand everything. And he didn't say anything else."

I unfolded the note and read it, "Remember our high school library? And the book in which you drew Hnyp? It's still there." I hid the note in my pocket.

"Thanks."

"Not at all. But tell me, is everything o…kay with Bodyo?"

Her voice was trembling.

"And why are you asking?"

"Because he said that if something happened to him, you would come to me." I was stunned. Tears glistened in her eyes, rolled down her cheeks, and got lost in her wrinkles. She looked at me in despair. She already guessed that something bad had happened. How could I fool her?

"You're right. Bodyo is gone."

"They killed him...," she sighed.

"Yes, they killed him...."

"That's why you came to me, Marko...." Tears ran across her cheeks.

"Yes, that's why I came to you."

"Well. Go with God." She wiped her face with the edge of her blanket. "And if they find that ... that cutthroat who killed him when I have already joined the better world, you must come to my grave and tell me his name. Do you hear me, Marko? You must do that, and I will get him even after I have died."

She broke into sobbing. I backed my way to the door, where when I reached it, I whispered:

"Goodbye."

The street was deserted and unfriendly. I walked to my car. Having made about a hundred steps, I heard the roar of a motor in the distance and hid behind a lilac bush. The car drove up to Bodyo's house and stopped. It was a dark blue Packard. Two guys came out of it. Apparently, I said goodbye to the old woman just in time. The door creaked plaintively. The papers they had secured might be of no value. Now they'll interrogate the old woman, and she'll probably tell them about me. I ran to the car and disappeared in an instant.

CHAPTER 7

I pulled over at the nearest telephone booth and tried to contact Obukh, but he wasn't in. My message about a robbery taking place on Horodotska Street was received, but from the secretary's bored voice I figured it would be too late by the time the police set off.

It was getting dark when I arrived at the Academic Gymnasium.[34] Hnyp was the nickname we gave to our history teacher – a tall, thin, and incredibly boring man, about whom we composed a song:

"What a squeak, what a creak? Here crawls creepy, creepy Hnyp!" He used to wear eternally squeaky shoes that would squeak even while he sat at the table. I parked and went inside. Classes were over, and the watchman was rattling his keys and locking doors.

"Can I help you?" He looked at me up and down warily.

"Is there still anybody in the library?"

"Oh, yes, yes ... Do you want to see Marta?" He shook his head. "There are so many of you suitors. It's time somebody proposed, but you keep coming and going."

"Actually, I've gotten the courage to do it." I smiled at him.

"Oh!" He rejoiced. "Then don't linger for too long. The girl is right in her prime."

I opened the door to the library and saw a girl I had never met before by the name of Marta. She was short and moderately endowed. She turned her plump, ruddy face to me and said,

"The library is no longer open."

"I know. But I'm haunted by a childhood memory."

"Did you go to school here, too?"

....

34   The equivalent of a high school in the U.S.

"Sure. Is Hnyp still teaching?"

She rejoiced:

"Haven't you forgotten him?"

"What a squeak, what a creak?"

"Here crawls creepy, creepy Hnyp!" Her eyes widened. "Not anymore. But he comes back once in a while."

"Wearing the same shoes?"

"He got fused to them. Are you here to share your memories?"

"I want to check on one book."

"What book? I'll bring it to you."

"No, no, I want to find it myself. It should be in the same place."

"Really? What kind of book is that?"

"*Grammar of the Ukrainian Church Slavonic Language.*"

"By Spyrydon Karkhut?" She wondered.

"Why are you so surprised?"

"Because this morning there was a gentleman here and he wanted to have a look at the same book. Although as long as I've been working here, no one has ever asked for it. It's not on our students' reading list. And he also wanted to find it himself. Very strange." She looked at me suspiciously now.

"It should be there on the top shelf."

"I know. But I won't climb the ladder. I fell off once."

"I'd be happy to do it for you."

I climbed the ladder, found the grammar, took it out, and saw a small notebook behind it. I covered the notebook with my palm and slipped it into my shirt pocket. Then I opened the textbook. The caricature of Hnyp was gone. Someone had torn it out. But I paid for my mischief – Father Spyrydon whipped me to his heart's content for committing sacrilege in his book. I put it back in place and climbed down.

"And what was that supposed to mean?" The girl asked. "What were you looking for there?"

"I once drew a caricature of Hnyp in the book. I wanted to see if it was still there."

"And?"

"Someone ripped the page out."

She looked at me in disbelief and sighed.

"It's not even funny. You know, I suspect you're not here to check on the book."

"On what then?"

"Not on what, but on who. Both the morning guy and you've come here for one purpose only – to have a look at me. Someone told you that there is a respectable girl eligible for marriage here. So, this is what all this fuss is about. You can't wait to get your parish, and a single man is not entitled to one. But remember," she frowned, "I won't marry a priest and I won't move to some village in the sticks."

I faked a sigh.

"What a shame. You were my last hope."

"Don't despair. I have a friend who would be on cloud nine to marry a priest. When will you come over again? I'll introduce you to her."

I thanked her, kissed her hand, and left my alma mater. I didn't manage to make it to the city center. Polish students had organized an anti-Ukrainian demonstration and were headed from Lozynsky Street to the monument to Kornel Ujejski,[35] where they gave several speeches, and then set off to Rynok Square[36] and Ruska Street, breaking windows in the houses of the Greek Catholic senior clergy, the Voloska Church, and the buildings of Ukrainian institutions and shops. I passed by two merchant women expressing their surprise at the destruction:

"Lookie, Pavlova, so much glass on the streets! Holy Mother of Jesus! Lookie – all of Ruska Street!"

"Holy Mother of God, they broke the windows in the Vuloska Church. Bloody Polish students!"

"Aha! And the Poles keep shoutin' there ain't no Ukrainians in Lviv, if that be so, whose windows would them students be breakin', huh?"

I wanted to see the girl from the dining room. I left the car in Khorunshchyna and walked up to the dining room just in time, because Yaryna had left and was striding toward me. She was very surprised to see me.

"Oh! Is it you? I thought you wouldn't come. Are you really here to see me?"

"Who else? You."

----

[35] Polish poet and politician of the Romantic period in the 19th century.
[36] The main market square of Lviv's old town in the center of the city.

She took me firmly by the arm, and we walked toward Rynok Square.

"And you've never told me your name." I introduced myself.

"Good," she replied. "Mar... Yar... And what do you do, Marko?"

"I'm a reporter."

"Get out of here. A night reporter?"

"Yes!"

"Oh, I've read your stuff. Why don't you sign with your real name instead of 'night reporter?'"

"Because sometimes I write things which might get me a whack to my head or a knife in my back."

"That's horrendous! You have a dangerous job. I've read how you spent evenings in dive bars tracking down robbers. Your future wife will be unhappy."

"Why would she?"

"Why wouldn't she? Spending evenings and even nights at home waiting for her husband. Who knows whether or not he'll come home. He might get stabbed with a knife or be beaten up so badly that he can't even get to his feet. That's awful."

"No, I've always been able to get back to my feet, unless...."

"Unless what?" She grew apprehensive.

But I had no desire to tell her about me lying drunk in a ditch.

"Unless I felt like lying down a little, to admire the stars...."

She laughed.

"Are you kidding me? From what I know about you, you don't have time to admire the stars, because you always have to rip and run. Where are we going?"

"I don't know," I said, because I really didn't know. I just wanted to be with this girl and chat about anything.

"Then let's go to the movies. *Dracula* is playing at the Apollo Theater. I love horror films, but I'm scared to watch them alone. Shall we?"

I didn't object. I didn't remember the last time I went to the movies. The film had already begun. The ticket-taker took us to our seats showing our way with a flashlight. Yaryna was holding on to me in the cinema, too. However, this time it was probably out of fear. I wasn't scared. It was rather funny, but I didn't disappoint her. I cuddled her. I could sit like that for a long time, but the show came to its inexorable end. After the film, I accompanied her to Lychakivska Street, thanking God that she lived down below the Church of St. Anthony. Going to those neighborhoods higher on the hill had always been dangerous. *Batyars* or other crooks could grab you, bringing lots of trouble into your life. I hugged her at the gate and wanted to kiss her, but she spun around and just waved her fingers to say good-bye.

THE FOURTH DAY
SUNDAY
SEPTEMBER 25, 1938

CHAPTER 1

Passing by the university, I saw a large poster on the building, "The First Day without Jews." A group of students were blocking the entrance and were checking IDs. Several reporters were hanging out nearby. Upon noticing me, they waved:

"Come join us! It's gonna be a sensation."

"What kind?"

"There will be a huge brawl of Jewish students with ours, the Nowy Wiek [New Century] reporter explained. "We've already seen some guys carrying sticks and knives in their hands."

"And where are the police?" I asked.

"They came and ran away," Józef Mayen from the Jewish periodical *Chwili* [Waves] muttered. "They're cunning...," he nodded at the students, "Various actions are taking place at the same time in the city. So, the police are running here and there." He took me by the arm and pulled me aside. "Someone is deliberately inciting them, you know? I saw money being passed out. One of the fighters from a previous scuffle was hanging around here, whispering and giving instructions. Then he disappeared. Because it must all look like a purely student protest. In fact, they just want to kick us out. Have you heard about Uganda?"

"I sure have. But is that something serious?"

"It only seems like it isn't. In fact, it's a complete plan. A young fellow from Warsaw came to our editorial office and tried to encourage us to write about what a wonderful prospect the resettlement of Jews in Uganda would be. He said there was money allocated for it, and he would also get his share. In a nutshell, it's a global scheme. Everything has also been settled with the Germans. There was an agent from the Soviet embassy here, who was also sniffing around."

"Why didn't you bring your photographers?" I asked.

"Boy, we did! But our guys had their cameras smashed on the spot. Only their guys are permitted to take photos. We aren't."

We said goodbye. I set off for Rynok Square. I could hear a whistle behind me. I didn't know what it meant and to whom it was directed, but in a moment more students ran out of the alleys and joined those at the entrance. On the way I didn't see any policemen. The market was flooded with women vendors and buyers. Attractive offers were heard from everywhere:

"Cabbage! Savoy! Fresh radishes!"

"Raspberries! The juiciest! Oranges the size of a melon! Three for one *zloty*! Take four of them, *Pan* – I'll take the loss!"

"Juice – fresh juice right out of the bucket! A clean glass – washed just yesterday!"

"Are you smelling it, ma'am? Get your nose out of here!? Hat lady! Haven't you seen savoy before? Watch out so's I don't sniff you with my broom!"

"The latest from the hit parade for a single *zloty*.: 'Tango Milonga', 'What does the lady have under her dress?', 'Why did you betray me?'"

"Buttermilk! Clotted cream! Egg pretzels!"

Young nimble smugglers were roaming between the rows of counters selling contraband. I bought German cigarettes from them and trudged to Batory Street to the General Police Headquarters, which had its premises in a new red-brick building surrounded by flowerbeds. The familiar scent of acrid cigarette smoke hovered inside. There was a meticulous order in Obukh's office. The desk wasn't cluttered with papers, like mine, and the folders were evenly stacked. I handed him the notebook. The rain started pattering against the window of the police station. The clock had just chimed nine a.m. The secretary was tapping the keys of the typewriter in the next room. Obukh opened the notebook and tried to figure out what those mysterious numbers and letters meant. They were supposed to stand for the names of those who were blackmailed by Tomashevych. In total, there were four pairs of letters.

"And what use can we make of this notebook?" he sighed. "How can we be sure that the initials correspond to the first and last name, and not vice versa?"

"Though, someone was really keen on getting it."

"They probably knew how to read it.... Wait. There are only four characters here. There were five shareholders. The fifth – is Tomashevych. So...."

"Can we hope that they're here? You have the list of the three recently deceased, don't you?"

Obukh took a folder out of a drawer and placed the list of the deceased shareholders on the table.

"Ye-es, what do we have here? Witold Pogorzelski ... Let's look for WP. Is it here? No. And PW? No. And Roman Korda? There is neither an RK nor a KR. Jan Fursa.... nothing like that."

He sighed heavily and lit a cigarette. I stared at the notebook, trying to figure out what was written there. The numbers were next to the dates.

"You know what? We have to check the dates of their death and the dates of payments. They wouldn't be able to pay after they're dead. Maybe that way we'll be able to understand who it was about. If the payments stopped after the date of death – that would be our shareholder."

"We can give that a try."

In fact, payments stopped about a month before someone's death. But it didn't give us any clue because the initials didn't match.

"Roman Korda died on May 6, and *Pan* TM's last payment was on April 12," Obukh reasoned. "What mysterious connection could there be between RK and TM? They don't seem to be shareholders."

At that moment, the door opened, and Commandant Gozdziewski and the Chief of the Counterintelligence Staff Konarsky entered the office. Their stern looks didn't bode well.

"What are you doing here?" the commandant asked Obukh.

"Tomashevych's notebook has been found."

Gozdziewski immediately moved to the table, snatched the notebook from the commissioner's hands, and began leafing through it.

"Where did you find it?" he asked.

"I didn't. A private detective did. He's dead now."

"Dead? What happened to him?"

"He was killed. Yesterday."

"And he didn't find anything else?" Konarsky asked, squinting his rapacious eyes.

"No."

"And what is the press doing here?" The commandant looked me up and down in a not particularly warm way.

"Actually, thanks to Marko, we obtained this notebook. Tomashevych was blackmailing someone. But it's still unclear who."

"Counterintelligence is in charge of this case," the commandant said. "I've forbidden you to stick your nose in there. The same applies to the press." Leaving, he turned at the door and added: "If you sniff out something else, come straight to me. And what about the robbery of the church in Vynnyky?"

"We tracked down two gypsies. The loot was confiscated."

Gozdziewski nodded and they both left. Suddenly the phone rang. Without taking his eyes off me, Obukh reached for the phone.

"This is the central police station speaking," a sharp female voice loudly reported. "The corpse of an elderly woman was found on Horodotska Street. Go there immediately."

"On Horodotska.... number...," Obukh took notes. "Is anyone there yet?"

"Yes, we've sent a doctor and a photographer."

"All right. We'll be there in no time."

"So, she was killed," I said.

Obukh flinched:

"Who was killed?"

"The mother of that snooper. I saw the same people who had killed Tomashevych go to her last night. And I called here, but they couldn't put me through to anybody."

"Yesterday was a hell of a day. Everyone was busy because of those students."

"Is everyone busy now as well? A fight with knives and chains is about to start near the university."

"And near the Polytechnic, and near the Academy of Veterinary Medicine, and near the Agricultural Academy in Dublyany, and near several gymnasia.... We're spreading ourselves thin! They are everywhere!" Obukh opened the door to the next room and shouted out: "Radomsky! Hey, Radomsky!"

The secretary sitting there jumped in place in surprise.

"Why are you shouting like crazy? Antek isn't here...."

"How come he isn't? Where is he?"

"He stepped out to grab some coffee."

"Damn it! Didn't he say where?"

"He did."

"Then why are you fooling with me?"

"I'm not fooling with you, and you should speak to me more politely. He is around the corner on Romanovych Street."

Obukh rushed to the street shouting to get the car out. I followed him. Indeed, there was Radomsky in the café around the corner. He was leaning over the counter flirting with the owner's daughter.

"Antek!" Obukh growled.

He looked back again with a sweet smile, which, however, was intended for the girl.

"Why are you all shook up? Am I being called in?"

"Yep! Quickly pay and let's go.

"Is he coming with us?" Antek nodded at me, getting into the car.

"He is, he is. He was the last to see her alive. Of course, other than the killers."

"Oh! Quite often he's the last one to see someone alive. What a lucky guy!"

The doctor and the photographer were hanging around the house in the yard. They seemed to have done their job: one had pronounced the victim dead on the scene, the other had taken photographs.

"Well, what's up there?" Obukh asked.

"The corpse of an old woman, close to eighty. Killed by a shot from a revolver through a pillow. The bullet went through her left eye and came out of the back of her head. The shot was made from above. The corpse will be taken out now."

Two orderlies carried the body on a stretcher and stopped in front of us. Obukh pulled the sheet off her head. It was impossible to recognize in the old woman's mangled face the same woman I had spoken to just the day before.

"Is it her?" Obukh asked me. I nodded.

"Take her to the car," the doctor told the orderlies, then lifted his hat. "Greetings, gentlemen. It's your job now."

The doctor and the photographer got in the car and drove away. Antek yawned and wrapped himself in his raincoat.

"Well," Obukh said, "let's go inside the house."

As could be expected, everything had been turned upside down there.

"What could they have been looking for here in this shanty?" Antek wondered.

"Don't talk too much. Look for a cartridge case."

Less than three minutes later, Commandant Gozdziewski appeared. He was accompanied by another police officer. They marched in decisively, inspected the room for a second, and the commandant asked:

"What are you doing here? Who was she?"

Obukh explained:

"She was the mother of a private detective who had been watching Tomashevych and his mistress. He had also broken into the villa and stole the notebook I gave you. After he had been murdered, the killers came here."

"But I forbade you to investigate the Tomashevych case. Have you found anything yet?"

"No," Obukh said, hiding the magnum cartridge case in his hand.

"All right. Then I ask you to leave. Corporal Nemet will investigate the murder. And what is he doing here?" He nodded in my direction.

"He knew her personally. We brought him to identify her."

"Well, you're dismissed then," he pointed to the door.

We obediently left the house and got in the car. Antek was driving. Meanwhile Obukh took out a folder with photos given to me by Kvartsyany from his hiding place. He might have studied them a hundred times. I didn't look at the photographs. I looked out of the window thinking that it would be good to hide Emilia somewhere. Considering the adroitness with which the killers cover their tracks, sooner or later they'll track her down.

"This is what bothers me," said Obukh, tapping his fingers on the picture of Tomashevych and Emilia in the company of an unknown man, an elderly, bald, fat guy. All three were sitting at a table outside. There were cups, a tray with snacks, and a partially imbibed bottle of *horilka* on the table. It looked like a friendly conversation. Tomashevych had some papers in his hand, which he was showing to the fat man.

"I wonder who he is?" Obukh pondered. "Maybe the fifth shareholder? In fact, this is the only photo where there is someone else in the frame. Although.... no, not the only one." He flipped through a few pictures and snatched the one he had been looking for. "Look. Isn't it the same gentle-man?"

In the photo, Tomashevych and the girl were walking arm in arm in the park. A man who looked like the fat guy was walking behind them at a short distance.

"Maybe he was Tomashevych's friend, maybe his enemy." Obukh said. "He doesn't seem to be watching them. They could have just met, chatted, and parted. Moreover, they were chatting quite calmly in the previous pho-to. I wonder what papers Tomashevych was showing him."

"It might have had something to do with blackmail."

"So, then ask Emilia. Show her this photo. She must have heard the conversation. And one more thing.... Today is Tomashevych's funeral. The service will begin in half an hour in the chapel at Lychakiv Cemetery."

"Are you suggesting that I go there first?"

"I can't. My superiors will definitely be there. I don't want to be seen there. But there will be lots of journalists anyway."

"I don't like going to funerals."

"Well, you may see someone interesting." Having sighed heavily, I had to agree.

I didn't get into the chapel, because it was chock-full. A rather respect-ably-sized throng had gathered on the street – some with flowers, some with wreaths, and some with cameras. I greeted the journalists I knew and stood to the side of the crowd. The chief of the counterintelligence staff, Konarsky, was standing close to me near the black Ford. He was wearing a black raincoat with his collar turned up and a black hat, tucked over his eyes, which were hidden behind sunglasses. This all looked funny, like in a B movie or spy film. I couldn't help but smile kindly at him, but I didn't notice any reciprocity.

Hammering sounds came from the chapel – they were pounding nails into the coffin. The crowd became agitated and parted, giving the way to those who were inside – close and distant relatives, friends, co-workers and, of course, the grief-stricken widow. She looked gorgeous in a black velvet dress and a navy-blue cape lined with down. The black veil fell on her bent face. She kept her black-gloved hands clasped in front of her. Then they car-ried out an expensive carved walnut coffin and carried it to a hearse drawn by four stallions adorned with black sultans on their heads. The coachman was wearing a black tailcoat and a black top hat. His grim, stony face showed no emotion. The hearse moved toward the cemetery, and the entire procession followed it. I inspected the audience closely, but those people weren't familiar to me. I saw no reason to stay any longer and was about to leave the cemetery when someone took me by the arm. I was surprised to see that it was Konarsky himself.

"*Pan* Krylovych, can I talk to you in private?"

"Do I have a choice?"

"No," he smiled. "Then let's go to my car."

I obediently followed him, and we sat in the back seat. The chief of counterintelligence stared at me with his piercing gaze, which made all spies and operatives lose consciousness. But not me.

"I see," he said, "that commissioner Obukh has dodged my order very deftly." To avoid putting himself on the line, he instructed you to collect evidence on Tomashevych's murder."

"Are there any doubts that he was murdered?"

"I'll tell you honestly – no. However, we do not want to air this awful story for the time being. We are interested in Tomashevych for another reason. And this reason is not his scams, machinations, or blackmail. We are interested in his contacts with the Germans and the Soviets. We are interested in the fact that he tried to sell them something for which they were willing to pay very hefty sums. Actually, we even know what it was. But we don't know where he kept it. We searched the villa and his apartment. And the apartment that was occupied by his mistress. However, all in vain…. There are rumors that he had another apartment. Have you heard anything about that?"

"I've heard the same thing you have. It's somewhere, but no one knows where."

"Well, why no one? Someone must know. We are not going to interfere with your investigation with Obukh's blessing, because, like I said, we are not interested in the person of the deceased. But should you hear anything about the secret apartment, I'd ask you to let me know. This is a matter of state importance," he stressed.

"Why don't you tell me what we're talking about?"

"These are certain documents German and Soviet intelligence are after. I won't tell you more. That's enough."

"So that's why he was killed? Because of the documents?"

"Maybe.... Maybe someone was working on trying to get him to turn them over."

"Didn't he give them away?"

"No, because German and Soviet spies are still here."

"So how could they have killed him?"

"But he wasn't killed," he said, watching with pleasure how impressed I was.

"How is that?"

"He died of a heart attack. Then they shot him in the mouth and put a pistol in his hand."

"I don't see the logic...."

"There is a certain logic. Suppose someone ordered his death. But the one who received the order was still pursuing his own interests – to obtain those documents. Tomashevych suddenly dies, and they haven't extracted the documents from him. And the customer, upon discovering that he died of heart failure, might refuse to pay. So, they mimicked a premeditated suicide. Is there any logic to that now?"

"There is now. Tell me, didn't your people hire Kvartsyany to follow Tomashevych again?"

He looked at me in surprise.

"Did someone hire him? I mean after Irena had done so?"

"Yes. By phone."

"No, we didn't," he shook his head. "Maybe the Germans, maybe the Soviets. Something wicked is brewing. We need to be careful."

"Will there be a war?" I asked what was on the tongue of every resident of Lviv.

He looked at me thoughtfully and nodded:

"There will be. But maybe it will pass us by.... I'll stay in Lviv for a few more days. Here are my phone numbers. If you have something interesting, I'll be glad to meet with you."

CHAPTER 2

No one answered the door. Neither Emilia nor her friend were in. Having walked around the house and peeped into the windows, I was about to leave when I heard someone calling me. I looked around. An elderly lady was waving at me from the window of the neighboring house. I approached her.

"Who are you looking for?" she asked in a low voice, looking around.

"Emilia."

"Quiet! Not so loud. And what's your name?"

"Marko."

"Come closer." She was scrutinizing me as if she were comparing me with a description she had received from someone. "Tell me, what kind of robe she was wearing when you first saw her?"

"Chinese."

"And what was the print?"

"Pines, huts, mountains and fog."

"Yes," she nodded and disappeared. In a minute she handed me a note. "She explains everything here. Someone came late last night. He knocked on the door, on the windowpane. They didn't open it. This morning they packed up and left."

The note gave an address in Vynnyky.

It was an old house, which was sunken into the ground up to the windows. Children were running in the neglected garden, happily squashing rotten apples and pears with their feet. Sometimes they slipped, grabbed the branches so as not to fall, and laughed wildly. Flocks of butterflies and flies darted off from under their feet. Both young ladies were sitting on a bench shelling beans.

"What happened?" I asked. "Did the nighttime visitor frighten you? That may have been some drunkard."

"No, he whispered so nastily, 'Emilia, come out!'" Emilia replied in a frightened voice. "He was not a random stranger. They found me."

I took out the photo and showed it to her.

"Who is this?" she shook her head.

"I don't know."

"But do you remember that encounter?"

"Yes, I remember it. He sat down next to us. He and Yanus were negotiating something. I couldn't figure out what. They spoke very quietly just in intimations. Nothing specific. Yanus gave him some papers.... I think those were newspaper clippings. He looked through them and gave them back."

"Did you see him again?"

"There was another time in the park. But they stepped off to the side. I couldn't hear their conversation. I only heard that the other guy was annoyed and cursed loudly."

"It's getting dangerous," I said. "The detective was killed. So was his mother."

"What will happen to me?"

"We can't stay here long," her friend said. "It's my grandmother's house. No one has lived here for a long time, and there's no way for me to hide here with my children. I won't be able to earn money for milk and bread without my sewing machine. I need to go home. But I can't leave Emilia alone."

I thought for a moment.

"She can stay with me. I'm never at home anyway. And I'll give you a ride home. If anyone asks, say that Emilia has gone to the countryside."

Emilia looked at me with surprise, but also with gratitude. At first, I drove her friend to Zamarstyniv, and then we went to my place. When we found ourselves at my building's gate, I thought the guard didn't need to know much about her. So, I asked the girl to wait for me. I would take the guard to the basement to show him where I presumably had seen a rat. Meanwhile, she needed to go up to the second floor. That's how she moved in with me – quietly and inconspicuously. Emilia had two large bags with her. I gave her a separate room, and she began to unpack. I went to the kitchen, scrambled four eggs with some milk and flour. I prepared a fluffy omelet, sprinkled it with dill, and served it on the table along with bread and butter.

"Oh, it looks delicious!" she said, smiling. "Do you know how to cook?"

"I can do everything, other than live without problems."

"And I can't.... Yanus hired a cook for me. She came in the morning, got my breakfast and lunch ready, and disappeared."

I cut the omelet into pieces and put it on plates. Emilia spread some butter on her bread and sprinkled it with a little bit of salt. I saw her eating delicately, as if she had come off the silver screen of a film about the English aristocracy. A girl who used to graze cows.

Obukh called.

"Well? Have you found her?"

"Yes. She doesn't know who he is. And they spoke hinting at things."

"And?"

"Now she's with me."

"Gosh, you are fast! Only don't rest but hustle over to the villa. Show the photo to the lady of the house and at the same time try to find out who else was a shareholder of the Association."

"Are you leaving already?" Emilia asked anxiously.

"I said that I'll be in and out all day long. But you're safe here. Just don't call anyone. There's some apple strudel in the pantry. Tea's on the shelf with sugar and honey next to it."

"You also know how to bake?"

"When I have inspiration."

"You are a treasure."

"I know."

She looked at me with admiration, and if I'd have said: marry me, she'd have thrown herself on my neck and covered me with kisses. Or maybe it just seemed that way to me. Many things appear to me that never really happen in reality.

CHAPTER 3

On the way to Bryukhovychi, I parked near Dzherelna Street, which was so bumpy that it was better not to drive on. Its crooked lanterns and sewer drains, clogged with leaves and shells, recalled [Emperor] Franz Joseph. An incredible mixture of scents swirled there, with every step changing its shades, which were alternately dominated by those of laundry, pea soup, and burnt charcoal. Disheveled heads peeked out of windows. In addition to the scents in the air, there was noise, which from time to time was pierced by someone's sharp desperate cry or curse: "Nasty bitch! Doctor's shiksa[37]! You sick pig! I hope you sleep on a bed of nails tonight!" From early morning to late at night the most dissolute prostitutes of Lviv traipsed along Dzherelna Street and the adjacent Shpytalna Street, as well as along the narrow and straight streets nearby: Tsekhova, Brygidska, Byka, and Pid Dubom. They were popularly called "rustlers" or "shufflers," because they no longer walked but shuffled. Dirty, ragged, with dissipated faces, often barefoot, they no longer provided their services in the best parts of town. In the summer they waited for their luck in the park on Vysoky Zamok [High Castle Mountain], on Stryyska Street, in the thickets of Lychakiv Park, and other similar places where bushes and abandoned buildings served as shelter for them. In autumn and in winter they camped there, where they could drink and keep themselves warm. Their clients were urban outcasts, workers, and soldiers, but only boozed up ones.

I walked past those monsters who had lost their human form. Some of them were exposing their bare, bony, bluish knees while others were waddling due to gross obesity. Their shabby dresses and ragged fur coats were

---

[37]   A Yiddish word, often used derisively, to describe a non-Jewish woman and a forbidden desirable other for Jewish men.

adorned with sequins and beads. Fake coral beads and necklaces dangled around their necks. Their tousled hair was garnished with faded autumn flowers, which they themselves faded into. Their lips spat out lustful, nearly incomprehensible gurgling.

I passed by several tent stalls and stands bustling with commercial life: Yuz Migl's barber shop, where no one got their hair cut or got a shave, but rather played blackjack, *ferbel*,[38] or read tarot cards. I passed by the fat and immortal Sarah Zuckerkandel, sitting on a three-legged stool and knitting mittens in front of her own store "Haberdashery and Cosmetics." Then I went down to the tavern "Under the Nightingales," into which a respectable gentleman fears even looking, lest cutthroats immediately assault him and putting a revolver to his head, shout, "your money or your life." The imagination painted images of terrible, filthy bandits stained with blood. In fact, the appearance of many bandits can easily compete with that of wealthy gentlemen. Quite a few of them are real dandies, especially "gigolos," whose looks favorably distinguish them from thieves and robbers. They are always taken care of by a Manka or Franka so that they have clean linen, ironed trousers, starched shirts, and polished shoes. Of course, the audience that gathers in these kind of dive bars frowns at every stranger but doesn't show aggression as long as he doesn't gawk, but behaves calmly and restrains from physiognomic studies, because such scrutiny doesn't appeal to the regulars: if you want to have holy peace, then they also want the same thing, everyone is their own master. This is the custom here. All these are gentlemen, decently dressed, with hidden knives and hooks, who are always ready to protect their private space.

From the earliest morning until eleven o'clock there is hustle and bustle, noise, and shouting there, because the "gielda" stock exchange – rules the roost. This is when stolen and looted goods are brought here to be sold at as profitable a price as possible. A group of Jewish buyers for the stolen goods shows up as well, and the bargaining begins. At eleven o'clock everything ends, and the gang takes a rest.

....

[38]   A popular card game of chance played by two to four players. The best hand consisted of holding all four aces. Many thanks to Svitlana Budzhak Jones for assisting us in finding information about the game.

When I walked down the steps to the tavern, a gramophone was creaking in the corner, and the enthusiastic sounds of "Ours – is Yours," "Ein und Zwanzig[39]," and "My Auntie's Your Auntie" emerged from the depths under the lamplight. A few prostitutes were swigging beer with gusto at the bar, casting interested glances at me. They didn't rush to approach me with tempting propositions, because they must have already sashayed a lot during the night.

But they were not the nightingales after whom the tavern was named, but a quartet of women of indefinite age with swollen faces, lavishly powdered and rouged, who played violins and trumpets with a kind of desperate insanity. From time to time, one of them rose to her unsteady feet and sang to frantic accompaniment, or rather howled obscene verses in a hoarse, drunken voice. Her howl, like that of a wolf, was so piercing that it could be heard in the street, and the inhabitants of the neighboring houses began to swear and curse.

Besides some lighted areas, the room was filled with thick smoke. It was not easy to see people's faces, but I needed to find Purtsel. Because of the curtain of smoke, I had to break that unwritten code of conduct in such establishments and walk between the tables, looking at peoples' mugs. Fortunately, Purtsel himself said: "Marko baby, you son of a slut! Why's you done come here t'day? You done be lookin' fer me? Sits yer heinie here. I'll pours you some *tsmaga* [vodka]. From Bachevsky's! It's not some swill."

I sat down next to him, had a polite sip from my glass and asked:

"Do you know a particular couple of guys – a white-haired stiff with a red mug and a worm-like fella, who keeps moving his legs like he wants to take a wee?"

"Why wouldn't I knows? Theys comes here. And why be yous needin' 'em?"

"I'm interested in who they work for."

"Oh, for some big cheese. With big dough. But I don'ts know whos he is."

"Didn't they work for Tomashevych?"

"For who? For the one who's shots himself? Naw-w. He daresn't be's involved with 'em. Naw-w... somebody from that branch a business with blackmarket risky stuff, coocaine.... But they, you knows, don't talks much.

....

39   Twenty-one in German.

Fews a dem starts gabbin' here. Let's me asks... "Brotsak!" He shouted to a blond-haired waiter with a nose like a potato. "Comes over here, I gonna gives yous some *tsmaga*."

"Sure!" he said gladly and immediately joined us at the table. "Who's that?" he nodded at me.

"That's my bosom buddy, you slut, you should know. Here, has a drink, and tells me about dem two dats comes here sometimes. One a dem's a beefy guy with blond hair and mitts like hammers, the other looks like he's about to wets himself."

"A pee-dancer?" Brotsak wiggled his short legs.

"Yep."

"Why wouldn't I know? Dyzyo and Heba. But they're sons of bitches. Better to stay away from those types. It was when.... 'bout a month ago, they had a run-in with the railroad guys.... Well, they got together for a rumble. The railroad guys thought that it'd be a fair fight – they'd smash each other's mugs a bit and then down some *horilka*. And those two pulled out blades and sliced 'em dead. No, those are bad folks."

"Don't you know who keeps dem under their umbrella?"

"A German guy."

"Come on! A German?"

"Yep, a German. During Austrian days he was in the army, rose through the ranks, then founded some kind of ass-oo-cia-tion."

"Of tavernkeepers?" I broke in.

"Maybe of tavernkeepers.... And afters the war he's been runnin' various fishy businesses."

"For example?"

"An underground casino, an underground distillery. He makes moonshine that's balls to the wall."

"And where is the casino?"

"In Zboiska."

"Have you been there?"

"Me?" He laughed. "No way, people like us aren't allowed nowhere's near. The place is there's only for guys with a thick wallet. But the Dyzyo and Heba are kiddos next to another fella, who works for hims. They calls hims 'The Doctoor.' He's, I'ma tellin' you, a real horror show. He knows how to top off a guy so there's no trace of hims left. Well, the late Ferbel once said he'd seen that Doctoor stick a spike as thin as a hair into one guy's eye. Right here – in this here pub. And he just squealed and got twisted into a Jewish pretzel."

Purtsel and I looked at each other.

"Well, you see?" Purtsel asked. "No wonder I ain't never wanted to drink wit 'em. Naw, you should be careful wit dem kinds a characters."

I said goodbye to the guys and went outside. I had hardly walked a few meters to my car, as the same people I had been talking about blocked my way – Dyzyo with his red mug and the worm-shaped Heba with a Mauser under his arm. I pretended to be drunk and incredibly happy:

"Dyzyo! Heba! How you doin'?"

They were stunned for a second, but quickly came to their senses. Burly Dyzyo took me by the collar and asked:

"So, where're you hiding that snatch?"

"Which snatch?" I didn't get what he was saying, although I vaguely guessed he meant Emilia.

"You really needs reminded which one, or you mebbe can guess yourself?" His threatening voice didn't portend anything good.

"Emilia?"

"Yes, Emilia. Where'd you hide her?"

"Why the hell would I need her? And why do you need her? She's so scared she won't tell anything to anybody."

"We don't give a fig about her. But the boss wants to see her. He's interested in Tomashevych's apartment. Not the villa, and not the building where he lived, cause there's got to be another one."

"And what's there?"

"There might be something. But that's none of your beeswax. Do you know where it is?"

"I've never heard of it. Neither Emilia nor Irena mentioned it. Otherwise, I'd have checked it out a long time ago."

"Irena may not have known. Tomashevych no longer lived with her. But that snatch with nice tits can tell us a lot. So?"

"So what? I never saw her again. The doorman said she had moved out somewhere."

"Aha, she moved in with her friend. But then she fled again. Because stupid Heba boy scared her."

YURI VYNNYCHUK

"Why me?" Heba was indignant.

"Because you're a stupid stink bomb. You began to scare her in the middle of the night. I shouldn't have let you go out on your own."

"Don't call me stink bomb," Heba gritted his teeth.

"Shut yer trap, you stink bomb."

"Why'd you shoot Tomashevych, if he'd already died?" I intervened in their quarrel.

"So, you know?" Dyzyo was surprised. "You hear that, Heba? *Pan* Reeporter knows something! If you just try writin' anything, we're gonna twist your head off like that." A knife flashed in his hand. "See? Now you'll come with us."

"Where?"

"You'll see. There I'll tell you everything what's happened."

At that moment, a bunch of guys led by Purtsel spilled out of the pub.

"Marko boy, why've they closed in on yous? Aah? Are you boys lookin' fer trouble?"

The *batyars* began to approach in a semicircle with knives flashing in their hands, too. Dyzyo and Heba figured they wouldn't be able to cope with a group of a dozen hefty guys and backed off without saying a word.

"We'll see you again later," Dyzyo hissed.

In a few minutes I was on my way to Bryukhovychi.

CHAPTER 4

The lady of the house answered the door herself. She was wearing the same gown but was not as sober as last time. She had a glass of wine in her hand.

"Ohh, look who's come to visit us! How delightful! I can't believe my eyes."

"I'm happy you're happy about my visit," I said, bowing and kissing her hand.

She took me to the living room and sat on the couch with her legs tucked under her, her round pink knees exposed without stockings. I sat down in the armchair.

"Would you care for a drink?" There was a bottle of champagne on the table and a large box of chocolates. I poured myself a glass and drank it. She didn't take her eyes off me. "What brought you to me?"

"This, here," I held out the photo. "Who is this?"

"Can't you tell a crook right away?"

"Do you know him?"

"I saw him a few times. More precisely, at all three funerals."

"Was he at Tomashevych's funeral?"

"There were a lot of people there. I didn't pay attention. There – check the album on the shelf." I got up and handed it to her. "Here are photos of members of the Association. Come here, sit down."

I sat down next to her, intoxicated by her perfume, by the elusive energy and mood she radiated, and admired her fingers opening the album. The group photos showed members of the Association dressed in swanky black suits and vests with pocket watches on their waists, with indispensable hats and mustaches. There was a photo of the stranger among them.

"So, he was a member of the Association, wasn't he? And don't you have any photos of the shareholders?"

"No, they never took pictures together."

"There is only one shareholder left, who took possession of the stone apartment buildings and taverns. Who is that?"

She shrugged.

"How do I know? Yanek didn't put me in the picture."

"Did he express any suspicion about the shareholders who had died under strange circumstances?"

"What was so strange about them? Just tragic accidents."

"Tragic, but in a short span of time. Six months. They seem to have been killed, just like your husband. It remains a mystery who lured your husband to the villa and who he was expecting with champagne."

She smiled.

"Do you think it's me? Because I drink champagne? It's hard to come across a woman who wouldn't like it."

"Emilia, for example."

"A country bumpkin."

"In the morning Tomashevych had two telephone conversations with women. One of them with Agnieszka. We don't know who the second woman was."

She turned her head sharply to me and looked intently. An ironic smile lingered in the corners of her mouth. She put the album down without taking her eyes off me, as though hypnotizing a rabbit or a frog. And I yielded to the hypnosis. I leaned toward her, pressed her against me and felt all the heat of her body, the taste of her hot lips and the trembling of her tongue. I felt our teeth clattering like glasses, and then her tongue tickled my palate. Her hand unbuttoned my shirt and stroked my chest. Well, we both wanted that. I pulled off her gown, and my palm squeezed her full, firm breasts. She leaned back for a moment, pressed something unfolding the back of the couch, then dropped her gown, and I saw her perfect alabaster body. I couldn't and didn't want to restrain myself and didn't think what Obukh might say about it. I succumbed to a wave of passion and was burning with uncontrollable desire. I felt her sharp fingernails dig into my back and travel all the way to my buttocks, then up and down again and again. It all ended very quickly, just to be repeated in a while but at a slower pace, without haste, without rushing, but still with the same sharp nails, from which my back was already burning.

And only then did I come to my senses and think about the reason for my coming here. All I learned was that the mysterious man was one of the members of the Association, but it is unknown which of the shareholders survived. She either didn't really know or was hiding it for some reason.

I started getting ready to leave.

"And where would you have to dash?" she asked, stretching out languidly.

"Unfortunately, I still have work to do. I honestly didn't plan on such a lavish interlude."

"No? But it seemed to me that you couldn't take your eyes off me that first night." She laughed, threw on her gown and poured some champagne. "Let's drink a toast."

I returned to the couch, took the glass from her hands, drank from it and said: "The detective you hired was killed. But he managed to find a notebook."

"What?!" She almost jumped in surprise. "Where?"

"In his office. You gave it a going-over, but not a thorough one, because he hid it in a sock. Now you have to kick your driver in the butt."

She was really stunned. Her hands were shaking. She gulped down her glass and poured some more for herself.

"So, you knew about the notebook." She was silent and just glared at me askance. She looked like an angry panther.

"And who has this notebook now?" She squeezed out of herself.

"The police."

"Did that idiot take it there himself?"

"No. He hid it at his mother's. And from her it ended up with the police." I didn't want to admit that it was me who had found that notebook.

"Have you seen it? What is in there?"

"Initials of those who were blackmailed by Tomashevych and numbers. Only four initials. We think they are shareholders. But the initials don't match."

It seemed to me that she sighed with relief.

"I've never seen that notebook, but I suspected it had to be somewhere, because Yan was too pedantic to keep it all in his head. We searched everything. Where was it?"

"Inside the leg of the desk."

"Damn it! We seem to have tapped on every millimeter of that table."

"Why were you looking for it? Did you want to take over the business?"

"No way! I don't get involved in dirty business." She lit up a cigarette and her fingers started trembling again. I got up and she didn't try to stop me. I set off for home.

CHAPTER 5

I didn't feel very well after my escapade with Irena. It seemed improper for me in relation to Yaryna, and although I wasn't going to confess my sin to her, I wanted to see her. I found her home alone. There was nobody at the pub, and in half an hour she was supposed to close up shop.

"Howdy!" I greeted her but noticed her frowning lips.

"What do you want?" she asked dryly, hiding her gaze behind her squinting eyelids.

"I want you," I said. "Has something happened?"

She was silent, as though plucking up her courage, and finally blurted out:

"It has. I, *Pan* Marko, am not waiting for those kinds of suitors. No, thank you. I'm not interested in birds of paradise.[40]"

"I don't understand, who is a bird of paradise? Can it be me?"

"Well, it can't be me."

"Could you explain in more detail?"

"Be my guest. Your buddies came to me. They asked about some Emilia that you're hiding. They asked if you had taken me to your place yet. And when I said no, they started laughing and said, don't worry, he'll take you there soon and...," tears welled in her eyes, but she didn't finish.

"They aren't my buddies," I said. "They are bad people."

"And who is Emilia?"

"The girl they're looking for."

"Did you hide her?"

"I did. What's wrong here? I have nothing going on with her. She's just an acquaintance of mine."

....

[40]   An idler, a scoundrel (author's note).

"They don't think so. And besides, they behaved like pigs ... one wanted to grab me by ... by ...," she placed her hand on her breast. "I broke free. And it is good that *Pan* Musyalovych intervened. No, *Pan* Marko, I don't want these kinds of troubles anymore. I'm better off marrying a priest."

"Oh!" it occurred to me. "Do you happen to have a friend Marta, who works in the library?"

"Aha!" Yaryna exploded. "Then you've already started to woo her! I knew it! Goodbye. Don't bother me anymore."

Feeling disconcerted I left. No, respectable girls aren't my cup of tea.

"You know, something weird happened today," the doorman started spitting out words as he opened the gate for me. "A gorgeous young lady came out of our building, passed by me without saying a word. And I was stunned because I couldn't remember letting her in. How is it she didn't come in, but came out?"

"With chestnut brown hair?" I asked in a trembling voice.

"Yes. She was respectably dressed. Not like some kind of strumpet."

"Did she have anything on her?"

"Naw, nothing. Maybe just a purse under her arm."

"When was that?"

"Two hours ago. Do you know her?"

"No. Only maybe she looks like somebody I know."

"But how is that possible, sir? How is it possible that I didn't let her in, and she came out of there?"

I spread my hands in a shrug and was about to go upstairs, but he stopped me.

"Wait. Here's a note for you."

"From whom?"

"A man dropped by."

I unfolded the note which read, "I'm waiting for you at Café De la Paix. It's in your interest." Signed with the initials L.K. I shrugged, thanked the doorman, and rushed to my flat. Emilia was not there. Only her things remained. I found a note on the table which read:

"I'm sorry, I had to leave. It's very important to me. I'll be back soon. Don't be angry. Think of an excuse for the doorman. Your Emilia."

"Stupid chick!" I cursed and started looking for a bottle.

There had to be half a bottle of wine left somewhere in the nooks of my pantry. I found it and started drinking. I lit a cigarette and thought it wasn't the condition in which I should be that day.

The phone rang.

"I've solved the riddle!" Obukh said. "All the initials are shifted by two letters. However, not according to the classical Latin alphabet, but the modern. Thus, Witold Pogorzelski is YR, Roman Korda is TM, Jan Fursa is LH. But who is NM? This is someone whose initials start with L and K. Well? What do you have to say?"

"Emilia's gone," I muttered.

"How come she's gone?"

"The little shit has taken off somewhere."

"This is not good. But maybe she'll come back."

"Yes, she has to, because she left her things."

I told him about my conversation with Konarsky.

"Interesting...," he pondered. "I learned about the heart attack yesterday. Good people informed me. But the documents that German intelligence is hunting for.... That is something new."

We said goodbye to each other. I went downstairs and told the doorman that when that mysterious young lady appeared, she should go to Café De la Paix.

"Oh, do you know her?" He winked at me, perhaps, secretly rejoicing that he had not seen a ghost.

"Not sure. But maybe she was looking for me."

He nodded understandingly. I put ten *zloty* in his hand.

"I sleep with one eye open," he said confidently. "Feel free to knock on the window."

De la Paix, as usual in the evening, was swarming with fishy guys solving problems, making deals, and drawing up plans. However, there were a lot of bridge players, of course, playing for cigarettes. The waiters scurried around at incredible speed, deftly dodging the seemingly inevitable collisions. I went to the bar and was about to order a bottle of chianti when a specimen of a guy, whom I wouldn't like to meet anywhere alone, approached me and wheezed out:

"The boss wants to shoot the breeze with you."

"Whose boss?" I wondered.

He shrank and nodded in the direction of the corner, where an older man with a big paunch was sitting. He was wearing a steel-colored wool suit and a light-colored shirt with a tie. There was a crimson handkerchief in his breast pocket.

"Your boss?" I specified. He nodded. "Then you should say: "My boss."

"Well, mine."

"Tell your boss he's not my boss. I'm my own boss. Understand?"

"Do you know who you're messing with?" He suddenly saw red. "Now, go there, or I'll drag you over by your collar!"

Of course, somewhere in a cozy place he could literally do it, but not here. I felt completely safe and just laughed, enjoying his helplessness and the way his hand twitched nervously in his pocket, clenching and unclenching his fingers on the hilt of the knife. I don't know what would have happened if the waiter hadn't approached us and said politely:

"I would ask *Pan* Night Reporter to come to that table. Someone wants to talk to you, if you please. *Pan* Leon is inviting you."

"Well, that's a horse of a different color, isn't it?" I winked at the waiter and went to the "boss."

The jelly-belly extended his hand, which was strung with rings like a spit with meat, and said:

"Leon Kallenbach. I already know your name."

I squeezed those stubby sausage fingers and sat down in a wicker chair. There were several plates with appetizers on the table.

"What are you drinking?" he asked.

"Since I've started with wine, I'll end with wine. Did you pass me the note?" He nodded in the affirmative, called the waiter, and ordered Madeira. Then he fit a cigarette in a long black mouthpiece, lit it slowly, and inhaled. The waiter brought the wine and poured some into my glass.

I gulped it down and poured myself some more.

The jelly-belly smiled.

"You've had a hard day, haven't you?"

"I can't remember ever having an easy day."

"So as not to beat about the bush, I'll tell you who I am. I'm Tomashevych's father-in-law, Irena's father. Understand?"

"Nice to meet you."

"Actually, I wanted to meet with you in circumstances other than this, but things have begun to get hot. You know, Tomashevych was a son of a bitch. He really poisoned my daughter's life quite a lot. But that's not the point. Neither my daughter nor I are going to miss him."

"Leon Kallenbach?" I got lost in my thoughts. If NM in the notebook means LK, then maybe it's him?

"What do you think about the murder of the four shareholders, including Tomashevych?" I asked him.

"So, do you think I killed four shareholders to take over the stone apartment houses and pubs? That is ridiculous. If I already own four dozen houses, then three more don't make a difference to my well-being. Likewise with the two pubs. I already have a dozen of them."

"Did he blackmail you?" I asked him.

"Not me. He blackmailed the shareholders. Each of them had some petty sins. He knew quite a lot about each one of them and managed to gather scandalous material. That was enough."

"So, you're not NM, are you?"

"Nonsense!" he flared.

"In Tomashevych's notebook all shareholders were noted by initials, but letters are shifted by two positions," I explained. "We came to the conclusion that NM is you, because your initials are LK."

"No, it's not me, because I'm not a shareholder. There were five of them. Four are dead. I don't know who the fifth one is. Do you have the notebook?"

"I had it. Now the police do."

"I see, you didn't waste your time. But I also learned something. The shareholders were the ones through whom the funds were transferred to a secret anonymous account. They were mediators and didn't suspect Tomashevych of anything. After the death of my son-in-law, my daughter and I visited his apartment on Legioniv Street. And there in the strongbox we found a folder with various photos and documents with which he blackmailed shareholders and forced them to meet with a courier. But they were not the main target of his blackmail. It turns out that he worked at Pilsudsky's headquarters during the last war. And there he stole documents that could compromise both the military headquarters and counterintelligence."

"So, he blackmailed the military?"

"Exactly. But this bastard did this through the hands of the shareholders. He first sent several copies of the documents to Pogorzelski, demanding that he send them to counterintelligence headquarters, and set a condition: regular receipt of funds for the promise not to publish anything."

"And they agreed without hesitation?" I was surprised.

"Well, I don't know whether it was without hesitation. But they paid. Once a month, a courier arrived from Warsaw and handed over the money. On the same day, the money was deposited in the anonymous account. After the sudden death of Pogorzelski, Korda began to receive funds, and after his death – Fursa."

"And now the fifth one should receive the money, right? Who is he?"

"This I don't know."

"When is the courier expected to arrive?"

"They always arranged to meet on the first Monday of each month at twelve at the restaurant in Hotel George. Fursa had told me this right before his death. The person who was supposed to receive the money would sit at a table, holding a newspaper upside down."

"Upside down? How stupid!"

"Not quite stupid. On the last page of the newspaper, at the very bottom, there is a solution to another criminal mystery. It is always printed upside down."

"Do you think shareholders were killed just like Tomashevych?"

"I have no doubt. I think they were killed by counterintelligence. As soon as they were spotted at the meetings with the courier. It was Tomashevych's crafty scheme. He understood that this kind of blackmail was a big risk. So, he substituted someone for himself."

"Why did he wait for so long after stealing those documents?"

"He had good reason to wait until those who depend on them hit a home run, become ministers, generals. At that time, they were only lieutenants, ensigns, and officers."

"Did you look through those documents?"

"What we found are not exactly documents. Those are just a few copies. Neither Irena nor I know where the originals are. But the fact is that a real bombshell is hidden there. For example, there is an acting minister's testimony, which he gave in Russian captivity, disclosing considerable secret information. That is, he turned out to be a skunk and a traitor. Our people got hold of the documents from the Russian headquarters. And there was this evidence. Tomashevych had been collecting these kinds of documents for a long time while working at the headquarters. Now it is an invaluable collection that can destroy many well-known people."

"Why do you think he chose the shareholders?"

"Because he had known them for many years. He knew about each of their weaknesses and sins."

"Why didn't he blackmail the fifth?"

"And who knows that he didn't? Maybe it was his turn after the death of the other four. But then Tomashevych drew a blank. The fifth shareholder must have guessed who was behind the blackmail. This is what I think. What if I hire you?"

"What for?"

"For you, bastard, to find that fifth one. And the folder with the original documents from the headquarters."

"Why do you need him?"

"I have some interest in him. My daughter's life is in danger. I also think that bastard killed my gardener. And then Emilia disappeared. I suspect that couldn't have happened without his participation."

"Emilia? Did you know her too?"

"Why not? She's my distant family. She was chasing after guys anyway. So Irena dressed her up like a doll and fixed her up with that creep. She called me today, and we agreed to meet. But she didn't show up. And that makes me very tense." He emptied his glass and had a bite of ham. Then he looked at me thoughtfully and asked: "Well, how much do you want for working as a gumshoe?"

"One hundred *zloty* a day."

"Oh!"

"Is that too much for you?"

"No, it's too much for you."

I treated him to one of those charming smiles that I used to enchant young ladies. He shook his head, reached into his pocket, and placed five one-hundred bills in front of me.

"You'd better stay within this budget. The clock is ticking." He wrote down his phone number and address on a napkin. "Any time of day or night."

"If I complete the assignment in less than five days, can I keep the change?"

He smiled.

"Don't worry. I'm interested only in results. But if you don't complete the assignment, you'll either get a new one or return the money. *Verstehen*[41]?"

CHAPTER 6

Upon arriving home, the first thing I asked the doorman was if Emilia had shown up.

"No, *Pan* Marko. She hasn't. However, there was a gentleman asking about you."

"What did he look like?"

"Well, he was really burly ... but very polite. He gave me one *zloty*. Apparently, he's a respectable man."

"With white hair and a red mug?"

"Yes," he rejoiced for some reason. "Do you know him?"

"Not very well."

I went up to my apartment and thought it was probably time to go to bed. But instead, I called Obukh and told him everything I had heard from Leon. He was especially interested in the documents that Tomashevych had stolen from the headquarters.

"It could really be a bombshell. But I didn't waste my time either and I've got something."

"What exactly?"

"Banking papers...."

He didn't have time to finish his sentence, as I heard the scraping of a key in the door. I thought it was Emilia, because she had a spare key. But when the door opened, I saw a revolver pointed at me. It was Dyzyo and Heba. The first stretched his scorched face in a mannered smile, and the second kept shrugging nervously, as if readjusting his sport coat and kicking out his legs.

"Howdy, kitty cat," said Dyzyo. "Would you be so kind as to invite us in for a visit?"

And without waiting for an answer, they both barged into the room. I put the receiver down with Obukh's voice still reverberating in it on the table and stood still. Let him listen.

"What, still haven't come to your senses?" Dyzyo asked. "Here, Heba, have a look-see if he's packin' a piece."

The short flunkie deftly searched me. My revolver was in the drawer.

"None?" Dyzyo was surprised. "Such an excellent reporter without a piece?"

"Yeah, no," Heba replied happily.

"His mommy must have forbidden him from playing with those kinds of toys, huh?"

They both laughed and put away their weapons in their pockets.

"Well, you little imp," the hulk said. "Get ready for a short walk in our brainy company."

"I don't get it. What do you want from me?"

"You'll find out there. The boss wants to see you."

"There's a hell of a lot of bosses who want to see me."

"And what did you want: you earned your own fame. Shake a leg!"

"I wonder how the doorman let you in?"

"How, how.... we said we were your relatives, ha-ha-ha-ha!" His own joke made him incredibly happy.

"And how did you get the key?"

"When you know a lot, you'll become as white as I am," Dyzyo laughed again.

I didn't like this laughter, but I obediently put on my shoes and slowly laced up. Heba suddenly shouted:

"Look, Dyzyo, he didn't hang up!"

"Oh, shit!" Dyzyo cursed. "Ask who it is."

Heba hopped up to the phone, grabbed the receiver and put it to his ear: "Hallo! Who is there?"

Apparently, he didn't particularly like the answer, because he made a wry face with his terrified eyes wide open."

"Well? What's up?" Dyzyo was losing his temper. "Who's there?"

"Your last hour!..."

"What bull are you shooting, you stink bomb?"

"It's not me! He told me so! And don't call me 'stink bomb' because I don't like it."

"Shut up, you stink bomb. Who was that?" Dyzyo asked me.

"The Police Commissioner. They're probably on their way here."

"Aha! That's what you did!" Dyzyo grabbed me by the arm and pulled me toward the door. "Hold still, otherwise it'll be worse."

Under their watchful eye, I went down the steps to the gate. The doorman wasn't asleep.

"So," he asked, "are you going to have some fun with your relatives? And yes, it's always nice to finally be able to get together after so many years."

"You're right," said Dyzyo, "The holy truth. Marko and I haven't seen each other for a long time. But now we're going to have a few. Good night."

"Good night, good night," said the doorman, opening the gate and glancing at me rather expressively. He seemed to have guessed that they were not relatives, and he even managed to wink at me.

A car was waiting around the corner. The albino sat in the back seat with me, and the worm got behind the wheel. I stared out the window, trying to figure out where I was being taken. Apparently to confuse me, having driven into Lychakivska Street, the car then drove through deserted streets, meandering left and right. From time to time, Dyzyo poked me in my side and drooled to distract me. I wasn't familiar with those small streets on upper Lychakivska Street, I had never been there and very soon I didn't know where I was. But it still made me happy, because if they were going out of their way that much to chat me up then, apparently, they didn't intend to kill me. On the other hand, it would have been easier to blindfold me. In a few minutes, Dyzyo hugged and pressed up to me in such a "friendly manner," that I could no longer see what was outside the window.

"Sit there, kitty cat, quiet and don't look around."

The car stopped near a tall building with barred dark windows and turned onto a gravel alley. The headlights hit the open garage door. The cottage was illuminated by wrought-iron lanterns. A statue of a young girl with a basket of grapes on her shoulder stood by the porch on a concrete hill. She had a rather sad face, and who wouldn't be sad, standing this way so still under the sun and rain.

"Get out," Dyzyo muttered, directing the flashlight onto the stairs leading to the porch.

Heba obligingly ran ahead of us and opened the door. We passed through an unlit entryway, and then the door to a spacious room opened right before me, with a bright light hurting my eyes. For a moment I couldn't see anything. Just then, in the depths I saw a fat bald man behind a massive desk with a marble countertop and crooked legs in the shape of a lion's paws. He was the stranger Obukh and I had seen in pictures in Tomashevych's company. He sat leaning back in a wide leather armchair and drummed his fingers on the table as if he were playing the piano. There was a bottle of whiskey to his right, next to it – two glasses, cigarettes, a lighter, and a Colt 45. An original still life. A huge red-haired cat, such a big smug pile of fur, was walking brazenly on the table. He moved his paws lazily, trying not to touch the glasses or the bottle, until he finally lay down and stared at me.

The fat tub of lard nodded in the direction of the chair and croaked out:

"Sit down, night reporter."

I sat down. Dyzyo and Heba were snorting behind me. The fat tub of lard straightened up, moved the Colt 45 closer to him, and cleared his throat, as if he were about to say something to me, but perked up and addressed his hatchlings:

"Scram, boys, we're going to chew some fat. But don't go too far. Wait in the next room. If you hear any suspicious sound – run in and shoot without warning." Waiting for them to leave, he continued, "To begin, Marko, I'd like to surprise you. Take a look at the bathroom."

I reluctantly stood up, feeling despair and fear rise in my heart, because I already suspected who I would see there, but what I saw terrified me, because I hadn't expected it. It was dark in the bathroom, I groped for the switch, turned it on, and light flooded the tub filled with water, in which a young woman's body lay, and it belonged to Emilia. Still, I thought I'd see her alive, not naked and dead. A blue stripe was visible on her neck. I felt my head spin and leaned against the doorjamb. Why is she in the water? The water was still steaming...

As if I were intoxicated, I returned to the room and crashed into the chair. The fat tub of lard smiled contentedly with the cat already perched on his lap and purring with pleasure as he stroked it.

"So, did you like our work?"

I was silent, shuddering. He pushed the bottle and a glass toward me. I poured myself some whiskey and downed it. Then I took a cigarette and lit it. The fat tub of lard didn't take his eyes off me. "Are you so naive that you thought you'd find her alive?" A persistent thought raced through my head. "She was doomed from the moment she left the house. Naturally. Calm down, you've done everything you could to save her. It's not your fault she didn't listen. It's her … her fault."

"Why have you brought me here?" I finally squeezed out of myself. "So that I could see this poor thing?"

"Not just for that. But she enters our program as a vivid example of what can happen to you. You, too, can one day end up in a bathtub like that. And then you'll be found somewhere in the woods or in a lake. But for now, I need you alive. I need you to do a small favor for me."

"A strange favor that's at the point of a revolver."

"Yes, yes, a favor. So far. I don't know if you've heard that Tomashevych blackmailed not only shareholders."

"No, I haven't," I lied.

"Then I'll tell you: he also blackmailed very important dignitaries. And it was no longer fun. He came up with a very cunning plan: by blackmailing shareholders, he actually aimed at blackmailing politicians and the military. Shareholders were only intermediaries for meetings with the courier. However, the days of their lives after the first or second meeting were numbered. And then he blackmailed the next one. Until he reached me."

"So, you are the fifth shareholder?"

He smiled, lit a cigarette, inhaled the smoke with gusto, and poured himself some whiskey.

"Yes, I'm the fifth one he stumbled upon," he said with a satisfied look on his face.

"How did you manage to find out that Tomashevych was blackmailing you?" I asked him.

"One day he met with me. I had some Geshefts [deals] with him. He showed me pictures of him being caught with that chick." He nodded in the direction of the bathroom. "And told me a touching story about how he was being blackmailed. And although they didn't demand anything yet, he was warned to prepare for some mysterious assignment. He also showed letters with threats. They were neither handwritten nor typed, but rather contained pasted letters clipped from a newspaper. A week later, the trial took place. The lawsuit was filed by Irena, and the same pictures were shown in court. Irena stated that she had found them at her husband's. She spoke about blackmail and threats and said that she was afraid for her own life. And after a while, I received the same letter with the same clippings and with the threat that the police would find out where my underground casino was located. On top of that, there were pictures from the bordello. And I have a beautiful patriarchal family! I really got angry. Who was behind that blackmail? And I started thinking. I don't know how long I would be racking my brains, but I was approached by a certain gumshoe, who I sometimes gave different things to do."

"Kvartsyany?"

"Yes. He said that a nice lady wanted to divorce her husband. It had to be done very delicately, without a hitch. And for this noble purpose she had hired him to follow all the escapades of her husband and his mistress and take pictures of them. I understood that she would prefer to honor him in the grave, and divorce was the best of bad options. I asked: 'Are you, by any chance speaking about Tomashevych?' 'Yes, Tomashevych.' 'But what concern is it of mine?' And he says: 'Quite by accident, I found these newspapers in Tomashevych's villa in the barn where they kept firewood.' And in front of me he set down a bunch of newspapers with words and letters cut out." He took a pile of newspapers out of the drawer and placed it in front of me. "Huh? How do you like it? At that point all the little wheels started spinning in my head. So, those letters were cut out by Tomashevych himself. And there was nobody mysteriously blackmailing him with photos, because those photos were available to his own wife. He lied to me."

"And then you decide to have a chat with him? And for this reason, you sent someone to make Emilia call Tomashevych. And before that, you arrange all the conditions for me to write a scandalous article. So, it's you in those bordello photos."

A very friendly smile lit up his face.

"Yes, it's me," he nodded.

"But Emilia didn't call. Then who?" He pretended to be quite surprised:

"What makes you think she didn't call? Because she said so?"

"No, because if she had listened and called, she would have been involved in the murder. She would have been on the same boat with you. Why kill her?"

"You're right," he agreed. "We found a woman to make the call."

"Agnieszka?"

"Maybe Agnieszka. Or maybe Irena." He was explicitly yanking my chain.

"So, the lady you brought with you rang the doorbell."

"Oh!" He brightened up. "How do you know that we brought her?"

"Oh, we've also dug something up. You brought her and took her away. You were seen driving a Packard. Four men and one woman. She called, then pressed the doorbell, and you broke in after her."

"Well, there's nowhere to hide dirty laundry," he flicked his hand. "Actually, this is exactly how it happened. But then there was an edifying conversation. We tried to find out what was behind it all. Who was interested in killing the shareholders. But Tomashevych evasively squirmed like an eel on a frying pan. At that time, I was not aware of him blackmailing the military. And he flatly denied blackmailing anyone at all. While my boys chatted with him, I rummaged in his office. And on the bookshelf, I found an envelope containing some interesting copies of documents, from which it became clear that his victims were people from Warsaw. These documents are of great importance and may be of interest to many."

"To whom, for example?"

"For example, to the Reich."

"Why would they need them?"

"In case of war, to grab a certain *Pan* General by the butt with the help of a folder testifying to his cooperation with the Bolsheviks in 1920. But those were just copies of four pages. Here he had to admit having blackmailed very respectable people. We tried to wrestle from him some information about where the originals were. He admitted that those were documents he had stolen from headquarters, but they had disappeared. He said he had not put those copies in the envelope and had not hidden them behind his books. He swore in the name of God he didn't know where the originals were. He said he used to keep them in the villa in the basement, and then they disappeared. I went down to the basement and really found, where he had told me, a hiding place under the floor – actually under one particular board. It was easy to remove, and you could easily hide a folder there. But there was nothing there. He was in tears, and I almost bought it, but ... my guys, when they taste blood, may not be able to control themselves. And although I ordered them to treat him delicately, they overdid it."

"Interesting! He was interrogated, although no marks of torture were found on him."

"Right. But what kind of marks are there, for example, on balls, when they are gently squeezed. Try it on yourself sometime," he laughed. "The pain is terrible, and no marks. Besides, I have a doctor ... Eh, I really have to introduce you! Doctor! Come here for a moment."

The door to the next room opened, and I saw a stranger who pretended to be a proponent of labor justice and then "saved" me from Dyzyo and Heba. His left hand was hidden in his pocket, his thumb out. With each step of his I could hear a quiet but unpleasant crunching sound.

"Well, I see you know each other," the fat tub of lard continued. "So. The doctor knows such spots on the human body that it is enough to insert a needle as thin as a hair, in such a spot, so that not just a man, but even an elephant howls in pain. Right, doctor?"

"Yes, boss. Do you want me to demonstrate?"

"No, no, we are having a friendly chat here. You may go." And again, that crunching sound. What did it remind me of?

Meanwhile, very slowly everything began to fall into place.

"But Tomashevych didn't die from having his balls squeezed," I said.

"No. Our doctor is also a dentist. He carefully unseals a tooth, inserts a long steel pin into the hole, and now this is the apotheosis, this is the peak of pain. Then the trumpet calls, the bright light is on, the actors come to the forefront and bow! In fact, during such a procedure, Tomashevych's heart failed. Who knew his heart was weak? Well, then they shot him in the trap."

"Why did they have to shoot him if he was already dead?"

"That's what pissed me off, too. Because at that moment I happened to be rummaging in the basement. I heard a shot, ran upstairs, but it was all over. They explained it by the fact that from the very beginning we planned to stage a suicide, so they brought the scene to a logical conclusion. Given their mental abilities, I was not surprised."

"You set up everything very cunningly. First, your doctor hands me the pictures of you in the bordello, then directs me to Stanislaviv, and then I write the article. Your accomplices pretend that they want to take the article back to stir me up. Meanwhile, the doctor saves me. I wonder what would have happened if your people had taken away the real article, not the fake one?"

"Well, we knew you were sly as a fox. But if what you are saying had happened, the doctor would have caught you and would have taken it away. We thought everything over."

"And then they pretended to be guarding me. I just don't understand why you killed Emilia?"

"You know.... We didn't mean to kill her. She could have stayed alive. Why not? She was so scared that she would hardly turn me over to the police. But she didn't want to complete another assignment of mine."

"Which one?"

"That's none of your business."

"Tell me.... This woman who was with you.... Was she present during the torture the entire time?"

He laughed contentedly.

"What do you think? That we chased her politely outside? No, she was sitting on the couch, sipping champagne, and munching chocolate. It was like a movie for her."

"And drank the entire bottle?"

"She was under stress. And none of us drank that swill. We drank our cognac and made sure to take the empty bottle with us."

"That babe is interesting, isn't she?" I asked ironically. "Sipping champagne watching her lover being tortured. Or maybe her husband?"

"He-he-he! Hold on! Don't try to catch me slipping up. I've told you too much anyway."

"Well, actually. Why the heck have you?"

"I'm telling you – I have to ask you for a small favor.... I'm interested in the folder with the original documents with which Tomashevych blackmailed the military. Kvartsyany swore that Tomashevych's wife didn't know where they were." He paused, shook the ashes onto the ashtray, and stared at the smoldering tip of the cigarette for a moment. "Then I sent Kvartsyany to the villa to look for that folder, taking his time calmly. He has a flair for such things. More than once he found something that the rest had overlooked, and he managed to sniff out stuff. When I call him the next day, he gives me a long song and dance about being ambushed and whacked on the head. And that's why, he said, he didn't find anything. He-he, but I, you know, wasn't born yesterday."

"He didn't lie. I saw him beaten up."

"And what? Didn't he find anything?"

The fat tub of lard squinted at me, and I guessed he knew everything.

"He did. The notebook."

"Oh, well! See? I know that the police have the notebook. But I don't give a shit – I'm not a criminal there, but an innocent victim. So, I pretended to believe him, and arranged for a meeting at his house. Because I was more interested in those papers. I didn't go myself, but sent the guys, Dyzyo and Heba. Well, they went too far again. Although I didn't mean to kill him. If I had sent the doctor, everything would have been done elegantly. But Bodyo decided to make some dough himself and didn't admit to finding anything."

"He didn't find any other documents. They got in his way."

"You see," he shook his head, "Now I believe that this was the way it was. But my boys still didn't believe. They tend to be very distrustful."

"But they whacked me good on the head and put a blood-stained hammer in my hand."

"Oh, yes, they are real jokers. Then they dashed to his old mother, and she gave them some worthless dogshit. I looked at it and chased them back to her with a kick. But someone got a jump on them and took away what she hadn't given us. Don't you know who it could be?" And again, that sly squinting eye. There was no point in dodging.

"That was me. Kvartsyany had warned her that I'd come. But it was just a notebook, which is of no importance to you."

He nodded contentedly.

"I knew you were a smart boy, and crafty. That's exactly the kind of guy I need – to find those documents."

"I haven't heard anything about them," I lied.

"It doesn't matter whether you've heard about them or not. Find them for me. Not for free, no. I'll reward you. A courier from Warsaw will arrive soon with the money.... You need to meet with him. You yourself understand that I can't send those dunderheads to the meeting – they frighten everyone with their appearance. But you have an intelligent face...."

"And the doctor?"

"Oh, doctor. I save him only for very sophisticated cases. And he will not be in Lviv that day."

"It seems you leave me no choice."

"I think so," he laughed again. "Unless you feel like swimming in the bathtub. And if you complete the assignment, you will receive ten thousand *zloty*."

"After I meet the courier, I guess I don't have to be reminded how brief my time on Earth is. And you know that perfectly well."

"No, no, don't be afraid. This time you won't take money from him. This time you will say that you are ready to return all the original documents and name the amount. And let them think about it. How to get that ransom is our business."

"And while they're thinking, will you contact the Reich? And also name the amount, but a much higher one."

"He-he-he," he laughed so loudly that the cat jumped off his knees and climbed back on the table, sitting down right in front of me. "And you, little bird, are quick! I immediately thought that you would be able to manage with this. After messing around with Irena."

Here he was already laughing, enjoying my surprise. Who could have told him about it? Not Irena. So, there must have been someone else in the villa. The driver? The bastard was sitting quietly like a mouse.

"If you killed an innocent boy, the detective, his mother, and Emilia, you won't leave me alive."

"No, no, we need you alive. Go have another fling with Irena, maybe you'll find out something else. Of course, in a very delicate way. Because if I visit her with the doctor, it won't be so delicate. But come with me, I'll show you something."

He led me to the next room, closed the door behind us. and went to the table. There was something like a suitcase on the table. He pressed a little button. There was a rumbling sound inside, and in a moment the dreamy sounds of my lovemaking with Irena – kisses, sighs, and passionate whispers. The old man watched with satisfaction what impression this would make on me. Of course, I was stunned.

"Superb, right?" He rejoiced, tugging at his pants that had slipped from his belly. "The cutting edge of technology. The Allgemeine Elektrizitäts-Gesellschaft-Telefunken tape recorder! It's not some Pompka & Vuzhik bike. He-he-he...," he giggled, leading me back by the arm, and when we sat down again on both sides of the table, he yawned wearily. He seemed to be getting bored with our conversation: "And this snatch of yours from the diner... What a cutie pie. If you try to screw us over, I'll hire her to wash the floor. Understand?"

What is not to be understood here? Everything was clear. The cat looked at me with its big eyes and, apparently, also understood everything. I stroked it, and it didn't mind it. Then I took it on my lap, and it purred with joy.

"A beautiful cat, isn't it?" The old man nodded, not taking his eyes off me.

Then, to weaken his focus, I said:

"All right, I'll do everything."

He really relaxed and leaned back in his chair. The muffled sounds of lovemaking could still be heard from the next room. Why didn't he turn it off? I got enraged and at the same moment threw the cat forcefully into his face. The cat meowed in horror. The old man squealed, waved his arms, and the cat flew to the wall. And I was holding the Colt 45 in my hand. I jumped up to the fat tub of lard, put the muzzle up to his scratched mug and hissed:

"Not a word! I think I have enough bullets for you and all your dunderheads."

He pursed his big plump lips with tiny bubbles of saliva. Fear alternated in his eyes with anger, then a spark of momentary decisiveness flashed but instantly disappeared. There, in the bathroom, I noticed a small ventilation window through which I could easily get out. It was the only window without bars on it.

"Get up!" I ordered.

He grunted and wiped his face with a handkerchief.

When he saw the blood on the handkerchief, he croaked:

"You won't get away with this.... No.... you won't...."

"Okay. I'll keep that in mind. Now, off to the bathroom." He froze.

"What are you going to do?"

"Don't worry. I'm not gonna do what you did to the poor girl."

I pushed him into the bathroom and closed the door behind us. He was scared for good reason. There was nobody in the tub. There was just some water on the tiles.

"Where did you take her?"

"If you behave badly, we'll plant her on you. And if not, then she'll be buried somewhere in the woods."

"Hands behind your back," I ordered.

He obediently put his hands behind his back, and I tied them with a towel. I pushed the second towel into his mouth, then turned my back to him and stunned him with the hilt of the Colt. The old man sank heavily onto the tile. I carefully supported him so that he wouldn't crash his noggin for good. Although, apparently, it was unnecessary. Then I quickly got to the window, easily climbed into it, and fell on the flower beds, losing the Colt. But I didn't look for it. In complete darkness, I ran across the yard to the car. The key was in the ignition. But there was another car in the garage – the blue Packard. I looked around and saw tools sitting on the garage shelves. I found tin scissors and punctured all the tires of the Packard with them. Then on the way to the car I looked at the house – Buzkova Street, number 8. Great. I got behind the wheel and turned the key with my heart pounding. The engine started obediently. I turned around and revved it up. In the mirror I saw the bandits fly out of the house at the sound of the engine. They didn't dare shoot because of the neighbors, and immediately rushed to the second car.

I drove into Lychakivska Street and stopped near *Pan* Svystun's Under the Star Pub, frequented by young bohemians, who couldn't afford such an artsy pub as Atlas. I had been there more than once. The owner of the pub was an old lame Ukrainian by the name of Svystun, who had high ambitions to catch up with Atlas, and in that endeavor went so far that he soon became a victim of crafty customers. Young writers found strong arguments to convince Svystun that it was thanks to them that he would soon become as famous as his pub. After all, they were all, according to themselves, future celebrities, and suffering from deprivation only now, but tomorrow.... Oh, tomorrow everything can change. Arranging various entertainment in the pub, the artists nourished the owner with pride, and he already saw himself as a famous patron, the guardian of talent. For this noble purpose, he often served free drinks to his guests.

Although it was late, the pub was full.

"Marko! How you doin'!" Old friends shouted to me. "Come join us!"

I would gladly do so another time, but no, not right now. I went to the bar, ordered a glass of *horilka* and asked if I could use the phone. Svystun nodded behind his back in the direction of a small pantry where there was a telephone. I closed the door behind me and dialed Irena's father's number. In a moment I heard his sleepy voice:

"Hallo! Who's the heck ringing me so late?"

"It's Marko. I found out what you asked for." He immediately cheered up: "Oh! And how?"

"I was abducted by his men, but I escaped."

"Remind me, how he was recorded in Tomashevych's notebook."

"NM. But the real initials are L.K."

"LK? Shit! And the ones who kidnapped you were a dumb white-haired hulk with a beet-red mug, and the other a worm?"

"Yes."

"It could only be Ludwig Krombach! Did they take you to their casino?"

"No. To some house. Buzkova Street, 8. You'll find them all there, because they don't have a car."

"Where the hell is that Buzkova?" I explained and added:

"Emilia is there."

"Alive?"

"No."

"Dirt bags!" He cursed.

"One more thing: Irena's driver works for him. He recorded our ah ... conversation and passed it on to him."

He cursed again and hung up. I downed the shot and called Obukh.

"Finally!" he rejoiced. "Safe and sound. I heard your conversation and ordered Radomsky to keep listening. Meanwhile, I grabbed a car and raced over to you, but it was too late. Now I've been sitting and waiting for news from you." I told him about my adventure, my conversation with Krombach, and gave him the address.

"But maybe you shouldn't hurry there," I added. "Let them shoot each other up a little there. You'll have less trouble."

"Son of a gun! I knew you were a cunning bugger! But as much as this!" He was seething from wrath.

"Please don't step in until the first shot," I warned in a calm voice. "Otherwise, you'll set me up. And then I won't be able to tell you much more interesting stuff."

"Go to hell!"

My buddies kept calling me, but I decided to spend that night in a different way and dialed Irena's number. She answered in a sleepy voice and was very surprised by my call.

"What happened?"
"Are you alone?"
"A-alone."
"Are you really alone?"
"Why? Why are you asking?
"I can't tell you over the phone."
"You can come over if it's really urgent."
"Okay. I'm on my way."

CHAPTER 7

I rang the doorbell. A growl came from inside. Irena opened the door and ordered her dog to lie down. She was dressed in snow-white pajamas, trimmed with white, foamy fur.

"You scared me with your call." She leaned close to me and wrapped her arms around my neck. We kissed and started moving, hugging each other, to the living room.

"I need a drink," I said, sitting down on the couch.

She brought whiskey and sat down next to me. I poured the liquor into glasses, and we drank it bottoms up.

"Well?" She placed her hand on my knee. "Say something."

"I had a very eventful day today. First, I had a meeting with your father, who asked me to find the fifth shareholder. And when I got home, I was kidnapped by some fishy characters. It turned out that they were working for the fifth one."

"Who is he?"

"He didn't tell me his name. But your father thinks it's Ludwig Krombach. Do you know him?"

She frowned and pulled her hand from my knee.

"I do."

"Those were his people who killed Tomashevych, Kvartsyany and his mother, your gardener, and Emilia.

"What? Emilia was killed?" She screamed.

"Yes. They kidnapped her when she was on her way to meet with your father."

"And where had she been before that?"

"I brought her to my place and ordered her to sit tight. Your father said she had called him and wanted to meet with him. He arranged to meet her in De la Paix. Is it true that she's your distant relative?"

She smiled.

"So distant that my father could make love to her."

"And he gave her to Tomashevych so easily?"

"But he never had any problems with that. My husband didn't know anything about her. My father and I fixed them up at a reception."

"Very interesting. And it was even more interesting when Krombach turned on the recording of our passionate lovemaking."

"What?" She was bewildered.

"Your driver recorded it and passed the tape to Krombach. So, he doesn't work only for you."

"Oh my God! I must get rid of him immediately. What a scoundrel!" She jumped to her feet and paced the room nervously. Suddenly she stopped. "Wait... but how could he do that? He wasn't there then. He had left just before you came. And he came back again in the evening, brought food, and in a few minutes, he was gone."

"He could have turned the recorder on, and then picked up the tape and passed it to the client."

"Why the hell would he need it?"

"Maybe just for fun."

"I'll fire him tomorrow."

After that, I told her my conversation with Krombach in detail.

"Oh my God!" she put her palms to her lips. "That's how it happened! Poor Yanus!"

It seemed to be the first time she uttered the name of the deceased the way Emilia used to call him.

"You know, what's surprising?" I said. "Why didn't he say where the notebook and those papers were? How could a person endure such torture?"

"I don't know.... I don't know...." She shook her head, wiping away tears.

"Maybe he didn't know where they were? Could someone have stolen them?" She raised her head.

"Who stole them? Who could have known about them?"

"Maybe the mysterious woman who was present at the torture and quietly drank champagne, snacking on candy and oranges?"

Irena closed her eyes and became immersed in her thoughts. Then she said:

"How little I knew about him.... Where did he ferret out such a monster? To calmly watch the suffering of a living person?"

"Could it have been Emilia or Agnieszka?"

"Emilia? Give me a break.... She once cut her finger and almost fainted. I can't speak for Agnieszka. I didn't know her closely."

The phone rang, Irena picked up the receiver.

"Hallo.... is that you, Dad? I can't hear you very well.... He's here.... Okay." I took the phone from her.

"We've got an issue here," Leon said out of breath. "We've shot those two, the albino and the worm, but Krombach escaped."

"And the doctor?"

"What doctor?"

"There was a doctor with them."

"I don't know. We haven't seen him. Emilia hasn't been found either. Everything was clean in the house. Not a trace. By the way, here's your friend the commissioner. I'll put him on the phone."

"Well, I'll tell you, you did the right thing by calling me," Obukh muttered, "but we were late anyway. Now you're in danger. Do you realize that?"

"Yes. And is the Packard in the garage?"

"No, it isn't. We found just the punctured tires. But they must have had spare ones. They managed to do that pretty quickly. I think you'd better spend the night there. Don't go anywhere in the middle of the night."

"But they can come over here."

Then I heard Leon shouting: "Hurry! Hurry! Get to the car!" The phone clicked and the conversation broke off. What did that mean? Did they see something? Krombach would definitely want to get revenge. The first thing they'll do is visit my house. But without finding me there, they might rush over here.

"Does your driver have the keys to the house?" I asked Irena.

"Sure. Why?"

"Well, nothing. If he's working with them, he may have given them the key. But whether they have the keys or not, no door is an obstacle for them anyway. We need to hide somewhere. I think they're already on their way here."

"What are you saying?" She became worried.

"They're looking for me because they know your father attacked them. That's why you're in danger, too. Get ready to go."

Irena still didn't believe me and was fussing around trying to choose what to wear as though she were going to a reception, so I had to get her to get a move on. I quickly turned off the light and looked out the window. It was dark everywhere, but anxiety was growing. The silence seemed rather ominous. Then there was a flash of headlights from behind the trees on the side of the road. Suddenly the dog growled. It had been lying quietly in the hallway but then dashed to the door.

"Is there a back door here?" I asked Irena.

"Yes. Why?"

"We have to get out of here right now. I think they're already here."

She was about to say something, but didn't have time, because the key was turning in the lock. The door swung open. The dog rushed forward, but the doctor with his suitcase came in first. He deftly sprayed something in the dog's snout. The dog yelped and lay down. Krombach and Heba with his arm bandaged followed the doctor. Apparently, Heba had just been wounded. Meanwhile, the doctor grabbed the dog by the neck and gave it a shot. Frightened, Irena rushed to me and pressed her body against mine, instinctively seeking protection, but I couldn't protect her.

"He-He," Krombach smiled, "the birds are in their nest. It's very good that I have you two together. You, you shitbag, treated my neck really well. It still hurts. Is that your gratitude for my sincerity? You set her daddy on me! And the police! What were you thinking? That I wouldn't manage to take care of them? From the legal perspective, you won't be able to get to me. Why are you frozen to the spot? Heba, go ahead and thank him for my neck."

The worm, smiling, pulled the Mauser out of its holster, approached me with his pee-dancing step, and slammed me behind my ear with the handle. The only thing I could do was try to predict the movement of his arm and expose my neck instead of the back of my head. Of course, I hissed in pain and fell on the carpet like a sack. I didn't pass out, but just pretended to be unconscious. Meanwhile, Krombach sat down in an armchair that creaked plaintively beneath him, poured himself some whiskey, drank it down, and handed the bottle to the doctor.

"You guys, drink some, too. We need to relieve the stress...." He was silent for a moment, then turned to Irena. "Well, don't you already know what's of interest to me? The folder with the documents."

"With what documents?" Irena muttered out horrified.

"Don't play me for a fool, kitty cat. I'm not your father. The folder with the documents with which your husband blackmailed the military headquarters."

"I don't know what you're talking about. He was the one who was blackmailed. He was threatened. How could it be the other way around?"

"The detective you hired found newspapers in your barn. Words and letters were clipped out. He pasted them and sent them to the shareholders, including me. Don't you know that?"

"You are forgetting that we didn't live together. All I wanted was to get rid of him as soon as possible."

"Not only that. But also, to get the villa back."

"What's wrong with that?"

"No, nothing. But, you know, sometimes I like to put two plus two together, three plus three, four plus four ... interesting combinations come out. I wonder why your Yanek didn't admit anything, even though my boys did the kind of experiments on him that even a big bear would admit to being a parrot. And for some reason he couldn't tell us anything, even under the threat of impending death. And just imagine –we didn't kill him! He died. Of a heart attack."

I was lying facing Irena and saw her fingers tremble. Apparently, she wasn't the one who witnessed Tomashevych's death. I was thinking frantically about what to do. Should I keep lying and pretending to be unconscious, or should I show some signs of life. I chose the first. I wouldn't be able to handle them both anyway, but this way I'd be able to listen. Maybe I'd hear something interesting.

"Irena, Irena...," the old man growled. "You're a cunning cheat. You've been in the shadows all the time. In fact, you're one of us. Aren't you interested in the death of the shareholders?"

"I?" she blinked with her long eyelashes. "I'm a shareholder?"

"Don't pretend to be an innocent chick. Of course, you aren't a shareholder. But when we were making our contributions, Tomashevych paid a hefty sum on your behalf and insisted that you get equal rights. Yes, you aren't a shareholder, but you are registered as the 'chairman of the supervisory board,' who has the same rights as the shareholders. That is – after the death of the other shareholders, all property and assets are transferred to you."

"This is the first time I've ever heard of that!" There was sincere indignation and anger in her voice. "I never interfered in Yanek's affairs. I don't know what agreements he concluded with you. Yes, I gave him quite a lot of money as my dowry. I never asked how he used it."

"Well, I can report to you: you and I are the last Mohicans of the nearly extinct tribe of shareholders of the Association of Tavernkeepers. After us – there's a desert and darkness. But the truth is: have you ever wondered what the sense of this struggle for survival is? Is it just the matter of a few stone apartment houses and pubs? And some plots of land in the boondocks? Is it worth so many deaths?"

"Are you asking me?"

"Sure, who else should I ask since Yanek went down?"

"I can answer you: I don't know what the matter is. Yanek never shared anything with me. By the way, the letters that Yanek received also consisted of pasted letters and words. But I didn't suspect Yanek at all. What kind of claims can you have against me?"

"Well, maybe not against you. But you could have guessed that there was something much bigger behind all this. And this is the folder with documents that your husband had stolen from headquarters. Where they are?"

"Good Lord! I've never heard of them."

"Do you understand that there is no one who could endure the hellish pain my doctor can cause and not admit to everything? Even to flying on a broom to Lysa Hora[42]? Do you understand that?"

Irena nodded in fright.

"I understand."

"And I don't understand how Tomashevych could withstand such pain and not admit where that shitty folder was?!" Krombach roared, then became silent for a moment as the frightened Irena had lost the remnants of

....

[42]   The name translates as Bald Mountain. A mountain next to Vysokyi Zamok (High Castle Mountain) in Lviv. Bald mountains in Ukrainian folk belief are places where witches and dark spirits gather.

control over herself. "I'm surprised ... very much surprised that he didn't even give us that lousy notebook! Which is really a dime a dozen. I just wanted to see when the payments were made. And he swore again that he didn't know where it was. That notebook suddenly disappeared.... He even denied having made the copies I found on the shelf behind the books. He said he didn't put them there. Who could have done that? Maybe you, maybe Emilia.... Maybe, hell if I know."

He sighed and fell silent, apparently staring at Irena, because I saw her fidgeting under his gaze.

"I have no answers to these questions," she whispered. "I also had been looking for that notebook and couldn't find it. And this is the first time I've heard about the documents."

"But that's not all, because there are still scores to be settled between me and your daddy. He's been trying to take over my businesses for a long time. Didn't you know that, too? So far, it hasn't crossed a certain line. But tonight, he attacked me."

"Do you wonder why?" Irena suddenly bristled up.

"Of course, I'm surprised."

"You killed his gardener and Emilia. Isn't that enough?"

"Oh my God! Wage war against me because of those slimy worms?"

"Then I'll try to explain better. That boy was his son. Outside of marriage, though. But his son. And he took care of him, loved him in his own way. And Emilia was our, albeit distant, relative, whom he also took care of."

"Oh! I didn't know that! Well, if someone had explained that to me as plainly as you have, I would have acted differently. But what can be done – since what's already happened can't be changed? Now I have no choice but to take you and this chump hostage and demand those documents from your daddy. I don't care where he finds them. But he must. Because I don't think this is Tomashevych's only nest. There must be another apartment where he could hide his valuables. And there's no way you don't know about it."

"I used to know everything about him. But that was two years ago. He could have arranged for at least ten apartments for himself during these two years. He had to meet with his mistresses somewhere."

"Well, yes ... yes ... what you are saying makes sense. And yet I have no way out of this. The police are already chasing me. Although no one has found and won't find Emilia's corpse. So, the murder took place exclusively in the imagination of your lover-boy. Give him a kick. Hasn't he come to his senses yet?"

I felt the tip of Irena's slipper poke me in my shoulder.

"Kick harder!" Krombach said, laughing. "It's not a ball, it's a guy. Otherwise, I'll ask the doctor to revive him."

This time the kick was stronger, but I kept pretending to be half dead.

"Heba, you overdid it. Doctor, do you have a shot to bring him back to his senses?"

"I sure have," the doctor said. "Do you still want to talk to him?"

"Of course." Here I became worried and stirred. "Oh, look, doctor, he has already come to life from hearing your voice!" Krombach rejoiced. "You work miracles."

I sat up but didn't get to my feet. I had to complete my performance. Sitting on the floor I rubbed the back of my head.

"He-he!" Krombach rejoiced. "So, now you know how it hurts, don't you? Irena, call your daddy. Stop winking at me. Your charms work on me like a poultice on a dead man."

Irena walked up to the phone.

"What should I tell him?"

"Tell him that if he doesn't give me the folder with the documents, my doctor will take care of your teeth. Or maybe even something else."

"Boss," Heba said suddenly, "I can make her talk if need be. I'd be happy to have my way with her."

"Hush, you stink bomb," Krombach waved him off. The doctor gritted his teeth. Irena dialed the operator.

"Please connect me to number 207-59."

There was a pause. Everyone froze attentively. Other than Krombach. He approached Irena and stuck his ear close to the receiver.

"What? Nobody's picking up the phone? Try again...." There was a click. "Oh, there he is...."

"Hallo! This is Irena speaking. Is that you, Yuzyk? Where's dad?.. Hasn't he come back yet? So late?.. When he comes back tell him to call me immediately... No, nothing's happened. That is ... yes ... something happened ... I can't say over the phone...."

Krombach snatched the phone:

"Well, why not over the phone? Yuzyk, tell Leon that Irena is in Krombach's hands. And if he doesn't bring the folder with the documents.... Don't ask which ones. He knows. So, if he doesn't bring it in an hour, Irena will start losing her teeth every quarter of an hour each. Got it? How many quarters are there in an hour? That's right, smarty pants, four. So, four teeth every hour. Bye for now." He hung up and looked at Irena's pale face. "What? Do you think I'm kidding? But you will have good company. This bozo," he nodded at me. "He'll be the first to start losing his teeth. Doctor, get your devices out."

The doctor rushed to lay out his dental instruments on the table with undisguised enthusiasm. He did everything with his right hand, his left still hidden in his pocket. This evoked in me an undefined anxiety. From time to time, he glanced at me, then at Irena, twisting a scalpel, a pair of forceps, or a long thin needle before our eyes, smiling contentedly in anticipation of fun.

"Eh," I said, "can't I have something to drink too? For disinfection," I tried to crack a joke.

"What? For disinfection?" Krombach burst into Homeric laughter. His entire body was shaking. "For ... for ... shite ... disin ... ha-ha-ha ... fection ... oy, I can't take itya. Ha-ha-ha-ha! Irena, go fetch a bottle. You gave me a good laugh! Disinfection is a serious matter."

He was still laughing when Irena put the bottle of whiskey on the table, where all sorts of horrible metalware had been lined up. I thought that if I were sober, I wouldn't be able to demonstrate courage and not panic. Irena was probably of the same opinion, because she also had a shot. Time passed slowly. The doctor was glancing impatiently at his watch, thoughtfully blowing out smoke from his nostrils.

"Boss," Heba said again, "it's a waste to spoil such beauty. And I'd frisk her for a bit, huh?"

"Shut up, you stinkpot," Krombach growled, "and don't prattle without permission. You can go to Kryva Manka [Crooked Manka] and make it with her as much as you want." Then he glanced at his watch. "Ten minutes left."

"It's nonsense," Irena said. "I don't know what kind of a folder it is and where it is. How could I possibly help you? If I knew, I'd give it to you."

"Someone must know. If not you, then your dad." Here I couldn't take it anymore:

"They found a folder in his apartment on Legioniv Street." Irena glared at me. "There were some documents from the folder with which Tomashevych had been blackmailing the military. But only copies. There were no originals."

"Oh!" Krombach rubbed his hands. "See, doctor, how nice? Little by little things are clearing up. There is already a folder with copies. And the originals will be here soon. What were you saying?"

"They'll sure be here, boss," the doctor gritted his teeth.

"There were no originals there," Irena said. "There were materials with which he had been blackmailing the shareholders. And a few copies. My dad and I searched everything. In the end, you can see for yourself. I can take you there myself."

"No, no, that won't work for me," Krombach shook his head. "If they could be there, you wouldn't invite me there. But they must be somewhere. Because someone hid them. If not your husband, and I'm more inclined to believe him, then it's you or your father."

"Check the shelves," Irena said. "That's all we've found."

Krombach jumped from the unexpectedness of what she said, went to the shelf, and picked up the folder. I looked at Irena in surprise. She hadn't told me anything about the folder, although I had learned about it from her father. Krombach flipped through the papers, but without much enthusiasm. It was clear that he was not interested in the photos with which the shareholders had been blackmailed. Several copied pages caught his attention. He ran his eyes over them, closed the folder, and tossed it on the shelf.

"It's not worth crap. These are the same copies I've already found."

"But that's all I have," Irena said.

Krombach shook his head nervously and glanced at his watch again.

"Well, it's time. Start, doctor."

I tilted the glass but didn't swallow. The doctor took the forceps in his right hand and clicked them several times. A smile spread on his mug. He approached me and took the left hand out of his pocket. Instead of four fingers, I saw iron prostheses clenching and unclenching with a creak. The oil, with which they were lavishly lubricated, sparkled in the light of the bulbs. Crunch, crunch, crunch... that's what I had heard before... It gave him great pleasure to watch Irena's and my terrified eyes.

"Well?" said Krombach. "So? Will you confess?" Irena burst into tears, an expression of unspeakable despair was reflected on her face. She began gasping for air and sobbed:

"I ... I ... Oh Lord...."

The doctor told me to open my mouth and raised the forceps to my lips. Crunch, crunch.... Irena shouted:

"No, no! I'll tell you!.. she didn't say anything, but kept sobbing and choking on her tears, muttering something indistinct.

"Well, open your trap!" The doctor growled. Crunch, crunch, crunch....

And I opened it, but only to spit a mouthful of whiskey in his eyes. He groaned, dropped the forceps, and rushed to look for water. Krombach pulled out his revolver and cursed.

"Tell me!" He growled at Irena.

CHAPTER 8

At that moment, one of the windows shattered. The door slammed open and shots were fired. Krombach, vomiting blood from his throat, fell on the floor. Heba managed to pull out the Mauser but didn't use it, because in a second he was already convulsing; and the doctor locked himself in the bathroom.

Irena's father together with several armed guys and Obukh burst into the living room.

"Surprisingly, just in time!" I expressed my astonishment. "Because I'd already said goodbye to my teeth."

"And that was in vain," Obukh replied, "we were watching from the outside waiting for the right moment."

Shots were fired in the yard.

"What's that?" I asked.

"*Pan* Doctor must have been trying to escape through the bathroom window," Leon said. "But we have guards everywhere. Boys," he turned toward his people, "clean up here and wait for us in the gazebo. Fetch a bottle in the credenza for your nice work." Then he sat down in the chair where Krombach had been sitting before and crossed his arms contentedly on his belly. His guys took out the corpses, rolled up the blood-stained carpet and left with it. Irena rushed to her father with her arms open for a hug.

"Thank you, daddy, I'd already said goodbye to my life."

"Well, it's over," Leon said. "Although we don't have the folder with the original documents that Tomashevych was hiding."

"Why do you need it?" Obukh asked.

"I don't need a damn thing. I'd return it to the courier."

"If that's so, then *Pani* Irena should help us." Obukh smiled at her.

"I?" She wondered. "How? I don't have a clue about that folder."

"Krombach demanded it, too," I said. "She doesn't know anything."

"It's commendable, Marko, that you played the role of *Pani* Irena's unso-licited lawyer, but I'll have to tell you something," Obukh said dryly.

I noticed Irena's fingers trembling again. Obukh took a clean glass from the credenza, sat down in a chair, poured himself some whiskey, and drank it down. We all watched his movements, not understanding anything, es-pecially not the longest of pauses. In the end, Leon couldn't hold back any longer: "Well? We're listening."

Obukh reached under the top of his shirt, pulled out several folded piec-es of newspaper with clipped words and letters, and handed them to Leon.

"Why are you giving this to me?" he wondered.

"Take a closer look at these clippings. I picked them up from Krombach's table."

Those were the same newspapers that Krombach had showed me. Leon unfolded the papers, looked at one side, then at the other, but only shook his head.

"I don't understand what you expect from me," Irena started fidgeting.

"Don't you see that these cut-out empty spaces are uneven, and round-ed?" Obukh asked.

"And here is the letter that Krombach received; everything is clipped evenly."

"Well...." Leon nodded. "I see. So what?"

"The only thing is that these words and letters were cut out by different people. These newspaper columns were cut not with regular scissors, but with a lady's. Scissors for ladies are known to be rounded."

Irena laughed:

"And I was wondering: what are you getting at? Scissors for ladies – that's quite a discovery! And I can't even imagine how you can cut out letters with ordinary scissors."

"But then I can. After all, these are capital letters from the headings, not from the text. They can be cut out with ordinary scissors. And in the letter to Krombach – pay attention! Everything is cut out with ordinary scissors. But that's not all. It might seem like these are the very newspapers that were used to blackmail shareholders. But in fact, these are all fairly fresh news-papers. Although no dates can be seen here, the content of the news shows that all these newspapers were published a week ago. Having made clippings with the ladies' scissors, someone wanted to convince someone that these newspapers were used for those anonymous letters. Who could that be?"

"I still don't get it," Leon shook his head.

My tipsy head failed to understand where Obukh was heading.

"I'll explain. If these are the same newspapers, then the cut-out places must coincide with the pasted words and letters. Right?"

"Yes," Leon sighed with relief.

"But in the case of the letter to Krombach, they don't match."

There was a pause. Everyone was digesting the news and its significance thoroughly. My head began to clear up a little.

"But you haven't seen any other letters," Leon replied.

"These pieces of newspapers have nothing to do with any anonymous letter," Obukh continued.

"What makes you so sure?"

"Because we know that the letters were almost identical. All shareholders received the same threatening letters. Including Tomashevych. But the words clipped from these newspapers weren't used for blackmailing."

"Interesting," Leon said, "I am speechless, but are you sure they have nothing to do with the blackmail?"

"Absolutely. The blackmailer made a mistake. He bought several identical newspapers, cut them into separate columns, made chaotic clippings, and decided that all that would make a corresponding impression on someone. In our case on Krombach. But due to the fact that some pages are duplicated, we can find out exactly what words were cut out. For example, 'Scandinavia,' 'university,' 'rain,' 'wind,' 'tram,' 'Ethiopia,'... What can this all have to do with the blackmail? I continue. These excerpts were brought to Krombach by the detective Kvartsyany. Where did he get them? Presumably in the barn. And who was in touch with Kvartsyany?" Here he looked at Irena.

"Why are you looking at me?" She wondered. "He was spying on Yanek."

"Yes, he was, but not on the villa. He had another task. He completed his intimate surveillance two months ago. He had no reason to hang around the villa, not to mention peeking into the barn. You gave him the newspapers."

"I? That's ridiculous!"

"You gave him these newspapers to show to Krombach. And you knew that Krombach just wouldn't put up with it. Having received an anonymous letter the day before, he found out who that mysterious blackmailer was thanks to you. And so, you could no longer doubt that he would want revenge. And so, it happened. You got rid of the husband you loathed through Krombach's hands. You knew that your husband had been blackmailing the shareholders. You also guessed that he had sent anonymous threats to himself. And when there were only two shareholders left, your husband and Krombach, you decided to take advantage of the situation and set Krombach on Tomashevych."

"Hey!" Leon said. "Don't forget this is my daughter! I will not allow her to be slandered. She knew nothing about the fifth shareholder."

"Of course, I knew nothing," Irena said. "And it seems to me that it's high time our guests left."

"And here is an anonymous account to which funds were transferred...." Obukh put papers from the bank in front of Leon. "Here it is noted when and how much money was deposited. The amount is always the same. And the dates fall on the first Monday of each month."

"It makes sense," I said. "Because the meetings with the courier took place on the first Monday of each month."

"What do I have to do with this account?" Irena was indignant.

"Only the fact that it's yours now. You killed two birds with one stone and took possession of all the shareholders' property. But the biggest gem you got is the 'pane'...."

"Which, dammit, 'pane'?" Leon muttered.

"Or 'window'...." Obukh paused, enjoying the father and daughter's reaction to his words. "You can call it whatever you want. Don't you know what we call 'panes' or 'windows'?"

"No, I don't," Leon muttered frowning.

"I think I do," I said. "That's a well from which oil is pumped."

"Yes," Obukh nodded. "But they aren't pumping yet because the shareholders had no idea that oil was found there. Only *Pani* Irena knew about it thanks to *Pan* Leon." Leon muttered something in discontent. "It was their little family secret. This 'window-well' is located on the outskirts of Drohobych. And it turned out to be the most valuable property of the shareholders."

Irena crossed her legs and smiled.

"You sure don't have any evidence, do you?" Leon asked, suddenly cheering up. "Take these bank papers.... What kind of proof are they? The account is opened not in a name, but under a password. Everything else is up in the air."

"Yes, I admit that this evidence is not enough to arrest *Pani* Irena for arranging for the murder of her husband. And I'm not going to do that. Not even for bringing the murderers here."

"Well, you're crazy!" Irena snorted. "Who brought them? Me? Those monsters?"

"I think that you lured your husband here with the offer of an amicable divorce agreement and quietly indulged in your favorite candies, admiring his being tortured. And although I asked *Pan* Leon to keep at least one of them alive, he was in too much of a hurry."

"Oh Jesus!" Irena shook her head sadly. Instead, Leon flared:

"Hey! Don't pass off your conjectures as facts! Under these circumstances, we couldn't have acted differently. I had to save my daughter. Irena had no contact with Krombach. Otherwise, I would have found out about it. Krombach wanted to make peace with me, but I didn't want to press flesh with the rascal."

"I'm not claiming. I'm just thinking out loud," Obukh said. "You see, I didn't call anybody from the police. Those who could testify against *Pani* Irena are already dead. For example, Kvartsyany won't be able to say how *Pani* Irena gave him payment in advance, which he then gave to Dyzyo or Heba on the condition that Tomashevych needed to die. Because she wasn't sure of Krombach's intentions. Who knows, maybe they'll come to terms with each other, and Tomashevych will get off the hook. So, she decided to take no chances. That's why, when Tomashevych had a heart attack, one of them shot him in the mouth so their fee wouldn't be lost. They received the rest of the money from Kvartsyany at his house. And *Pani* Irena made copies of the documents and put them on the shelf so that Krombach could easily find them and learn what her husband was really doing."

"God, what a boundless stretch of imagination," Irena waved it off.

"And don't worry," Obukh said. "You're safe. All I'm trying to do is to get this infamous folder through which several people have been killed. And perhaps many more fates will be smashed. Someone may end up committing suicide."

"I want to get these documents no less than you do and give them to the courier," Leon said.

"What for?" Obukh shrugged. "So that the courier would take them to Warsaw, and a scandal breaks out there? No, they must be destroyed. These people, who had been taken prisoners by the Muscovites, had to testify under threat of death, of which they are now certainly ashamed. But would each of us be such a hero to withstand the fear of death?"

"Let it be your way," Leon agreed. "We don't have them anyway."

"I think you're wrong. *Pani* Irena has them."

"Your fantasies again!" Irena said. "When will you finish weaving these intrigues?"

"As soon as I get the folder," Obukh said firmly. "Well? I'm waiting."

"I don't have the folder," Irena said, looking away.

"Then I'm calling the police. You'll be detained on suspicion of plotting to kill your husband. And while the investigation continues, you'll sit behind bars in the company of prostitutes and thieves. And just so you know, we have a witness – your driver. I had a nice chat with him yesterday. He saw you cut out the newspapers and hand them to the detective."

Irena laughed:

"God, what cheap tricks!"

"Oh, I think I can guess why you laughed," Obukh became livelier. "Because he could hardly have spied on you cutting out the letters, and he wasn't present at the meeting with the detective. You were there yourself. But he was watching you. He also worked for Krombach. And that's not all. He has other interesting evidence. He'll be with me tomorrow morning. If you plan to try to catch him overnight, then your hopes are in vain. He won't be hiding at home, but at an address known only to me, where he'll be picked up in the morning by a police car."

Irena stopped laughing. Leon frowned.

"You've just said that you're not going to accuse my daughter."

"That's right. As soon as I get the folder, you won't see me again."

"What makes you think that Irena's got the folder?"

"Because nobody else can possibly have it. Krombach's men interrogated Tomashevych with such passion that it's impossible to believe that the man wouldn't indicate where the documents and the notebook were hidden. And he still didn't confess. Or just had nothing to confess? Because *Pani* Irena found both the notebook and the documents and hid them.

The notebook is known to have been found in a table leg. This table has an interesting story. Two and a half years ago, it was purchased by *Pani* Irena herself from the furniture company Budylovych & Co. I didn't hesitate to visit them and talk to the carpenter who had made the table. When placing her order, *Pani* Irena emphasized that two hiding places should be made in the table. One in the leg, and the other under the tabletop. That was before *Pani* Irena filed for divorce. But she still concealed this little trick from her husband."

I glanced at Irena, who was sitting red-faced, biting her lip. She lied when she said she had been looking for the notebook, and it came as a surprise to her that someone had managed to find it.

"Irena!" Leon turned to her. "Is it true? Did you even hide it from your own father?"

"I think *Pani* Irena will now show us this mysterious mechanism that pushes the tabletop apart," Obukh said.

Irena took to her feet, lingered for a moment, then went to the study. We all followed her with curiosity. Having come up to the table, she placed her hand under the tabletop. Something rumbled, and the tabletop began to move apart, forming a hollow in the middle. There was a black folder.

"You can take it," Irena muttered. "I wasn't going to use it anyway."

"Why," shrugged Obukh, "you've made great use of it. Tomashevych was hiding the folder and the notebook here in the villa. Namely in the basement under the floor. He had no secret apartment. These are just rumors that *Pani* Irena skillfully spread. If you hadn't hidden the folder, Tomachevych would have given it to Krombach, and he wouldn't have had a heart attack. However, that might not have saved his life, because you bribed the killers. And Krombach himself, having meticulously planned his revenge and having incited the reporter against Tomashevych, later confessed to your driver that he wouldn't kill him until he received the folder."

Leon took the folder from Irena's hands, unfolded it, flipped through it, and handed it to Obukh.

"I give it to you on one condition: everything that has been said here stays between us. You know me...." Here he glared at me. "I know how to get revenge. No police will save you if you don't keep your promise."

"All right," Obukh agreed. "I vouch for Marko. Let's get going."

"Let's take that folder, too," I said, nodding at the shelf. "That's what Tomashevych blackmailed the shareholders with along with several copies of the documents from headquarters."

"Take it, take it," Leon gestured with his hand. "We don't need that garbage."

"Yeah," Obukh smiled, putting the two folders together. "Now you have the kind of fortune that you don't need to worry about your old age in retirement."

Leon stepped closer to him and said in a low voice:

"I think you'll be discreet enough not to spread any information about the 'pane'?"

"Don't worry," Obukh assured him.

While we were walking to the exit, the dog finally recovered and raised its head, carefully examining everyone present, and Irena squeezed my hand:

"I'll be waiting for you," she whispered.

I gave her my charming smile and replied:

"And the courier will be waiting for you."

She glared at me with anger and pressed her sharp claws into my palm.

It was daylight outside when Obukh and I left that snake pit. The birds had already awakened, and a car was humming somewhere. Leon's men were sitting in the gazebo. When we appeared, they perked up and watched closely where we were going. Two corpses, covered haphazardly with a blanket, were lying to the side. The doctor was lying next to the wall, where he was hit by bullets. His hand with the iron claw was unnaturally twisted. We walked a few meters toward the forest and chose a small meadow.

"Give me the matches," Obukh said, then rolled up a few sheets of paper and set them on fire. Time and time again he tossed in the rest of the documents, and finally the folders themselves. We waited until everything turned to ashes and went to the car.

"Something tells me that you were bluffing," I said. "Both about the driver, and about Irena."

"Of course, I was bluffing. We have nothing on them. The old man didn't know that his dear daughter had arranged the murder of her husband. We detained her driver. He's in our cell, where you were. However, I don't think we'll learn anything more than he's already told us."

"And what did he say?"

"He doesn't know where Irena was that day when her husband was tortured. He didn't see her at all that day. Although this is a special case, because she only called him from time to time."

"And what's next?"

"Nothing. We'll release him tomorrow. Leon will take over Krombach's Casino. Irena will start pumping oil. Money will pour down from heaven."

"And who will go to meet the courier?"

Obukh looked at me like at a palm tree under the snow.

"And what concern is it of yours? It's no longer our business."

"Someone has to tell the courier that the folder has been destroyed, and the blackmail has stopped."

"Yeah?" Obukh shook his head in surprise. "Well, actually ... of course ... but, it won't be us, will it?"

I nodded. Meetings with the courier ended badly.

The car was rolling down quiet muddy streets where there were no pedestrians yet, but street sweepers with shovels and brooms had already appeared.

Obukh parked in front of the Videnska [Viennese] Café on Legioniv Street.

"Let's have some coffee," he suggested.

I didn't object. A cup of coffee with cognac was exactly what I needed after a sleepless night. Over coffee, I remembered the promise I had made to Bodyo's mother: I was obliged to go to her grave and tell her the names of the murderers.

THE FIFTH DAY
MONDAY
SEPTEMBER 26, 1938

EPILOGUE

The doorman was sweeping leaves into a pile in front of the gate.

"Oh, you've finally come," he said. "And she's already waiting."

"Who?" I didn't get who it was, and a motley array of all the young ladies from my hectic life dashed through my head.

Who could be waiting for me and moreover in my apartment? Maybe Yaryna? Or maybe, Agnieszka? Or, God forbid, Irena? Did the doorman give her the key? Is it someone from old times? Oh, I've given keys to so many. Some didn't return them, and I had to make new ones. But the doorman just smiled mysteriously and winked in a fatherly way.

I dashed up to my apartment. The door wasn't locked. I entered the hall and smelled the intoxicating scent of perfume. She was lying in the bedroom on the bed, covered with a checkered blanket. Her lush hair was falling in waves across the pillow. Upon seeing me, she smiled and slowly pulled off the blanket, exposing her graceful body with full breasts and breathtaking thighs.

"Come over to me," she murmured, running her tongue over her lips. "I'll warm you up."

Then she bent her left knee, and I felt like I was losing my senses. I started to take off my clothes. In a second we were already entwined in a warm embrace, although at the same time I was haunted by the thought it's not her, it can't be, she's dead, dead, dead ... it's a dream ... intoxicating and mad ... just a dream....

Then she cuddled up to me and whispered:

"I was forced ... forced ... I didn't want to ... I called Leon, I thought he would help me. I made a mistake not listening to you. When I left the house, they grabbed me, took me to Krombach and began to interrogate me about Tomashevych's other apartment. I didn't know where it was. They believed me, because it didn't make sense for me to hide something. Krombach said to give them the key and sent his two guys for you. And he told me that he had nothing to do with me, that when he sent Heba for me, he only wanted me to pass some news to Leon from him. Because Leon doesn't want to talk to him at all. They had a falling out once...."

"And those marks on your neck?"

"Krombach told me to run the bath. I burst into tears thinking they wanted to drown me. He said that he needed me like a hole in the head. He just needed to scare you. When the car approached, I took off my clothes and got into the tub. The doctor rubbed my neck with something and ordered me to lie still. I didn't believe till the end that I would remain alive."

"And after that?"

"When you went to the other room, the doctor told me to scram. I grabbed my clothes and he showed me out into the corridor. There I got dressed. We waited a moment for you to leave. And then he took me there through another door. I was sitting neither dead nor alive listening to your purring. What were you doing to her there that made her moan so much? Huh? I want some of the same...."

Those were the last words I remembered, and then her face began to dissolve before my eyes. It all melted like a wax candle, covered with a mist, because I was falling into a deep, drunken sleep, actually on the very bottom of the dark and warm ocean.

I woke up at noon. The scent of coffee and the rattle of utensils wafted from the kitchen. I began recalling the crazy night and no less crazy morning. Who's there in the kitchen? Emilia ... Emilia ... she's alive ... Why do I need her? Thoughts intertwined, swarmed, and swirled. How weak I am! I'm not in any condition to overcome my instincts. I had Yaryna from *Pan Musyalovych*'s dining room. I had her ...and then didn't... Why do I need Emilia? But Yaryna is a respectable girl. You can only marry these kinds of girls, not make love to them. But am I ripe for marriage? What wife can come to terms with my lifestyle, my nighttime exploits, my meddling in scandals, and risks I take to my life?

Emilia ... why not? Anyway, she doesn't have a place to live. I started to get dressed.

"Are you up?" Her voice came from the kitchen. "I made coffee and scrambled eggs. If you want, I'll go shopping, because even a mouse would starve to death here. There isn't even any fresh bread. But I found some stale bread, soaked it slightly, and fried it as well. It's good that at least there's some cooking oil here. Well, where are you?"

She fried stale bread ... Well, well, I'll be all right with this kind of girl.... I went to the bathroom, washed up, shaved, brushed my teeth, and appeared fresh and walking on air.

Emilia hugged me, kissed me, and began to purr:

"But promise me ... promise me you'll quit smoking. I can't stand the scent of tobacco ... And shave your mustache, because it tickles me."

ABOUT THE AUTHOR

Ukrainian writer **Yuri Vynnychuk** was born in 1952 in Stanislav, Ukraine. The city is now called Ivano-Frankivsk (affectionately known as "Frankivsk" by the local inhabitants). Vynnychuk's father was a doctor for the anti-Stalinist and anti-Nazi Ukrainian partisans during World War II, and his uncle on his mother's side Yuri Sapiha was killed by the Soviet secret police (the Cheka) in 1941. Vynnychuk was named in memory of his murdered uncle. In 1973 Vynnychuk completed the Stanislav Pedagogical Institute where he developed the reputation of a prankster. At that time he became involved in student publications as well as in the literary underground. In 1974 the KGB conducted a search of his house but found no materials that would have incriminated him in the eyes of the Soviet regime. In order to avoid inevitable arrest, he moved to the larger city of Lviv, where he hid at apartments of several friends, constantly covering his tracks from the all-seeing eye of the KGB.

Until 1980 Vynnychuk was blacklisted and not allowed to publish in official sources. Till then he published works under the names of various other writers and ghost wrote books on occasion. He eked out a living from the honoraria from his various pseudonymous publications, a practice which, by habit and by design, he continues to this day. During the 1980s he held readings of his works in the apartments of friends and became well-known for his satiric poetry and stories about a mythical country called Arcanumia – a land where the streets and, in fact, everything, are paved with fecal matter. Any association of Arcanumia with the Soviet Union or Soviet Ukraine, of course, would have been purely coincidental. "The Island of Ziz" ("Ostriv Ziz") is the best-known story from this cycle. From 1980 on, Vynnychuk was allowed to publish his articles and translations in the Ukrainian periodical press. He made a number of enemies among the Soviet literary establishment for his merciless attacks against hack writers. In 1987 Vynnychuk was instrumental in the creation of a stage singing and performance group "Ne zhurys'!" (Don't Worry!), which rose to swift popularity in Ukraine. After a tour to Canada and the United States in 1989, Vynnychuk decided to leave the group and devote his time exclusively to literature. Off and on he has continued to participate in concerts with the group. Under Mikhail Gorbachev's *perestroika-perebudova* and subsequent Ukrainian independence, Vynnychuk emerged from the underground (always keeping one foot there even to this very day) to occupy an eminent place in the new Ukrainian literature. His collection of fantastic stories *The Flashing Beacon* (Spalakh; 1990) sold out almost immediately. He also published a collection of poetry *Reflections* (Vidobrazhennia; 1990) and compiled and edited two anthologies of Ukrainian fantastic stories from the 19th century. His pulp fiction novellas *Maidens of the Night* (Divy nochi, 1992) and *Harem Life* (Zhytiie haremnoie, 1996) enjoyed extraordinary popularity. His love of storytelling and of his adopted hometown is combined in several volumes – *Legends of Lviv* (Lehendy Lvova, 1999), *Pubs of Lviv* (Knaipy Lvova, 2000), and *Mysteries of Lviv Coffee* (Taiemytsi lvivskoi kavy, 2001). His fantasy novel *Malva Landa* (the heroine's name) appeared in 2000 and a collection of fantastic tales *Windows of Time Frozen* (Vikna zastyhloho chasu) in 2001. And his novel *Spring Games in Autumn Gardens* (Vesniani ihry v osinnikh sadakh, 2005) won the 2005 BBC Ukrainian Book of the Year Award. His collection of autobiographical works, *Pears a la Crepe* (Hrushi v tisti, 2010) also was nominated for the BBC Prize. His book *Tango of Death* (Tango smerti) won the 2012 BBC Ukrainian Book of the Year Award and has been garnering an extraordinary amount of attention both in Ukraine and in European circles, particularly in German and Czech translations. The plot of *The Apothecary* (Aptekar), that appeared in 2015, harkens back to seventeenth-century Venice and Lviv. *The Night Reporter* (Nichnyi reporter) appeared in 2020 and is the first in a trilogy of crime novels featuring the same protagonist. Other more recent of his novels include: *The Censor of Dreams* (Tsenzor sniv; 2016), *Lutetia* (Liutetsiia; 2017), *Blood Sisters* (a sequel to the novel *The Apothecary*; Sestry krovi; 2018), and the novel *The Keys of Maria* (Kliuchi Marii; 2020; co-authored with Andrei Kurkov). *The Fantastic Worlds of Yuri Vynnychuk* is also available from Glagoslav.

ABOUT THE TRANSLATORS

Alla Perminova is a practicing literary translator, an independent researcher and an educator based in Barcelona, Spain. She received her doctoral and postdoctoral degrees in translation studies from Taras Shevchenko National University of Kyiv where she worked as a full professor for 15 years. She is Oleh Olzhych National Literary Contest first prize winner (1997), Fulbright senior scholar (The Pennsylvania State University, 2012-2013), the co/author of 70 scholarly articles, co/translator and/or editor of 15 books, presenter of over 30 talks at international conferences. Her personal philosophy as a translator and a researcher is discussed in her book *A Translator's Reception of Contemporary American Poetry* (in Ukrainian, 2015), in which she promotes the reception model of literary translation.

Michael Naydan is Woskob Family Professor of Ukrainian Studies at The Pennsylvania State University and works primarily in the fields of Ukrainian and Russian literature and literary translation. He has published over 50 articles on literary topics and more than 80 translations in journals and anthologies. He has translated, co-translated or edited more than 40 books of translations, including *Selected Poetry of Bohdan Rubchak: Songs of Love, Songs of Death, Songs of the Moon* (Glagolsav Publications, 2020); the novels *Sweet Darusya: A Tale of Two Villages* and *Tango of Death* (both with Spuyten Duyvil Publishers, 2019); *Nikolai Gumilev's Africa* (Glagoslav Publications, 2018); Yuri Andrukhovych's cultural and literary essays, *My Final Territory: Selected Essays* (University of Toronto Press, 2018); and Abram Terz's literary essays, *Strolls with Pushkin* (Columbia University Press, 2016). His novel about the city of Lviv *Seven Signs of the Lion* appeared with Glagoslav Publications in 2016. He has received numerous prizes for his translations including the George S.N. Luckyj Award in Ukrainian Literature Translation from the Canadian Foundation for Ukrainian Studies in 2013.

ABOUT THE ARTIST

The artist Olha Fedoruk hails from the city of Lviv, a place that she loves dearly. A number of her works focus on the unique beauty of the city, including a series of artistic meditations on the poetry of one of its most famous past inhabitants – the poet Bohdan Ihor Antonych. The cover painting that she provided for this volume is entitled "The Old City" and her painting "Night over the Old City" is used as the background for the back cover.

Olha studied decorative scheme at Ivan Trush State College of Decorative and Fine Arts, and decorative ceramics at Lviv National Academy of Arts. She works as a graphic artist and painter. She has had eleven personal exhibitions. Her most recent exhibition took place in Ukrainian National Museum in Chicago together with her daughter, photographer Oksana Kami. Olha has exhibited her paintings and graphic art in Ukraine and abroad. She is a member of the National Union of Artists of Ukraine.

HERSTORIES: AN ANTHOLOGY
OF NEW UKRAINIAN WOMEN PROSE WRITERS

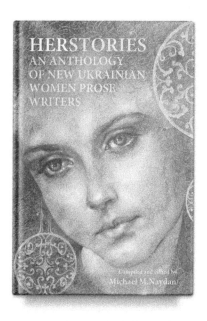

Women's prose writing has exploded on the literary scene in Ukraine just prior to and following Ukrainian independence in 1991. Over the past two decades scores of fascinating new women authors have emerged. These authors write in a wide variety of styles and genres including short stories, novels, essays, and new journalism. In the collection you will find: realism, magical realism, surrealism, the fantastic, deeply intellectual writing, newly discovered feminist perspectives, philosophical prose, psychological mysteries, confessional prose, and much more.

The volume will include 18 contemporary writers: Lina Kostenko, Emma Andijewska, Nina Bichuya, Sofia Maidanska, Ludmyla Taran, Liuko Dashvar, Maria Matios, Eugenia Kononenko, Oksana Zabuzhko, Iren Rozdobudko, Natalka Sniadanko, Larysa Denysenko, Svitlana Povaljajeva, Svitlana Pyrkalo, Dzvinka Matiash, Irena Karpa, Tanya Malyarchuk, and Sofia Andrukhovych.

Buy it > www.glagoslav.com

The Complete
KOBZAR
by Taras Shevchenko

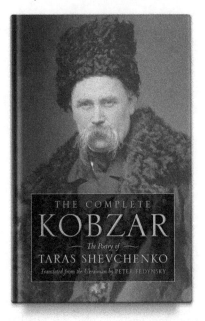

Masterfully fulfilled by Peter Fedynsky, Voice of America journalist and expert on Ukrainian studies, this first ever English translation of the complete *Kobzar* brings out Ukraine's rich cultural heritage.

As a foundational text, The *Kobzar* has played an important role in galvanizing the Ukrainian identity and in the development of Ukraine's written language and Ukrainian literature. The first editions had been censored by the Russian czar, but the book still made an enduring impact on Ukrainian culture. There is no reliable count of how many editions of the book have been published, but an official estimate made in 1976 put the figure in Ukraine at 110 during the Soviet period alone. That figure does not include Kobzars released before and after both in Ukraine and abroad. A multitude of translations of Shevchenko's verse into Slavic, Germanic and Romance languages, as well as Chinese, Japanese, Bengali, and many others attest to his impact on world culture as well.

Buy it > www.glagoslav.com

SEVEN SIGNS OF THE LION

by Michael M. Naydan

The novel *Seven Signs of the Lion* is a magical journey to the city of Lviv in Western Ukraine. Part magical realism, part travelogue, part adventure novel, and part love story, it is a fragmented, hybrid work about a mysterious and mythical place. The hero of the novel Nicholas Bilanchuk is a gatherer of living souls, the unique individuals he meets over the course of his five-month stay in his ancestral homeland. These include the enigmatic Mr. Viktor, who, with one eye that always glimmers, in a dream summons him across the Atlantic Ocean to the city of lions, becoming his spiritual mentor; the genius mathematician Professor Potojbichny (a man of science with a mystical bent and whose name means "man from the other side"); the exquisite beauty Ada, whose name suggests "woman from Hades" in Ukrainian, whose being emanates irresistible sensuality, but who never lets anyone capture her beauty in a picture; the schizophrenic artist Ivan the Ghostseer, who lives in a bohemian hovel of a basement apartment and in an alcohol-induced trance paints the spirits of the city that torment him; and the curly-haired elfin Raya, whose name suggests "paradise" in Ukrainian and who becomes the primary guide and companion for Nicholas on his journey to self-realization...

Buy it > www.glagoslav.com

The Fantastic Worlds of Yuri Vynnychuk

by Yuri Vynnychuk

Yuri Vynnychuk is a master storyteller and satirist, who emerged from the Western Ukrainian underground in Soviet times to become one of Ukraine's most prolific and most prominent writers of today. He is a chameleon who can adapt his narrative voice in a variety of ways and whose style at times is reminiscent of Borges. A master of the short story, he exhibits a great range from exquisite lyrical-philosophical works such as his masterpiece "An Embroidered World," written in the mode of magical realism; to intense psychological studies; to contemplative science fiction and horror tales; and to wicked black humor and satire such as his "Max and Me." Excerpts are also presented in this volume of his longer prose works, including his highly acclaimed novel of wartime Lviv *Tango of Death*, which received the 2012 BBC Ukrainian Book of the Year Award. The translations offered here allow the English-language reader to become acquainted with the many fantastic worlds and lyrical imagination of an extraordinarily versatile writer.

Buy it > www.glagoslav.com

Hardly Ever Otherwise

by Maria Matios

Everything eventually reaches its appointed place in time and space. Maria Matios's dramatic family saga, *Hardly Ever Otherwise*, narrates the story of several western Ukrainian families during the last decades of the Austro-Hungarian Empire, and expands upon the idea that "it isn't time that is important, but the human condition in time."

From the first page, Matios engages her reader with an impeccable style, which she employs to create a rich tapestry of cause and effect, at times depicting a logic that is both bitter and enigmatic. But nothing is ever fully revealed—it is only in the final pages of the novel that the events in the beginning are understood as a necessary part of a larger whole, and the section entitled Seasicknesspresents a compelling argument for why events almost always have to follow a particular course.

Buy it > www.glagoslav.com

The Frontier

28 Contemporary Ukrainian Poets - An Anthology

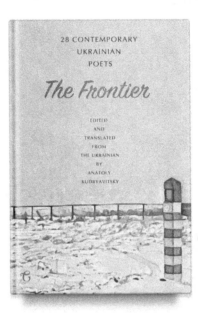

This anthology reflects a search of the Ukrainian nation for its identity, the roots of which lie deep inside Ukrainian-language poetry. Some of the included poets are well-known locally and internationally; among them are Serhiy Zhadan, Halyna Kruk, Ostap Slyvynsky, Marianna Kijanowska, Oleh Kotsarev, Anna Bagriana and, of course, the living legend of Ukrainian poetry, Vasyl Holoborodko. The next Ukrainian poetic generation also features prominently in the collection. Such poets as Les Beley, Olena Herasymyuk, Myroslav Laiuk, Hanna Malihon, Taras Malkovych, Julia Musakovska, Julia Stahivska and Lyuba Yakimchuk are the ones Ukrainians like to read today, and each of them already has an excellent reputation abroad due to festival appearances and translations to European languages. The work collected here documents poetry in Ukraine responding to challenges of the time by forging a radical new poetic, reconsidering writing techniques and language itself.

Edited and translated from the Ukrainian by Anatoly Kudryavitsky.

A Bilingual Edition.

Buy it > www.glagoslav.com

The Lawyer from Lychakiv Street
by Andriy Kokotiukha

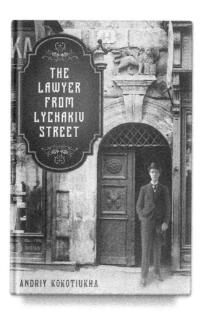

At the beginning of the twentieth century, 1908, a young Kyivan, Klym Koshovy miraculously flies the coop and escapes from persecution by tsarist police to Lviv. However, even here he is arrested – near the corpse of a well-known local lawyer, Yevhen Soyka. The deceased had dubious friends and powerful enemies in the city. Suicide or murder?

The search for truth leads Koshovy through the dark labyrinths of Lviv's streets. On his way – facing daring pickpockets, criminal kingpins and Russian terrorist bombers. And Klym is constantly getting in the way of the police commissioner Marek Wichura. The truth will stun Klym, and his new loyal friend Jozef Shatsky. It will forever change the fate of the enigmatic and influential beauty Magda Bohdanovych.

Buy it > www.glagoslav.com

Dear Reader,

Thank you for purchasing this book.

We at Glagoslav Publications are glad to welcome you, and hope that you find our books to be a source of knowledge and inspiration.

We want to show the beauty and depth of the Slavic region to everyone looking to expand their horizon and learn something new about different cultures, different people, and we believe that with this book we have managed to do just that.

Now that you've got to know us, we want to get to know you. We value communication with our readers and want to hear from you! We offer several options:

— Join our Book Club on Goodreads, Library Thing and Shelfari, and receive special offers and information about our giveaways;

— Share your opinion about our books on Amazon, Barnes & Noble, Waterstones and other bookstores;

— Join us on Facebook and Twitter for updates on our publications and news about our authors;

— Visit our site www.glagoslav.com to check out our Catalogue and subscribe to our Newsletter.

Glagoslav Publications is getting ready to release a new collection and planning some interesting surprises — stay with us to find out!

Glagoslav Publications
Email: contact@glagoslav.com

Glagoslav Publications Catalogue

- *A History of Belarus* by Lubov Bazan
- *Children's Fashion of the Russian Empire* by Alexander Vasiliev
- *Empire of Corruption: The Russian National Pastime* by Vladimir Soloviev
- *Heroes of the 90s: People and Money. The Modern History of Russian Capitalism* by Alexander Solovev, Vladislav Dorofeev and Valeria Bashkirova
- *Fifty Highlights from the Russian Literature* (Dutch Edition) by Maarten Tengbergen
- *Bajesvolk* (Dutch Edition) by Michail Chodorkovsky
- *Dagboek van Keizerin Alexandra* (Dutch Edition)
- *Myths about Russia* by Vladimir Medinskiy
- *Boris Yeltsin: The Decade that Shook the World* by Boris Minaev
- *A Man Of Change: A study of the political life of Boris Yeltsin*
- *Sberbank: The Rebirth of Russia's Financial Giant* by Evgeny Karasyuk
- *To Get Ukraine* by Oleksandr Shyshko
- *Asystole* by Oleg Pavlov
- *Gnedich* by Maria Rybakova
- *Marina Tsvetaeva: The Essential Poetry*
- *Multiple Personalities* by Tatyana Shcherbina
- *The Investigator* by Margarita Khemlin
- *The Exile* by Zinaida Tulub
- *Leo Tolstoy: Flight from Paradise* by Pavel Basinsky
- *Moscow in the 1930* by Natalia Gromova
- *Laurus* (Dutch edition) by Evgenij Vodolazkin
- *Prisoner* by Anna Nemzer
- *The Crime of Chernobyl: The Nuclear Goulag* by Wladimir Tchertkoff
- *Alpine Ballad* by Vasil Bykau
- *The Complete Correspondence of Hryhory Skovoroda*
- *The Tale of Aypi* by Ak Welsapar
- *Selected Poems* by Lydia Grigorieva
- *The Fantastic Worlds of Yuri Vynnychuk*
- *The Garden of Divine Songs and Collected Poetry of Hryhory Skovoroda*
- *Adventures in the Slavic Kitchen: A Book of Essays with Recipes* by Igor Klekh
- *Seven Signs of the Lion* by Michael M. Naydan

- *Forefathers' Eve* by Adam Mickiewicz
- *One-Two* by Igor Eliseev
- *Girls, be Good* by Bojan Babić
- *Time of the Octopus* by Anatoly Kucherena
- *The Grand Harmony* by Bohdan Ihor Antonych
- *The Selected Lyric Poetry Of Maksym Rylsky*
- *The Shining Light* by Galymkair Mutanov
- *The Frontier: 28 Contemporary Ukrainian Poets - An Anthology*
- *Acropolis: The Wawel Plays* by Stanisław Wyspiański
- *Contours of the City* by Attyla Mohylny
- *Conversations Before Silence: The Selected Poetry of Oles Ilchenko*
- *The Secret History of my Sojourn in Russia* by Jaroslav Hašek
- *Mirror Sand: An Anthology of Russian Short Poems*
- *Maybe We're Leaving* by Jan Balaban
- *Death of the Snake Catcher* by Ak Welsapar
- *A Brown Man in Russia* by Vijay Menon
- *Hard Times* by Ostap Vyshnia
- *The Flying Dutchman* by Anatoly Kudryavitsky
- *Nikolai Gumilev's Africa* by Nikolai Gumilev
- *Combustions* by Srđan Srdić
- *The Sonnets* by Adam Mickiewicz
- *Dramatic Works* by Zygmunt Krasiński
- *Four Plays* by Juliusz Słowacki
- *Little Zinnobers* by Elena Chizhova
- *We Are Building Capitalism! Moscow in Transition 1992-1997* by Robert Stephenson
- *The Nuremberg Trials* by Alexander Zvyagintsev
- *The Hemingway Game* by Evgeni Grishkovets
- *A Flame Out at Sea* by Dmitry Novikov
- *Jesus' Cat* by Grig
- *Want a Baby and Other Plays* by Sergei Tretyakov
- *Mikhail Bulgakov: The Life and Times* by Marietta Chudakova
- *Leonardo's Handwriting* by Dina Rubina
- *A Burglar of the Better Sort* by Tytus Czyżewski
- *The Mouseiad and other Mock Epics* by Ignacy Krasicki

- *Ravens before Noah* by Susanna Harutyunyan
- *An English Queen and Stalingrad* by Natalia Kulishenko
- *Point Zero* by Narek Malian
- *Absolute Zero* by Artem Chekh
- *Olanda* by Rafał Wojasiński
- *Robinsons* by Aram Pachyan
- *The Monastery* by Zakhar Prilepin
- *The Selected Poetry of Bohdan Rubchak: Songs of Love, Songs of Death, Songs of the Moon*
- *Mebet* by Alexander Grigorenko
- *The Orchestra* by Vladimir Gonik
- *Everyday Stories* by Mima Mihajlović
- *Slavdom* by Ľudovít Štúr
- *The Code of Civilization* by Vyacheslav Nikonov
- *Where Was the Angel Going?* by Jan Balaban
- *De Zwarte Kip* (Dutch Edition) by Antoni Pogorelski
- *Głosy / Voices* by Jan Polkowski
- *Sergei Tretyakov: A Revolutionary Writer in Stalin's Russia* by Robert Leach
- *Opstand* (Dutch Edition) by Władysław Reymont
- *Dramatic Works* by Cyprian Kamil Norwid
- *Children's First Book of Chess* by Natalie Shevando and Matthew McMillion
- *The Revolt of the Animals* by Wladyslaw Reymont
- *Illegal Parnassus* by Bojan Babić
- *Liza's Waterfall: The hidden story of a Russian feminist* by Pavel Basinsky
- *Precursor* by Vasyl Shevchuk
- *The Vow: A Requiem for the Fifties* by Jiří Kratochvil
- *Duel* by Borys Antonenko-Davydovych
- *Subterranean Fire* by Natalka Bilotserkivets
- *Biography of Sergei Prokofiev* by Igor Vishnevetsky

More coming . . .

CPSIA information can be obtained
at www.ICGtesting.com
Printed in the USA
BVHW070014090223
658191BV00023B/682